# DYNASTY

## II

DUTCH

www.dcbookdiva.com
www.myspace.com/dcbookdivapublications

ISBN-10: 0984611002
ISBN-13: 978-0984611003
Library of Congress Control Number: 2009936476

Paperback Edition, December 2010

**Publisher's Note**
*This is a work of fiction. Any names historical events, real people, living and dead, or the locales are intended only to give the fiction a setting in historic reality. Other names, characters, places, businesses and incidents are either the product of the author's imagination or are used factiously, and their resemblance, if any, to real life counterparts is entirely coincidental.*

Edited by: A. Slye
Graphic Designer: MWS Designs

**DC Bookdiva Publications**
#245 4401-A Connecticut Ave
NW, Washington, DC 20008
www.dcbookdiva.com
facebook.com/dcbfanpage

twitter.com/dcbookdiva

# DUTCH

# DYNASTY

## II

DC BOOK DIVA PRESENTS

# CHAPTER 19

Ty gripped the pistol tightly and looked from Guy to Vee in total shock. His emotions were wired and his adrenaline was running high. Guy was speechless. He felt the tension and rage exuding from Ty as he stood above him. When he saw Ty adjust the aim and tighten his grip on the pistol, he knew what was about to go down. The grieving father in Guy wanted it to happen, but there was another part that wouldn't allow it, the part of the absentee father he saw in Hawk's accusing eyes.

Without warning, he raised his arm and hit Ty's forearm hard, a split second before Ty pulled the trigger. *BOOM!*

The sound of the gunshot filled the room as the bullet pierced the wood on the ceiling. Guy noticed that throughout the episode, Vee didn't blink an eye. Guy had thought Vee had come prepared to die, but Vee aired the confidence of a man that knew he wasn't going to die that day.

"Yo, Pop, what the f- ?" Ty curled his lip aggressively, but couldn't finish the question. He had never cursed at his father. "Why you stop me?"

Guy glanced at Hawk Bill and calmly replied, "Because I can. Now sit down, Tyquan."

Ty glared at his father until Guy met his look with a glare of his own.

"I said SIT…DOWN!"

Ty reluctantly complied. Guy leaned back in his wheel chair, rubbing his hand over his face. *Shantelle's son? His son? Kev? Vee killed Kev? A son killing a son?* Although Guy didn't believe in karma, he couldn't get the thought out of his mind. *What goes around comes around.* The world he had created with manipulation, deception and murder had come full circle in the form of the man before him. He sighed heavily and looked over at Hawk Bill.

"Hawk, talk to me. Where is Shantelle?"

Hawk replied, "She still up in Troy?"

Hawk had seen the look in Ty's eyes. The barrel was still aimed at Vee, but the bullet would have to go through him first. Ty had fully intended on killing him.

"I saw him comin' outta momma's house, and you know I never forget a face, Guy. Done too much dirt for that. I remembered him from when he was Ty's lieutenant," Hawk said, cutting his eyes at Ty. "I knew Ty had said Vee was the one that killed Kev, may God rest his soul. Guy, I was ready to kill him myself. So-"

"Then, why you didn't?" Ty interrupted angrily. "He comin' outta yo momma's house and you ain't do shit?? Get the fuck outta my face! Pop, you hearing this shit?"

Guy eyed Hawk directly. He had known the man for too long and knew his ways. Hawk was many things, but a liar wasn't one of them.

"Go 'head, Hawk," Guy said, ignoring Ty's exasperation.

"Wasn't no way I was gonna kill him until I knew what the fuck he was doin' at her house. If he knew, then who else knew? So I followed him all the way to Troy. I didn't see the connection at the time, 'cause I wasn't thinkin' about nothin' but my momma. I caught him in the McDonald's after the visit and that's when he told me."

Nobody spoke as Guy sat with his hands tented in front of him, weighing out everything Hawk Bill had said. Although Hawk could tell Guy believed him, he also saw his hesitation.

He knew all about Guy's pride and that his love for Kev was a major factor. Hawk broke the silence in the room.

"How long have we known each other, Guy?"

Guy looked at him and calmly replied, "A long time, Hawk."

"And nigga, I done stood by wit' you back-to-back ever since grade school. Yo daddy," he continued and nodded at Willie, "and my daddy, may God rest his soul, was the same way. I'd die for you and your family. You know that. I love Kev too, and I know this some mind blowin' shit. To be honest wit' you, I don't know what I'd do in your shoes. But I know what I'm askin' you to do." Hawk placed his hand on Vee's shoulder. "This boy's your blood...my blood...OUR blood. You can't turn away from that."

"Blood don't make you family," Ty growled.

"If it don't, then somethin' wrong", Hawk shot back.

Everyone waited for Guy to speak, but it was Vee who broke the silence.

"I ain't come here to plead for my life."

"I can't tell", Ty snidely remarked.

"Then why did you come?" Guy was interested to know.

"I came," Vee began, first eyeing Ty and then looked over at Guy, "Because the woman that raised me had once told me that the chickens always come home to roost." Then Vee smirked wickedly, "What kind of man lets a woman take a charge for him then leaves her for dead?"

Guy wheeled his chair around the table, stopping in front of Vee. "Is that what she told you? That I left her for dead?" Guy was incredulous. "I tried to get Shantelle the best lawyers, but she refused my money." Guy shook his head at the memory. "I didn't leave her for dead. But...you... killed my son."

Vee dropped his eyes and for a split second in remorse. He then looked Guy directly in his eyes. "I can't change the past and neither can you. You think it didn't fuck me up to know that the same nigga that wanted me dead was my own brother??" He shook his head and continued, "I did what I had to do, so regardless, if I walk outta here alive, nothin' will ever change that."

Ty jumped up from the table and said accusingly, "Kev wanted you dead because you tried to kill Pops! He said you admitted it!"

"If he did, then he lied." Vee looked towards Guy. "I didn't spark the war."

Guy's head began to spin. Too much had happened too fast. He needed time to think and sort things out. "Hawk, I'ma talk to Shantelle, but not on those prison phones. Make arrangements to get her a cell phone as soon as you can."

"Done.", Hawk assured him.

"And Hawk, this isn't over. He's your responsibility. When I make my decision, I don't wanna hear no 'I don't know where he is' shit. You stand up for him, you stand in for him", warned Guy.

"Don't worry, Guy", spat Vee suddenly, "Don't need nobody to stand in for me. I won't be hard to find, but I won't be empty-handed, neither."

Guy smiled to himself. He would've replied exactly the same. *Yeah, that's my youngster,* he thought to himself. Out loud he said, "That's good to know", and turned his chair around towards the door to the back office.

Ty threw his arms up in the air. "That's it?? This nigga killed Kev and tried to kill you!!"

Ignoring Ty, Guy rolled himself through the door of the back office and slammed it shut behind him.

Ty grilled Vee with a hateful glare and marched around the table to face Vee eye to eye. Vee, unruffled, returned the gaze with calm.

"Nigga," snarled Ty, "I promise you…you a dead man."

"Don't make no promises you can't keep", retorted Vee.

Ty smiled. "You never miss your water 'til your well runs dry." They stared at each other a moment longer. Each knew damn well the other was dangerous, and in spite of it, there was a grudging respect between the two former friends.

Ty then eyed Hawk Bill coldly, and then brushed past Vee with an intentional shove with his shoulder.

*"Daaaddy!" a nine-year old Ty cried. "K-Kev sh-shot m-me!"*

*It was Memorial Day weekend and Guy had taken the kids over to Mine Well Park for the annual Webtown Throwdown. Every year the city of Goldsboro invited Guy to host the festival and he always looked forward to it. There were endless grills aligned all around the baseball diamond supplying hot dogs, hamburgers and chicken. There was beer and liquor for the adults and juices and sodas for the kids. The park also had a swimming pool that converted to a 'ballers' pool party well into the wee hours of the night.*

*When Kev shot Ty with the B.B. gun, they had been playing around with their friends and cousins while Guy was laughing and drinking with Scatter, Hawk and a few others. Gloria was sitting at the picnic table with the other wives and girlfriends, while Debra hosted her own table of women close by. When Ty cried out, Guy scowled while Debra immediately jumped from her seat and opened her arms out to the crying boy.*

*"Awww, come here, baby," she cooed.*

*"Deb, sit yo' ass down!" Guy barked.*

*"But Guy, Kev shot –" Debra began, but Guy cut her off angrily.*

*"Bitch didn't you hear what the fuck I said??" He glowered at her until she reluctantly sat back down. Guy strode to the sniffling boy and crouched down. "Ty, stop that damn cryin', you nine years old, not nine months! Now move your hand and lemme see…"*

*Ty moved his hand away as Guy lifted up the leg of the boy's shorts. An angry red mark met his eyes. "Nigga, you alright", Guy said gruffly. "What you call me for?"*

*The boy blubbered out, "C-c-cuz Kev shot me."*

"And all you gonna do is stand there and cry?" taunted Guy. "What, you scared of your brother? You a punk? A sissy?"

Ty shook his head.

"Boy, I can't hear no head shakes. Are you a punk??"

"No!!" yelled Ty, his face now dry.

"Okay then, what you gonna do?"

"I'ma, I'ma....." Ty hesitated and looked at Guy for guidance.

"You gonna kick his ass, right?"

"I'ma kick his ass!!" Ty answered and the men laughed while the women shook their heads in disapproval.

"And you better not lose, neither one of you!" Guy looked them both sternly in the eye.

Ty balled up his fists and ran straight at eleven-year old Kev. Although Ty was half Kev's size, his fury could not be underestimated. Ty butted his head into Kev's stomach, knocking the wind out of him with one big whoosh and both children tumbled to the ground.

"Kev! Get yo' ass up, boy!" Guy yelled in encouragement, while Gloria rolled her eyes in disgust.

Kev rose and rolled onto Ty while swinging at him wildly at his face. Ty was able to duck from most of the punches and jabbed in several of his own. If it weren't from the furious looks on their faces, one might think the boys were playing a game of 'patty-cake'.

"Fight him, Ty!" Guy urged.

Ty aimed a viscous kick at Kev's groin and Kev bent over in obvious agony. Ty used the opportunity to rain Kev with multiple blows, while Kev cried in frustration.

"Godammit Guy, that's enough!!" Gloria yelled and rose to her feet. Chuckling, Guy broke up the fight and held them apart by their wrists.

"See what ya'll did?? Don't you ever let nobody do that to either of ya'll without you both jumpin' in. You hear me?" Guy looked at each of their faces expectantly.

"Yes, sir!" they both said in unison.

"Ya'll are brothers, you know what that means? It means no matter what, you look out for each other. Now hug!" Kev and Ty looked at each other and reluctantly hugged.

Guy then said, "Now Kev, go get me that B.B. gun." Kev retrieved the gun and handed it solemnly to Guy. After looking the gun over carefully, he aimed and - pop! He shot his son Kev in the left kneecap. Kev sucked his breath in with an audible hiss, but knew better than to cry.

"You know why I shot you?" Guy asked the bewildered boy.

"Because I shot my brother?" Kev asked in a small voice.

"No! Because you don't never give up yo' gun to no damn body, 'specially if it's loaded. Now go play." Guy chuckled to himself as he watched them scamper off. I'ma make real soldiers outta them two, he thought to himself.

Although Ty and Kev never knew what it was like to be poor, they were never fed with silver spoons, either. Although both Gloria and Deb had beautiful homes in affluent neighborhoods, both were still close to the projects; West Haven Housing Projects in Gloria's case and Green Haven Housing in Debra's. Guy ensured the boys were not in need yet made them work for what they wanted. First it was just chores around the house but as they got older, they would go to Guy's landscaping business and even work in the blazing sun when called on. Guy would also take them to one of his construction companies, where they were taught how to put up sheet rock and paint.

One evening, when Guy and the boys were at Debra's for dinner, Kev and Ty complained to their father about the sweat, dirt and the exhausting work they had to undergo every day.

"What the hell you mean you tired of bein' dirty? What's wrong with doin' an honest day's work?" Guy exploded.

"You don't come home dirty", mumbled Kev while pushing at his mashed potatoes with a fork. Guy smiled.

"That's because I'm the boss and bosses don't get dirty."

"Well, we wanna be bosses, too!" exclaimed Ty. Guy looked over at Debra, who just shook her head in exasperation.

*A few months later, while driving back from Wilson, Skat-
ter told Guy that Kev and Ty had a hangout called "The Funhouse."*

*"The Funhouse? What the fuck is 'The Funhouse'?"*

*"Some type of lil' kid shit," replied Skatter. "They got vid-
eo games and shit. Plus, they sellin' ecstasy and weed."*

*Guy was fuming. "Show me this fuckin' funhouse," he
snarled.*

*The Funhouse was an old two-story plantation-style build-
ing on Carolina Street. Though it was a quiet street, it was si-
tuated right across the street from West Haven. Guy figured
this was Kev's doing.*

*They parked where they could see the youngsters go in and
out of 'The Funhouse' where loud music emanated from inside.*

*"Them lil' niggas definitely yo sons," Skatter chuckled.
"They runnin' a tight operation…a fuckin' junior liquor store."*

*Guy shook his head, trying to maintain his composure. Af-
ter a moment he calmly instructed, "Skat, get on the phone and
get a team over here now."*

*Guy had decided to give his boys a lesson in 'Crash-
Landing 101.*

*The place was packed with teenagers. The sounds of Juve-
nile's Ha was playing loudly from the stereo while two
youngsters smoking blunts played the Madden '98 video game
on a large screen TV. Young girls were scattered all over the
room, half naked and high on 'X'. Some were dancing and
kissing in the middle of the living room amidst a Purple Haze
smoke-filled room. Two dudes dressed in blue guarded the
door while Ty and Kev sat at the kitchen table counting money. Various colors of Ecstasy pills peppered the table among
several bags of Purple Haze.*

*"Fifteen, sixteen, sixteen-fifty, seven hunn-ed…" Ty
counted. "Shit, that's our re-up right there. The rest is pure
profit."*

*Kev smiled. It had been his idea to open up the spot. A
young mother on Section 8 Kev was seeing allowed him to use*

the downstairs of her home for dealing. Kev was about to turn 18, while Ty was only 15 years old. They were making more money than they had ever seen in their young lives.

Suddenly, they heard a female scream and the angry sound of male voices.

"Get down on the fuckin' floor!"

As Ty, Kev and several others ran towards the back door, they saw it had been broken in and two masked men were aiming AR-15s at them.

"Where you think you goin'?" snarled one of the intruders. He snatched the bag of money from Ty's hand and shouted, "Lay down!"

One of the teens, Dino got down instantly. Ty and Kev hesitated until one of the masked men placed his gun at Ty's head.

"You think I'm playin', huh? Get down or I'ma lay you down!"

Ty barked, "Nigga, you better kill me 'cause if not, you'z a dead muthafucka!"

The gunman then swung the weapon over to Kev's head.

"Fuck you, pussy!" Kev growled, "You know who the fuck I am? Simmons, nigga!"

The gunman chuckled. "What? You really gonna die for this sorry-ass shit??"

No one said a word.

"Then you both some goddamn fools!" said Guy as he entered from the living room.

"Pop??"

"What the ---??" Both boys were flabbergasted.

Guy looked at them both with disgust and instructed his team. "Get this shit outta here. Police come in, we all goin' to jail behind these two hard-headed muthafuckas. And get all them kids outta here."

When Guy was alone with his kids in the kitchen, Kev summoned up some courage to speak. "Pop, we---", he began.

"Don't say shit!" Guy spat and then sat down. "So upset wit' you, I don't know what to do." Guy crossed his legs, and stared hard. The boys had their heads hung down in shame, as if waiting for judgment. "What? You think you tough, huh? Because you was ready to die for some bullshit? You bad now??" The boys remained silent.

"Answer me!!" Guy thundered.

"Pop, I...."

"We were only..."

Both had tried to speak at the same time, but since Kev knew Ty was the better speaker, he backed down to let him do the talking.

"We just...we ain't gonna let nobody take nuthin' from us", mumbled Ty.

"So, all your life is worth is a few pills and a couple a hundred dollars?"

"No, but---" Ty stammered.

"But what?!"

Ty then raised his to look at Guy's.

"Once we let somebody take somethin' from us, they gonna keep takin' and takin', til we ain't got nuthin'."

Though Guy felt a tinge of pride in the answer, he wasn't about to let it go.

"Money can always be replaced. You can never be replaced. You die for family or a worthy cause, not money, not pride. You understand?"

Kev and Ty stood still, stone-faced. Then Ty spoke.

"Is that what you would do? Or is you just tellin' us that?" Guy couldn't help but smirk at the audacity of the question. "I been robbed before. Goes with the territory...the same territory ya'll ain't got no business bein' in. What the hell is on your mind, Kev? Ty?"

Neither would look Guy in the face.

"Oh, now you can't talk, huh? Somebody better say somethin'."

"We wanted to make some money."

"What?"

"We wanted to be bosses."

Guy didn't know what to think. On one hand he was sick at heart because he didn't want that life for his sons. On the other hand, he couldn't help but feel that his sons were truly boss material.

"Like this?" Guy laughed cruelly. "Sitting in a hot ass spot, drugs everywhere, music blaring, under-aged kids getting high? I thought I told you bosses don't get dirty."

Guy shook his head and began pacing the room, thinking. It was clear what path his sons had chosen. They have the heart and the attitude necessary to follow that path, but do they have the stomach? What he did next was partly a test and a deterrent.

"Come on," he grumbled and the boys meekly followed their father into the living room, where Skatter and the other gunmen were waiting patiently. Guy winked at Skatter slyly.

"Skatter, when you gonna have that money you owe me?" Skatter answered without missing a beat.

"Man, Guy, I almost got it. Just gimme a little mo' time!"

Guy took the gun from Skatter and turned to Kev and Ty, who were watching his every move.

"So, you wanna be bosses, huh? Well, bosses got choices to make. You see this man? The one ya'll call Uncle Skatter? I grew up wit' this man, known him all my life. So, he think just 'cause of that, he can play wit' my paper."

"Guy, man, I---"

Guy cut Skatter off.

"Shut the fuck up!!" Guy grabbed another pistol from one of his gunmen and handed them to the boys, one each.

"Now ya'll bosses. Can you look at a man you both love and respect in the eye and take his life if his hands call for it?" Guy asked them intently.

Kev and Ty stared at Skatter without a word, weighing their responses. This was a man who had been there for them throughout their formative years. They did indeed call Skatter their uncle and loved him deeply.

"Well, can you??" demanded Guy.

"I can", Ty spoke first.

*"Yes," Kev followed suit.*

*"Then show me," Guy gravely instructed. "Kill the mother-fucker."*

*There was no hesitation on Ty's part. He reacted so quick-ly, even Skatter had to blink with surprise. Kev was right be-hind his brother, both pulling the triggers with an empty click.*

*Guy's sons had passed the test. On the other hand, Guy had failed. The way he had tested his sons was the same way he had been tested as a boy. His heart was bursting with pride and at the same time was breaking to pieces.*

*"Graduate high school. If ya'll feel the same way...."Guy began. "The Funhouse is officially closed."*

# CHAPTER 20

Sami pulled up to his store in a low key brown van. It was a bright sunny day, the type of day that made Sami feel that God was smiling. However, he was about to find out God was not smiling on Sami that day.

"Mornin' Leroy, how are you doin' today?" he said cheerfully.

Leroy was homeless and Sami often employed him to do odd jobs such as sweeping the front of the door of the shop and washing the display windows.

"Hope you got some work for me," he grumbled, only slightly louder than the way his stomach was growling.

"Yes, yes. Come in, I'll get the broom."

As he and Leroy entered the store, they were warmly greeted by a cute red-bone behind the counter. "Good morning, Sami."

"Good morning, Tisha," Sami replied while handing the broom to Leroy. As soon as Leroy walked outside to sweep, two Mexicans entered the store.

"I need to speak to Sami," the shorter one said.

Warily, Sami replied, "He's not here. Can I take a message?"

He wasn't sure he liked the vibe the two men brought into his store.

"Yeah, you can tell him this," the other Mexican answered as he pulled out a sawed-off shotgun from beneath his flannel shirt and cocked it.

Boom!

Tisha screamed.

He cocked it again.

Boom!

Both Sami and Tisha fell with their chests wide open like piñatas.

The shorter Mexican knelt by Sami's dying body and aimed a .357 at his head.

"Ty said to tell you it's nothing personal. It's just that you were in the way."

Brain matter and blood suddenly exploded and splattered the wall as Sami was put out of his misery. The blood slowly began to form an ungodly halo on the floor around Sami's body. Tisha lay behind the counter, her eyes wide open in shock and horror as she gasped for breath. A second shot rang and Tisha was still.

When the Mexicans exited the store, there was no sign of Leroy.

Vee rode shotgun as the chick from Durham, Felicia, sped the rented Pontiac down Highway 85.

"J, I'm tellin' you, shit is on fire in Durham!" Felicia shook her head in disbelief.

"The police caught feelins' over Banks' family gettin' stabbed up like that with the Wolf Pack's name written all over it."

Vee sighed as he looked out the window. He should've seen this coming. The senseless slaughter of an entire family is something the D.A. lives for in order to fulfill ambitions of getting to be mayor or a judge. Unfortunately his anger had gotten the better of him. Banks' treachery had to be dealt with severely and now it was coming back to haunt him.

"Get off right here," he instructed Felicia. She clicked on her turn signal and swerved into the right lane to exit the highway.

As much as he tried, Vee couldn't stop thinking about Guy, his father. He didn't know how Guy would react, but he just couldn't leave Hawk Bill to stand in for him. Hawk Bill was his mother's brother and Vee's uncle and had never run from a fight, no matter the odds. Every time he was called, he would come with all he had.

When Felicia rounded the corner to Sami's store, Vee frowned with puzzlement. *The store closed in the middle of the day? Sami never did that.*

"Park right here," he instructed Felicia to a spot a little further up the block.

Vee got out, walked down to the store and tried the front door. It was locked. He cupped his eyes and peeked through one of the front windows. He noted the white chalk outline on the floor made by the police and wondered what happened. At that moment a young boy dressed in red was pedaling slowly by. Vee called out to him.

"Hey, lil' man, let me holla at you!"

The boy looked around and turned his bike towards Vee.

"What's up, man? Got that haze, yo. Big bags, too!" the little boy exclaimed eagerly.

He couldn't have been a day over eleven.

"Naw, Shorty, I'm straight. You live around here?"

The boy looked at him suspiciously.

"Why?"

Vee jerked his head towards the store. "You know who got killed in there?"

The boy looked Vee up and down as if to say, who are you, the police or somethin'?

"I don't know shit," he spat and tried to pedal off. Vee reached out and grabbed the handle bars.

"Nigga, do I look like the police? If I was, your stupid ass woulda *been* locked up. Trying to sell me some haze. Dumbass nigga!"

Vee was seething, and just looking at those cold eyes made the boy realize he had made a bad mistake.

"My bad, yo. Just that cops have been all over the place since Sami and that chick got killed in there."

"Sami?" echoed Vee with shock. The boy nodded.

"Like, two days ago. Broad daylight. Gangsta as fuck!" bragged the boy.

Vee felt sick. Sami was his goose who laid the golden eggs, his connect, his pipeline. A hustler without a connect was like an addict without a dealer. The hustle is that addictive.

As he watched the boy pedal away, Vee suddenly understood his brother Ty's words. *You never miss your water 'til your well runs dry.* Ty was trying to tell him he was going to murder Sami. That way, if a war was inevitable, Vee's resources would be stagnant.

*You got that one, Ty, but best believe I'm a holla back.*

After Felicia dropped him off in Raleigh, he took a cab to his Bentley and headed for LaGrange. He knew for certain that was one place where no one could find him.

When he arrived, he grabbed a large duffel bag and went straight to his stash spot under Ms. Sadie's shed where he kept $750,000 in cash. After filling up the bag with the money from the safe, he went inside.

Once the situation with Guy played itself out, Vee planned on heading for Baltimore. He just couldn't get Cat out of his mind. He was still hurting from the way she rejected him, cursing at him and seemingly hated him. He had to find her and make things right again.

Vee smiled to himself when he thought of the first time they had met. She was so vibrant, aggressive even. It had been

Cat who approached him. He remembered when they had first made love and when she announced she was pregnant. He remembered the birth of his son Takeem. All those warm fuzzy memories were now cold reality. Takeem was dead, Cat was gone, his connection murdered. Hell, even Ms. Sadie had disappeared. Although the bag he carried helped to make him feel invincible, at that moment he felt trapped. There seemed to be no escape from the pain of loss and separation he felt. Vee glanced down at the stacks of money in the duffel bag. He caught a faint whiff of the musty odor of money when it has been enclosed for a long time. Suddenly Vee felt like an old man, alone with his money. The ringtone from his cell phone brought him out of his reverie. He didn't recognize the number, but something told him to answer it anyway.

"Yeah."

"Victor, this is…um…" The words both were thinking at that moment was "your father." Instead, what came out was, "Guy Simmons."

"I know." Vee replied without emotion.

"I, ah, talked to your mother…" Guy began awkwardly. The guilt he felt for Vee was not as strong as his love for Kev, but it was significant enough to affect him deeply.

"I wish things could have been different. I don't know why your mother hid this from me. I would've taken care of you, regardless."

Vee listened only half way. Not having known your own father and then to find out he was also the father of your enemy was crazy, but Vee had more pressing concerns on his mind. "Yeah, well, it is what it is," he shrugged.

"Yeah."

There was more awkward silence.

"Guy…"

"I'm still here."

"Well, look, I'm kinda in the middle of somethin' right now. Wassup?" Vee wondered why Guy was calling him. There was no turning back now, regardless of blood, because blood had been spilled. He was definitely not expecting a Ricki Lake reunion.

Guy took a deep breath.

"I…I acknowledge you as my son, but I can never embrace you. Therefore, in spite of what you did, I'm a let it go. But…I never want to see you again."

Vee's insides were boiling for reasons he couldn't understand. Why did he feel so upset for being rejected by a stranger? He covered his emotions and gave a dry laugh.

"*You* acknowledge *me*? What the fuck that supposed to mean, huh? Acknowledge *this*. I ain't got no father and you ain't got but one son. If you wanna keep him, you better keep him on a short fuckin' leash."

The words stung Guy. He realized at that moment he didn't have a son, no one to carry on the Simmons legacy. Although he loved Ty, he wasn't a Simmons. He gave Ty an ominous warning.

"I'm not going to argue with you, Victor. I've had my say. Stay away from my family, and we'll stay away from you. Test my resolve if you want to."

"Motherfuck the Simmons!" Vee sneered and severed the connection.

Guy gripped his cell phone and lowered his hands to his lap. In one hand he held a photo of him holding Kev when he was seven or eight years old. Making this decision to give Vee a pass had been painful. To look at the man who had murdered his only son and then let him just walk away took everything Guy had. He was a man who prided himself on taking care of his family and although he hadn't known Vee his whole life, he still felt he owed him something. He thought about Vee's angry words and had a feeling it wasn't over yet. He remembered Shantelle's words, *Yes, Victor is your son. Deal with it.*

Guy realized how bitter she had become but didn't know the half of it.

"Bitch, either I can go in or go over you. Either way, I *will* see Guy."

Guy heard Gloria's angry words in the other room and immediately turned his chair towards the door. The middle-aged maid had answered the front door in surprise.

"Mrs. Simmons! I—"

Gloria cut her off.

"I'm here to see Guy."

"Um, Mrs., ah, Simmons instructed me that Mr. Simmons isn't to see anyone," the maid said timidly. She knew the mighty force Gloria was and protested meekly when Gloria pushed her way inside. "Mrs. Simmons, I don't think---"

"Where's Guy?" Gloria demanded.

"Bitch, have you lost your mind??" Gloria looked up and saw Debra starting down the half-moon stairway in the hall. "Who the hell do you think you are, bustin' up in my damn house?!"

"I'm here to see Guy. Don't make me see you, too," Gloria hissed as Debra walked towards her.

"Didn't you hear Catherine? Guy's resting. Now get the fuck out, before I put you out!"

Gloria stepped up to Debra and balled her fists.

"Bitch, either I can go in or go over you. Either way, I *will* see Guy."

Debra tried to understand that Gloria was grieving, but it still took everything she had to keep in control.

"Debra!" Guy suddenly appeared, wheeling his chair from the patio.

Debra was about to protest, but withdrew when she saw the dead-serious look on Guy's face.

Gloria approached and began to wheel Guy to the study. When Debra started to follow, Guy commanded, "Let me speak to Gloria alone."

Gloria felt a keen satisfaction when she shut the study door in Debra's face. *I'm still the first lady, bitch.*

As soon as the door was shut, Guy wheeled himself to the large bay window that overlooked his many acres of land. Gloria stood silently next to him for a minute and then she noticed the photograph of Kev in his hand. She gently pried it from his fingers and stared at it. She ran her fingers lovingly over it and noticed it was wet with what had to be Guy's tears.

"I—I'm sorry, Glo," Guy began. "I failed you, I failed Kevin."

Gloria could hear the pain in his voice and she thought about comforting Guy, but the anger wouldn't allow it.

"Then make it right, Guy." Guy knew what she meant. "TyQuan told me what happened, Guy. How could you?! How could you let the man that murdered Kevin just…just… walk away?"

Guy was heated with TyQuan. He knew why he had told Gloria, so that she would do what she was doing now, trying to change Guy's decision.

"Ty shouldn't have discussed business with you," he replied.

"Business?? No, it was MY business!" Gloria retorted.

"He's my son, Gloria."

"And Kev was MINE! Yours…or have you forgotten?" Gloria shot back, tears in her eyes.

Guy studied her intently and quietly asked, "What do you want from me, Gloria?"

"Justice. Honor Kev's memory."

Guy chuckled.

"You mean blood. Don't try and sugar-coat it. You want Vee dead."

"You're goddamn right I do! I want him to suffer like Kev suffered. I want whoever his triflin' ass mama's heart to ache like mine does! I want the muthafucka dead!!" Gloria thought her heart would burst.

"You once told me that wouldn't bring him back, Glo." Guy reminded her.

"At least he'll rest in peace!" She was also reminding Guy of his previous words.

Guy lowered his head and shook it back and forth. Then he looked back up at the hurting woman and his gaze softened.

"Glo, I know you're in pain but I am, too. The decision I made wasn't easy, but I made it and I stand by it. Vee may not be your son, but he is mine. If it had been Kev, I'd be telling Vee's mother the same thing."

Gloria returned his gaze and softly said, "Guy, I don't care about nobody's mama, okay? It ain't Vee, it was Kev and Kev is my only concern. I've taken a lot of shit from you for a long time. I put up with more than any fool would. I lied to my family for you, Guy…my FAMILY,' she stressed and Guy knew she meant Eddie's murder. "I'm asking you…no, I'm begging you, please. Do something for me. Sacrifice for me, for once in your goddamn life. Do something for other than yourself."

The room became eerily quiet as Gloria waited for Guy to respond. He was thinking how he would give her anything but that, and he knew she wouldn't accept anything less. He sighed heavily, wishing things could've been different.

"Glo, I can't."

Gloria held up her hand.

"Save it. I don't even want to hear your sorry excuses. I love you, Guy, but I can't accept…no, I won't accept this." Then she looked Guy dead in the eye. "If you won't do anything about this, then I will."

They held each other's gaze, both steely-eyed. Then Gloria headed for the door and left, her ultimatum hanging heavily in the air.

# CHAPTER 21

*T*y had never before been with two women at the same time. Now, here he was at 16, standing in a room at the Holiday Inn eagerly anticipating his first ménage-a-trois.

"Lemme see ya'll kiss," he instructed, and he licked his lips with lust. The women, in the throes of Ecstasy (X), embraced and began a tongue dance which was visible at first, then disappeared within the recesses of their mouths.

Ty had met the two "ladies" at a club in Goldsboro, where he and Kev had relocated their operation. This time they were more careful so Guy wouldn't find out about it.

Pam had light skin and was thicker than government cheese. Her low rider jeans seemed to be bursting at the seams from her 41-inch ass. The dip in her jeans revealed she wore no panties underneath.

Kiki was a shade darker than Pam with a skin tone like a dark chestnut. Her short cropped hair reminded one of Toni Braxton. Her ass was plump and her titties were juicy and firm with nipples that stuck out like elevator buttons. What really caught Ty's attention were her grey cat-like eyes which were mesmerizing.

Kiki slid Pam's jeans off giving Ty a full view of that glorious big ass. As she palmed it and spread her cheeks wide, Pam had slid her hand inside Kiki's capris and was finger-fucking her already wet pussy.

"Oooh, Fu-uck", Kiki gasped and came with a shudder.

The X was putting all their senses on edge, making every sound, touch and smell a vastly sexual experience. The girls stripped each other down while Ty watched, smoking a blunt of Haze. He gripped the front of his jeans and felt his dick throbbing hard.

He finally couldn't resist joining in when the girls twisted into a "69" position. He placed the blunt on the table and dropped his pants to his knees. The sight of Pam's pretty ass and Kiki's lizard-like tongue parting the lips of Pam's pussy, darting in and out had Ty's dick swollen and throbbing.

He rammed his dick straight up inside Pam's pussy with such force, she screeched loudly and came so hard, she milked it all over Kiki's face. Kiki eagerly lapped away at it like a starving kitten. Ty punished Pam's pussy while sliding two fingers in her ass as she bucked and writhed with pleasure.

"Beat it, Daddy. Fuck this pussy hard," Pam begged and dug her nails hard into Kiki's thighs. She then lowered her head to feast on Kiki's juices.

Kiki licked Ty's balls while he was fucking Pam. The feeling had Ty in a zone so good, he doubted he would ever fuck just one girl at a time again. He was hooked!

"Come in my mouth, baby, please," Kiki moaned. "Fuck my mouth like it's a pussy!"

Ty felt the oncoming eruption and quickly complied, filling her throat and mouth with his thickness, thus making Kiki gag. As he fucked Kiki's mouth, Ty finger-fucked Pam's pussy and ass until she came from both at the same time. Before long, Ty erupted deep in Kiki's throat and didn't stop pumping until she had swallowed every last drop.

"Point five muthafuckas, who fadin' that?" Big JD gruffed while shaking the dice in his hand. He and four other dudes were crouched around a corner store on Nash Street. They called him Big JD because he was just that, Six-foot-five and 240 lbs of jailhouse muscle and grimy attitude. He was notorious in Wilson for being a stuck-up kid, hustler as well as an all-around troublemaker.

Kev and Dino pulled up in Kev's brand new money-green Acura NSX. It had been a graduation gift from Guy, even if Kev's graduation was still a month away.

"Yo, JD, what up, dawg?" Kev called out as he hopped out of the vehicle, quickly followed by Dino. JD looked over his shoulder when he heard his name, simply grunted and continued to roll the dice. Kev was sensing a bad vibe and walked up to the dice game.

"JD, what up?" Kev repeated the greeting.

"Ain't nothin", JD replied casually and released the dice. "Jump Judy! Uumph!." The dice rolled and stopped on two threes.

"Double up, nigga," said another dude whom Kev knew as Nate Rogers.

"Money on the wood, yo", JD replied, rolling again.

"Yo, J, I need to holla at you for a minute," Kev piped in.

"I'm busy. Holla at me later," JD grumbled.

Kev was starting to feel aggravated. JD owed him money for 2 lbs. of Purple Haze and 1,000 "X" pills and hadn't returned any of Kev's calls.

"Naw, J, I need to holla at you now," Kev said firmly.

Kev hadn't seen JD turn his back and go for his waist. When he turned back around, he held a snub-nosed .38 aimed at Kev's throat.

"Or, what?" JD growled with a menacing sneer. "Huh? Or what?"

Kev and Dino were caught off guard. JD had always been friendly up until he didn't return Kev's calls. He had always shown respect and bigging up Guy. He had even rocked Kev to sleep as a child.

"Damn, JD, is it like this?" Kev asked softly.

JD patted Kev down and the Dino. He laughed out loud when he realized neither carried a gun. JD lowered his weapon and called to his buddy, Nate.

"Yo, Nate, these stupid mothafuckas ain't even strapped." The crowd of gamblers laughed cruelly at the expense of Kev and Dino.

"You ain't getting' shit, pussy. Now get the fuck outta my face!" spat JD. Kev saw himself rustling JD. Fuck his size, fuck the gun, he told himself. He smiled inwardly and a new thought invaded his mind. Murder.

"You got that, J, word up, dawg. I don't want no problems wit you," Kev made himself sound scared.

JD puffed his chest out. "Nigga, you can't be a problem for me. Now get the fuck outta here 'fore I run your pockets!"

Kev dropped his head as he and Dino headed back to the car. As they got in, JD shouted, And tell your punk-ass daddy to suck my dick!!" He laughed and the others joined in.

Kev pulled off and JD returned to his game. "Bitch-ass nigga made me forget my point." Nate chucked. "You shoulda killed them niggas."

"Fuck them Goldsboro niggas." JD snorted.

Fifteen minutes later, JD learned the wisdom of Nate's statement. Kev and Dino tip-toed around to the back of the store armed with Tech Nine submachine guns. They each wore a ski mask and were thirsty for the respect they deserved.

Kev barked, "JD! Can I holla at you now?"

JD spun around and stared death right in the face. The gun-fire that followed made it seem as if World War III had begun right there on the corner in Wilson.

Kev had never caught a body before, but there was no hesi-tation in his trigger finger as he sprayed all five men down like a gardener hosing his lawn. When JD hit the ground, blood was spilling from his mouth and soaked his shirt. Kev stood over him, a sneer on his face.

"Please…please Kev," JD begged and coughed up a load of blood. "Don't…don't kill me."

*Kev smirked behind his mask, relishing the power held over JD at that moment.*

*"Now, nigga, suck MY dick," he spat and then emptied the clip in JD's face until it was nothing but a mangled piece of flesh, brains and blood.*

*Kev and Dino then disappeared as quietly as they had come.*

*"You kil--," Ty began saying too loudly, so he lowered his voice and leaned across the table over his steak and egg breakfast. "Get the fuck outta here," he said incredulously.*

*He and Kev were having their breakfast at the Waffle Shoppe the morning after the killings. Kev had told Ty everything that happened with JD. Ty downed his orange juice and said, "Damn, I hate that I missed that shit. Bro, how did that shit feel?"*

*Kev shrugged and continued eating his pancakes. He wanted to appear nonchalant as if it was no big deal.*

*"Man, it is what it is," he replied calmly. But Ty saw right through him and playfully threw a piece of scrambled egg at Kev.*

*"Nigga, quit frontin' like you cold blooded! You was probably scared as a muthafucka!"*

*Kev laughed.*

*"Yeah, but that shit felt good as a muthafucka, yo!"*

*Damn, and I thought fuckin' two bitches at a time was somethin'. Ty shook his head in wonder. "Damn, I wanna kill a muthafucka."*

*"Later for that, it's something else that—." At that moment the waitress arrived at their table.*

*"Good morning. Will there be anything else?"*

*Kev casually looked up and his eyes registered a pleasant surprise. "Karrin?"*

*"Hi Kevin,"* she replied cheerfully. Kevin had arrived soon after Ty and had not seen the waitress.

*"I-I didn't know you worked here,"* Kev stammered.

*"Part-time",* she replied with a smile.

*"Then I'ma start coming full-time",* Ty winked.

Kev shot him a disapproving look, but Ty didn't catch it. He had already been flirting with Karrin since he arrived. She was GORGEOUS! She had an Egyptian-bronze skin tone and pouty lips. She reminded Ty of Megan Goode. Her hour-glass figure looked like a Coca-Cola bottle despite the loose-fitting waitressing uniform.

Karrin smiled again and rolled her eyes.

*"Anyway, good to see you, Kev."*

*"You, too,"* he replied.

Ty couldn't help but stare at the sway of her hips as she walked away.

*"You know her, Kev? I know you smashin' that!"* he said with a knowing wink.

*"Now, yo, shortie ain't like that. She's good peeps. I used to holla at her cousin,"* Kev explained.

*"Then hook a nigga up. I'm tryin' to see them juicy lips wrapped around my –"*

Kev cut him off more aggressively than he meant.

*" I SAID she ain't like that. She a church girl, Ty."*

*"Shit, that's where all the freaks are,"* Ty chuckled. He suddenly got up and went across the room towards Karrin, who was in the midst of taking down another table's orders. When she turned around, she was startled at Ty's presence in her face.

*"Excuse you,"* she said with a sassy giggle.

*"Next year, this time, it'll be our first anniversary. How we gonna celebrate it?"* Ty asked with a sexy dimpled smile.

*"TyQuan, please",* she replied and rolled her eyes. She went around him to the counter. Ty followed suit, right behind her.

*"Oh, so you know my name."*

*"Who don't know you, boy. Wit' your ho-ish self."* Karrin remarked and went inside the kitchen door. Ty followed her into the kitchen,

*"Boy! What are you doin'?,* she asked looking around in panic.

The cook looked up with curious eyes.

*"First of all, I ain't a ho...unless the female acts like one. It's clear to me I'm in the presence of a beautiful young woman worthy of my respect. Second, I ain't a boy, I'm a man, the man for you,"* Ty said seriously.

*"Ahem, excuse me, sir. You're not supposed to be in here, "* the cook said nervously. Ty promptly ignored him.

*"Now, I already checked with Miss Cleo and she said I'd meet the woman of my dreams today, so don't fight destiny,"* Ty winked.

Karrin giggled. Indeed she knew what kind of person Ty was. She dug his style and heard that his dick game was crazy. Still, she didn't want to be just another notch under his belt.

*"How do you know she was talkin' about me?"* she asked flirtatiously.

*"Well, if you give me your number, we can find out."*

The cook interrupted the tête-à-tête.

*"Sir! You must leave now! Ms. Templeton, tell your friend here that if he doesn't leave—"*

*"555-7310",* she told Ty quickly. *"Now go, before you go to jail, boy."*

Ty winked and then stepped in smoothly to kiss her cheek. *"Happy Anniversary."* He left.

Dino drove Kev's NSX, while Kev rode with Ty. He wanted to question Ty about what happened with Karrin, but had more pressing issues on his mind.

*"Nate Rogers was there,"* Kev said.

Ty stared at him intently.

"At the dice game?"

Kev nodded.

"Did you…?"

Kev's silence confirmed Ty's suspicions.

"Shit", mumbled Ty.

They knew the severity of the situation. Nate Rogers was a nephew of BayBay Rogers, a heroin kingpin based in Wilson. He was also one of the last of Guy's major rivals. Although Rogers' organization was not as widespread as the Simmons', BayBay wasn't a man to trifle with, even if he was currently locked up in the Federal Penitentiary.

Ty and Kev knew killing Nate would be seen as a total act of disrespect. Everyone knew Guy had been itching to get BayBay out of the way, so this murder would seem like the first step on the road to war.

"We gotta tell Pops", Ty suggested and Kev nodded his head in agreement.

"He gonna know we ain't wait 'til graduation like he told us", warned Kev.

"It is what it is at this point, Big Bro."

The two rode in silence for awhile and then Kev had to ask.

"What happened wit' Karrin?"

"What you think?" Ty quipped with pride. "Bitches can't resist Baby Brah, yo. I thought you knew."

Kev inwardly cringed at Ty's calling Karrin a bitch.

"Don't play shawty like that," Kev replied, trying his best to sound casual. "All the chicks you got to fuck with, what you need another one for?"

"Next day, next pussy, Kev", Ty chuckled, then looked seriously at Kev.

"What up, bro? You ain't feeling shawty, are you?"

"Naw", Kev lied.

"You sure? 'Cause if you are, I'll fall—"

"Naw, dawg. I just know her family. They the type that like to settle down, one on one. And I know you, lil brah, you's a heartbreaker." Kev tried to play it off.

Indeed, Ty was just as Kev described, while Kev was the exact opposite. His desire to be true to a woman came from the pain he saw his mother go through due to Guy's womanizing ways. Kev promised himself he would never be like Guy in that aspect.

As for Ty, he was exactly like Guy. His mother was a kept woman, so Ty saw nothing wrong with playing the field, as long as you took care of the responsibilities that go with it. Women were his play things and he planned on making Karrin one of them.

Dino waited outside while Kev and Ty entered Gloria's house. As soon as they walked in the door, they heard Gloria and Guy screaming at each other.

"Did you do it?? Answer me, Guy!"

"Glo, what the hell is wrong wit' you?! What the fuck are you talking about??"

"Nigga, you know goddamn well what I'm talking about! Did you fuck her, Guy? Did you fuck my sister??!"

Ty and Kev were frozen in the living room. They both had heard their mamas argue with Guy before, but not like this, with all this intensity.

"Go ahead, now Glo. I ain't got time for yo bullshit!"

"Did you???"

"Yes, godammit, yes! You happy now? You heard what you wanted to hear?"

"You triflin' son of a bitch!"

"Glo, get the fuck off me."

As they heard the fight become physical, Ty and Kev ran up the stairs. They found Guy and Gloria in their bedroom, Gloria was tussling with Guy. Suddenly Guy back handed her to the floor.

"Pop!!" Kev shouted angrily and headed towards Guy.

"Stay outta grown folks' business, boy", Guy growled.

Kev then redirected his attention to his mother, who was rising unsteadily from the floor.

"You ain't have to fuckin' hit her!", he screamed.

Guy just sat and glared at Kev.

"Don't get involved, baby. I'm OK", Gloria said, now standing with her mascara streaking all over her face mixed in with her tears.

"I always got back-up, baby. Gloria Bell always comes out on top. Then she looked at Guy and hissed, "I done took all I'ma take from you, nigga. You…you killed my brother!"

Confused, Kev and Ty looked at each other.

"Oh, you didn't know, Kev? You didn't know your triflin' ass daddy killed my brother Eddie after Eddie took his raggedy ass out the goddamn gutter?" Gloria was yelling now.

"Aw-right Gloria, that's enough." Guy had his fists balled up. He hated to be reminded of the love Eddie had shown him and of the treachery he was repaid for it.

"No, nigga, I had enough! You fucked my sister, Guy! What else can you do to me??" she cried. Kev attempted to embrace his mother, but she pulled away, angrily wiping her tears with shaking hands. Then she straightened and announced, "I want you out of my house!"

"Your house?" Guy sneered.

"That's right, nigga. MY house, where I raised your son! Or are you gonna take this from me, too? Go stay with your goddamn whore, Debra!"

Ty bristled at the remark. He didn't appreciate Gloria calling his mother a whore. He gritted his teeth and let it go.

Guy took a deep breath and went towards the door. Gloria watched him with slitted eyes, staring holes into his back.

"This marriage is over", she whispered.

Guy swung towards her and replied, "Bitch, it been over." Then he left the room with Ty right behind him.

The little bit of strength Gloria mustered had deflated like a punctured balloon and she sunk to the bed in tears. Kev sat next to her trying to comfort her the best he could.

"It's gonna be okay, Mama. I'm here…I'm here." He rocked her gently in his arms.

"I know, baby, I know. I just …I need to be alone right now, okay? I love you, baby, but right now…." Her voice trailed off and she began to sob inconsolably.

Kev hated to leave his mother like that, but honored her request. He kissed her softly on her cheek before leaving. When he got downstairs he saw Guy by the wet bar and Ty sitting on the couch. Kev and Guy's eyes met. Never before had Kev felt such rage towards his father, and Guy could sense it.

"You got somethin' to say to me, boy?" Guy growled. He downed his drink and set the glass down with purpose.

Kev stood less than three feet from Guy. As enraged as he was, he still loved and feared his father.

"You dead wrong, Pop. Mama been good to you all these years." Kev shook his head in disgust. "You dead wrong."

"I been dead wrong before", Guy shrugged. But he saw the pain in his eyes and he softened a bit. He placed his hands on Kev's shoulders.

"Don't worry. Your mama divorces me at least once a year," he chuckled, trying to lighten the mood. Kev's expression didn't change.

"Now…what's this major problem Ty was telling me about?"

Kev took a deep breath and blurted out the whole story. Guy was stunned and just shook his head in disbelief.

"I TOLD you, wait until graduation!" he thundered. "Did anyone see you?"

Kev shook his head. "I don't know….but Pop, that ain't it. One of them nigga's name was Rogers. I…I killed BayBay's nephew."

From the look on Guy's face, Kev knew he had fucked up.

# CHAPTER 22

Debra turned her black Mercedes CLK into Ty's condominium parking lot. After hearing what transpired between Gloria and Guy, she immediately called Ty and told him she was on her way. Her grey ostrich sling-backs click-clacked on the concrete with a purpose. Before she could ring the doorbell, Ty swung the door wide open.

"What's up, Ma?" he asked and then kissed her on her cheek.

She whizzed into the living room and when he closed the front door, demanded, "How the hell you let Vee walk out alive?"

"Let him?" Ty echoed. "I didn't let him do nothin'! Pop let him! I tried to murder that nigga, but Pop stopped me."

Debra ran her manicured nails through her auburn highlights. She always kept the grey out of her hair, she didn't want to look old.

"Why?? Didn't you hammer into his head that Kev said he had tried to kill Guy?"

"Ma, I saw that nigga kill Kev wit' my own eyes! I told—"

"I'm not interested in Kev, TyQuan." She sighed in exasperation. "Did Guy believe you when you told him what Kev said?"

Ty shrugged and sat down.

"I don't know. He was so fucked up over Vee being his fuckin' son, he probably shut everything else out. Like Kev wasn't his son, like I wasn't..." Ty shook his head in frustration.

Debra sat next to her son and grabbed his hand.

"Don't even think about it, Ty. You're just as much Guy's son as Kev was."

"Yeah, but you said yourself he would've never let me take over the family business." Ty reminded her with bitterness.

Debra gently turned Ty's face to hers.

"But you are, baby. Kev's gone. So now Guy has no choice. But Ty, he has to believe that it was Vee that tried to kill him. Let Vee wear it and our problem will be solved."

*Our problem?* Ty thought. But after thinking about it, he realized that in helping Debra with the cover-up, he was just as guilty.

Ty nodded. "I got you, Ma. I'll do my best."

"No, Ty." She looked at him in the eyes. "Do it. Don't worry, baby, I'll be working him from my angle. And you know, Mama don't miss." She winked.

Ty chuckled.

"Yeah, you good. I'll give you that. But we still don't know where the girl is that was wit' Pop."

Debra smiled wickedly. "I lied."

"Huh?"

"I had to, baby. At the time, I didn't expect Kev to get killed. But I had planned on removing him, too."

Ty couldn't believe how triflin' his mother was. But he was power hungry, and was able to accept it. "What will you do next, Ma?"

"No, baby. What *won't* I do." I've been Guy's second wife for too long, in spite of the fact I wear his last name. And you've been his second son. I ain't put up with all his bullshit to come in second, Ty. Period."

"So what did you lie about? You know where she is?"

"You think I'd leave a detail like that to Brah Hardy? Of course I know where she is...and so do you."

"Hello, Victor, How are you?" Mrs. Richards warmly greeted Vee with a hug at the front door of her home. "Phillip, Victor's here!" she called out. Cat's father, came downstairs and shook Vee's hand firmly.

"How you doin', son? How've you been?"

I'm good, Mr. Phillip. Thanks for asking." Vee replied.

Mrs. Richards' eyes searched Vee's face and framed it with her hands. "You don't look so good, Victor. You haven't slept, have you?"

Vee lowered his gaze.

"Baby, Kionna will be back. The Lord will see to it," she said soothingly.

"Yeah," mumbled Vee with little faith, especially since now he knew his fate.

Mrs. Richards kindly took him by the hand.

"Come on in, baby. We were about to have dinner."

Vee ate heartily, it had been awhile since he'd eaten a home-cooked meal. The family atmosphere warmed him, like a man who'd been out in the cold for a very long time. After dinner, Mr. Richards took Vee out to the back porch to talk. He handed Vee a beer, then popped his open.

"'Preciate that, Mr. Richards," Vee said while popping his open. He took a long swig.

"No problem, son. So…how did you like dinner?"

"It was good," replied Vee. He could tell Mr. Richards had something on his mind.

"Vic, I just wanted you to know that we don't blame you for what happened to Kionna."

Vee nodded solemnly.

"And I definitely don't want you to blame yourself. Kionna loves you with all her heart…I know," Mr. Richards chuckled. "Because you remember how things used to be between us."

Vee smiled and replied, "No doubt."

Mr. Richards continued. "But when my baby girl stood up to me and said, 'Daddy, I love Vee and I don't care what you say or do, we gonna be together." He shook his head. "My baby Kionna always been a feisty one. Wherever she is, I believe she's okay."

"I don't know, Mr. Richards. I just feel like I should've been there. She wanted me to stay, but..." Vee's voice trailed off. If ever there was a moment in his life, he wished he could turn back the hands of time from when he left Cat and Taheem in Baltimore.

"When doesn't a woman want her man to stay home? But what's done is done, Vee, and I don't need you to beat yourself up. I need you to find my baby girl." Mr. Richard's eyes misted over.

"I fully intend to." Vee looked the man in the eyes.

Mrs. Richards walked in at that moment carrying the cordless phone.

"Excuse me, gentlemen. Victor, Karrin's on the line, she wants to speak with you." She handed Vee the phone.

"How you doin' Karrin?"

"Hey, Vee, How are you?"

"I'm making it. You?"

"Same here. I'm worried sick about Kionna, and Vee, I'm so sorry about Taheem," Karrin said with tears in her voice.

When he heard his son's name, Vee felt as if a cold, invisible hand had gripped his heart.

"Thanks," he mumbled into the phone.

"I was just calling Aunt Marie and she said you were over there. I just wanted to say hi and let you know that if there's anything I could do...let me know. You got my number?" When he said no, she gave it to him and Vee locked it into his cell phone while he gave her his.

"I just wanted you to know," Karrin added softly, "I don't hold anything against you, you know?"

Vee indeed did know. She was talking about the fact he had killed Kev.

"Aw-ight, ma, hold your head."

"You do the same. And Vee…you're in my prayers." Vee hung up.

Vee pushed the Bentley up Route 85 North, listening to Cat's favorite CD, Mary J.'s "My Life",

*How can I love somebody else*
*When I can't love myself enough to know*
*When it's time to let go…*

It was the same song that was playing when they first met. He played the same song three times in a row, savoring the bittersweet memories. Wherever Cat was, he was determined to find her. He only hoped she wouldn't reject him, too.

Vee picked up his cell phone and scrolled to Tre's number. He picked up in the middle of his Daddy Yankee's "Carolina" ringtone.

"What up, Jay? What's good?"

"Ain't nothin' my nigga, how're you?" Vee answered.

"You know me, fam, tryin' to touch this paper."

"I feel you. Yo, I'm 'bout to swing through, like tomorrow night. That cool?"

"Come on, Jay, you ain't even gotta ask. Just text me when you get here, aw-ight?"

"No doubt."

"Be safe, my nigga."

"Done."

Tre hung up as he approached the stop light. When it turned green, he started to pull off, but a scraggly dressed female staggered by, making him slam on brakes. "Stupid bitch!" He cursed loudly. The woman glanced in his direction. Recognition flashed briefly through Tre's mind, but he couldn't place the face. He watched the woman disappear around the corner. It was obvious that she was on drugs, so Tre shrugged it off like, "Probably served her back in the day". He didn't give it another thought. If he had, he would've recognized her as the girl Vee had with him.

It was Cat.

After leaving the hospital, she had wandered Baltimore in a daze. Lost, cold and alone she ended up in a soup line and fell into a conversation with a conning dopefiend name Lisa. Cat didn't want to go home. To her, the reality of her past was too painful. So she couldn't go back. She allowed Lisa to take her in, reel her in and eventually turned her on to her pimp, Jerome. Cat was still beautiful, and Jerome saw a goldmine. He worked on her mind while Lisa worked on her veins. It has been said about Heroin, once is too much and a thousand times is never enough......Cat was chasing her thousandth. Insatiable, hopeless, loss and turned out, just another slave of King Heroin.

Gloria hated to fly. She was one of those that believed if God wanted humans to fly, he'd had given them wings. However, she hated long bus and train rides even more.

Gloria looked out of the plane window at the New York City skyline below her. The way the sun was shining on the city made her think the buildings looked like they were studded with diamonds. Although she had lived down south for over twenty years, Gloria was a Harlem girl all the way.

Although she was happy to be back in NYC, she was unhappy at the circumstances. Gloria had given Guy seven days, seven whole days, without a word from him. He hadn't even called to check on her, or even take her out or to scratch that itch only he could reach. Reluctantly, she decided her only recourse was Tito and the Bell family. She knew Guy would be furious at the fact she had stepped outside of his boundaries in order to take care of the pending problem. However, she was dead serious when she had told Guy "If you don't do anything about it...then I will."

The intercom on the plane began to splutter. "This is your captain speaking. I hope you had a pleasant flight, and welcome to New York. Thank you for flying Delta."

Gloria fought her way through the throngs of people at JFK Airport. All the airports in New York were like international bazaars, with people of every culture imaginable. It seemed like people were laughing, crying, saying their goodbyes in every language on earth.

"There she go! Aunt Glo! Aunt Glo, over here!" Gloria heard her niece Brooklyn call out amongst the crowd.

Gloria searched for her and finally saw her standing with Asia and their mother Theresa, who was Gloria's sister-in-law. She waved excitedly and quickened her steps towards them.

"Hey, ladies!" exclaimed Gloria before being engulfed in a four-way hug. Then Gloria hugged each individually.

"Girl, look at you, looking too good! Hey, is that--?" Theresa questioned with admiration at Gloria's outfit.

"Oh, girl, this is so last year's..." Gloria preened and swirled around so they could get a better look. "Do I have to teach you people everything when it comes to fashion? Don't worry, the best-dressed bitch is back to guide you."

Theresa cracked up and struck a pose of her own.

"Girl, please, she never left."

Both shared a girlish giggle as Asia and Brooklyn looked on patiently.

"It don't matter what you wear, ain't nobody checkin' for you old hags," Asia deadpanned.

"Old hags??" Gloria echoed and stood with her arms at her waist. "You must ain't ever heard of the term cougar, have you? Little girl, I'll take yo man!"

"O-kayyy!" chimed Theresa, laughing hard.

"Ma, you might need my man, then maybe you won't be so bitchy." Asia laughed.

The foursome left the airport in a Benz limo, heading straight for Madison Avenue. While they balled out on black cards, they caught up on each other's lives, and then they had lunch at Tavern on the Green.

"Mmmm….Lord knows I shouldn't be eatin' these", Theresa moaned. She took a bite out of the chocolate covered cherry she held daintily between her forefinger and thumb. She then followed with a sip of Dom Perignon. "But girl, chocolate and champagne? I mean the real champagne, none of that American bullshit. This shit's got me in heaven."

She offered a cherry to Gloria, who politely declined.

"Oh, and did I tell you about this one?", Theresa asked. Brooklyn sucked in her teeth and thought, *here we go.*

"Oh? And what she done now?"

"Ain't what she done, it's who she's doin'!"

"Who?" asked Gloria, her curiosity piqued.

"A rapper!" Theresa spat out in disgust. "Guess who his daddy is? Melvin Coombs!"

Gloria scrunched up her face, trying to remember the name.
"Melvin Coombs?"

You remember, fine ass Melvin. Used to hang out at the Gold Lounge. Used to be up all over you when he ever saw you."

The light of recognition lit up in Gloria's eyes and she laughed.

"Oh, yeah, the one Guy was about to whup at The Hubba that night. I remember."

"Let me find out you had three niggas out here fighting over you, Aunt Glo," Asia quipped.

"Mmm-mmm, that's her 'lil boyfriend," Theresa added.

"He ain't no rapper, Mother. He owns the label and I told you, he ain't my boyfriend. He just somethin' to do," Brooklyn mumbled and stared out the window.

Gloria clucked her teeth. "Listen to you, 'somethin' to do." I know you don't mean what I think you mean."

Theresa jumped in. "I'm tellin' you, Glo, this generation…I don't know what the hell happened. They don't believe in nothin', ain't got no fight in 'em, unless it's against each other. You'll see. Harlem done become Blood Central. All these kids runnin' around here like they crazy." Theresa shook her head in disgust. "And the white folks? They takin' over Harlem, callin' it SoHar."

"So-what?"

"SoHar, as in South Harlem. You know ain't nobody but a cracka thought of that name. Harlem ain't nothin' like when we ran it, Glo. When we walked them streets knowin' our shit ain't stink, runnin' up in The Hubba and the Gold Lounge."

"Oh and don't forget the Tiger Lounge," Gloria interrupted, laughing.

Oh yeah, what was that spot on the corner of 155th and Macombs Pl?"

They both thought for a minute and simultaneously said, "The Flash Inn!" They leaned on each other, laughing. Then Theresa put her arm over Gloria's shoulder.

"I missed you, big sis that I never had," she winked. "I'm glad you're home."

Theresa could sense Gloria's sadness under her smile and was doing her best to comfort Gloria and make her feel welcome.

"Yeah," Gloria began. I just needed to get away, you know? Had to get outta that house."

Theresa nodded sympathetically.

"I really wanted to see Tito while I was up here. Is he still around?"

"Naw, Auntie, Tito in Philly," answered Asia.

"Well, shit, call him! Tell him to get his ass up here and kiss his Aunt Glo!"

Although Gloria was laughing, Asia could sense an urgency in her aunt's voice and understood why. She knew the situation regarding Kev. So, she pulled out her cell and dialed Tito up.

"What up, A?" Tito answered, in a voice that implied he was busy.

"Aunt Glo just came up here and said she wants to see you."

"Aw-ight, tell her I'll be home in a few days."

"You sure?" Tito could detect the insinuation in Asia's voice. Tito thought for a minute. He wanted the deal with the Simmons to go down ASAP, especially considering why he was in Philly.

"Well, check, baby," he told Asia. "I can't leave right now. Just bring her up here tomorrow."

Gloria couldn't hear Tito but she sure heard Asia's scream of delight.

"A new fur?? For real??"

"Who getting' a new fur?" Brooklyn suddenly grabbed the phone from Asia and yelled, "Get me one, too!"

Tito smiled and shook his head, bemused at the extortion by his little sisters..

"You some bullshit," he replied.

"See you tomorrow...", Asia sang out, then clicked off. She turned to Gloria and said, "He wants us to take you up there tomorrow."

Gloria cackled when she realized what Asia was up to. "You too much, girl."

The next day, Tito and his Philly lieutenant Nazir, met Asia, Brooklyn and Gloria in Atlantic City. It was just too hot in Philly at the moment. One of his stronger teams had been raided and arrested. Tito smelled a rat in his operation. The same thing had happened in Connecticut to another branch of his organization the previous month. It seemed like his whole operation was beginning to show some major cracks. *When it rains, it pours,* he thought to himself.

They met at Asiya's, a Muslim restaurant owned by Nazir and named after his wife. Atlantic City was a stronghold for a syndicate called The Black Reign, which was under the Bell's umbrella, but operated as a separate entity.

The restaurant was closed for renovations, so it was completely empty when they arrived. After they all met and gave the obligatory hugs, Nazir commented, "Word, Asia, you get more beautiful every time I see you."

"No, Nazir, I'm Brooklyn, that's Asia," Asia lied playfully. Nazir looked puzzled, then laughed.

"Naw, sweetness, believe me, I can tell ya'll apart."

Brooklyn threw her hands up in a fighting stance.

"Oh, so what you tryin' to say 'bout me? I'm the ugly one or somethin'?" Everyone laughed. Tito turned to Nazir. "Yeah, word, I'm glad you came. Please take them over to your furriers and get 'em outta my hair." Nazir, Asia and Brooklyn left, with Nazir still blatantly flirting with Asia.

Tito took down a couple of chairs that were stacked on one of the tables and offered one to Gloria. "How are you, Aunt Glo? You look good," he said warmly.

"So do you, Tito. Every time I see you, you get more and more like Eddie," she beamed at him. Tito humbly took the compliment. Eddie had been killed when Tito was too young and didn't have much recollection of him. He had seen a bunch of photographs of Eddie, though.

Tito saw Gloria struggling with her thoughts and he reached across the table to take her hand. "What's wrong, Auntie? You know I'm here for you."

The tenderness of his voice and the warmth of his touch were too much for Gloria to bear. Her eyes became clouded with tears.

"I...I don't know what to do, Tito," she sobbed.

Tito handed her the napkin dispenser that was sitting on the table.

"Don't cry. Just tell me what's going on and let me help you."

Gloria dabbed at her eyes and sniffed loudly.

"I'm sorry, baby. Things have been crazy since Kev passed." She paused and Tito waited for her to continue.

"Ty knows who killed Kev. He was there when it happened." Tito nodded. He already knew, because Asia and Brooklyn had been there, too. Gloria took in a deep breath.

"Ty...Ty had a chance to kill the boy, but Guy stopped him and told him no."

"No" Tito echoed in shock. "Why?"

"I don't know," Gloria lied straight-faced. She was too embarrassed to tell Tito that Vee was Guy's son.

"Did you ask?" Tito was incredulous and leaned in towards her.

"Yes, but Guy just told me to mind my own business, as if Kev ain't my business!" She was getting angry all over again.

Tito was deep in thought. *Why would Guy give the man who killed his son a pass? Was he getting soft? Tired?* Tito needed to know, it may be something he could use to his advantage.

"I can't believe Uncle Guy would do that!" Then he looked at Gloria. "Do you know who the guy is?"

Gloria smiled inwardly. "He ain't hard to find."

Tito sighed. "Aw-ight...let me speak to Uncle Guy, then—"

Gloria interrupted. "For what? I just told you Guy let him go, just let him walk away
   scot-free!"

"I know. But Aunt Glo...if he wouldn't tell you, maybe he'll tell me," Tito reasoned.

"And when he tells you the same thing, then what?"

"What can *I* do?" Tito asked, exasperated now.

Gloria leaned into the center of the table and gritted, "You can find the son of a bitch that killed my son, Tito. Then you kill his ass!"

Tito leaned back in his chair, clearly upset.

"Auntie...please, don't ever say my name and the word 'kill' in the same sentence, again, okay? I know you're upset, but you can't talk out loud like that."

"Kev was your cousin, Tito," she reminded him.

"I know...and believe me, I would like to see his memory done justice. But-"

"Do you, Tito? Do you really? Or is it you just don't want to make waves with Guy so's you can salvage that precious little deal with him?"

Tito looked away.

"Oh, you think I didn't know what Aruba was about? You think I don't know what you want? Tito, I been around this game before you were even thought of, okay? Yo mama was still skipping rope, okay? I know how this game is played. I always believed family was more important to you than money." Gloria sat back against her chair.

It was true Tito didn't want to do anything to mess up his deal with Guy, but he also knew there was more to the story than what Gloria was telling him. If anything, he would gun down a whole church congregation with their hands folded in prayer to get what he wanted. But he would never do it half-cocked.

"Come on, Auntie, that's some deep shit to say, you know me better than that."

"Well, maybe you just scared of Big Bad Guy Simmons," she taunted.

Tito stood up slowly.

"As far as I'm concerned, this conversation is over. You want something to drink?" he offered.

"Nigga, ain't shit over! My son is layin' in the goddamn ground and you his blood and won't do shit?"

Now it was Tito's turn to get pissed.

"It's the nature of the goddamn game!" he shouted. "we ain't crossin' guards, and the lead we speak through ain't pencils! Kev knew that, Auntie! It comes with the territory. You want somethin' done, then go see your ex-husband!"

"So…it's okay my son is dead, huh? He knew, right? Well, SO DID EDDIE! He knew, too. Guy killed your goddamn father! Now what? You still wanna talk to him??"

Gloria regretted that tirade as soon as she said it, but there was no turning back now. The look in Tito's eyes confirmed it.

"He did WHAT?" he boomed and closed the distance between them. Instinctively Gloria backed away from his anger. She had never seen that side of him before.

"Say it again!" Tito demanded.

"Tito, I'm sorry! I didn't know-", she cried.

"You knew! You-" he couldn't finish the sentence.

Gloria braced herself for the blows he was about to unleash upon her. Instead, he turned around and walked to the back of the restaurant.

# CHAPTER 23

Standing up, Ty looked at his mother and thought, *what the fuck?* "Ma, are you fuckin' crazy? Karrin ain't cut out for no shit like this!" He began pacing the floor. Debra sat back on the couch and crossed her legs while smoothing out her dress. She allowed Ty to vent because she knew it was a lot for him to take in.

*"Karrin??"* he said more to himself.

"Baby, you'd be surprised what a woman in love is capable of." Debra replied checking out her manicured nails.

"Ma, this shit…this shit is crazy! Why you ain't tell me before? Why'd you believe we had to find a bitch that didn't exist?"

"Because, I didn't want you acting off on emotion and doing something we'd both regret."

"What? Like killin' her??"

Debra nodded, then stood up and went to him with her arms spread wide open.

" A lot of things happened that weren't supposed to happen, like you finding me with Brah, and you killing him. Guy living and Kev getting killed…no plan is fool-proof."

"But you said you planned on removing Kev, Vee just beat you to it."

Debra walked over to the bar and began pouring them both a glass of Remy Martin.

"That worked in our favor. It just wasn't as clean as I would've liked," she replied and handed Ty his drink. I just don't throw things together and pray for rain, Ty. Believe me, I've been working on this for awhile now. I used the two people I knew would do anything for you and me. Brah, in my case, Karrin in yours." Debra sipped her drink.

"But how…how could Pop not know it was Karrin?" Ty asked, confused.

"Because women are chameleons, TyQuan. We can be one person one day, and another totally different one the next."

She giggled. "Didn't Karrin look a little darker when you saw her after the shooting?"

Ty remembered thinking that very same thing when he saw her at the hospital.

Debra continued.

"She tans well. The rest was the magic of makeup, colored contacts and a wig. At first she wasn't having it. Like you said, she isn't cut out like that. But once I explained how with Guy and Kev out the way, nothing would stand in your way, and nobody would object to you two being together. I played on her love for you and yours for her, too. But, I made her think that you would've never acted on your love because of your loyalty to Kev and your love for your father."

"That's true." Ty interjected.

Debra smiled.

"The best game is always a half truth. After she was on board, it took nothing to get her to set Guy up for Brah, then set Kev up the next day and then-"

Ty cut her off.

"Kill her." He was beginning to learn how his mother thought. "And then kill her, right, Ma? Then you probably gonna make a way for me to find out- maybe even tell me yourself. You'd do it cryin' and tellin' me how Brah had used you to get to get back at Pop, knowin' that I woulda blew his brains out, closing the door on the truth forever. Ty shook his head both in admiration and a slight feeling of disgust. "God-damn, you good."

"Somethin' like that," she answered, although Ty had it right on.

"So I'm just another pawn, huh, Ma?"

"A pawn to be made king. Sometimes we have to do for the ones we love, when they won't do for themselves. I bet you don't remember how I used to get you to eat your vegetables." She giggled, lost in the memory. "I used to cut up the carrots and and broccoli in tiny orange and green chunks, then bake them inside a pound cake. You used to love pound cake." Ty chuckled. "I still do."

"But you sure hated them vegetables."

"I still do." They both laughed.

"I used to call it 'Candy Cake' and you always begged for more. Bein' on top gonna taste good to you too. Just goes to show, the end always justifies the means," Debra was serious now.

Ty downed his drink while thinking on Debra's words. He knew he belonged at the top and it felt damn good. It was where he belonged. He remembered the words he and Kev had said to Guy when they was little. *We wanna be bosses, too!* Ty had proven who the real boss was.

"What about Karrin?" he inquired.

Debra picked up her purse and car keys from the coffee table and stood up.

"Karrin loves you, TyQùan. There's nothing she wouldn't do for you and she's already proved it without you even know-ing. Sacrifice without acknowledgment is the true sacrifice. You need a woman like that on your side, baby."

"Yeah…I know…but I told Pops-"

"Never mind about Guy. Like I said, I'll take care of him. He knew you two were together before Kev did. Regardless, Ty. It's up to you. If you gonna be with her, fine. But if not, she's gonna feel played and scorned. So, either keep her close or…kill her."

Debra then coolly walked out.

"Bishop Langston! How good to see you again." Detective Atkins shook Skatter's hand enthusiastically. Skatter smiled to himself. They were standing in front of Mt. Zion A.M.E., the largest black church in Goldsboro. Beneath the bishop's designer suit lay the heart of a stone cold killer. Because of his prior criminal records, Guy wasn't able to get Skatter membership to the Masonic Lodge where he was a member. Instead, he helped him establish a legitimate business up front by getting him elected as Bishop at Guy's church. Everyone liked Bishop Langston, politicians, businessmen and policemen.

However, he was still Guy's chief bodyguard and all-round right-hand man. When Guy called, Skatter would put down his bible, loosen his tie and do what he did best- deprive muthafuckas of their lives.

"Good to see you, too Brother Atkins." Skatter knew Atkins was the lead investigator in one of the numerous murders Skatter was responsible for. He also knew they would never be solved.

Detective Atkins and his wife turned away and Skatter went inside the church. He saw Guy coming up the aisle helping his mother with Gloria next to him. Willie was on the other side of Gloria. Skatter smiled at the family scene which quickly faded when he glimpsed two masked men entering the church from the rear. Looking over Guy's shoulder he noticed another entering the front door of the church. All were armed with sub-machine guns.

"Skatter!"

"Guy!"

The warnings were followed by each pulling out their Heckler 9mm from their waists. Guy then roughly shoved his mother and Gloria between the pews and let off three shots at the man in the front of the church. The shots lifted the masked man off his feet, and was dead before he hit the ground. In the meantime, Skatter squeezed off his two shots at one of the men in the rear, spinning him around like a toy top, riddling his back with bullets and severing his spinal cord.

The church was in full pandemonium. People ran in all directions, praying, screaming, hiding in the pews. One man fell screaming after a bullet meant for Guy hit him in the back. Then, Guy saw what he would never forget. The death of his friend Skatter as a barrage of bullets riddled his body.

"Skatter!" Guy yelled as his and Skatter's eyes met. Skatter slowly sank down to the floor. Guy ducked behind a pew as bullets tore off chunks wood from the pew, scattering wood chips all over Guy's head. His instincts from his stint in Vietnam suddenly kicked in and all of a sudden he became calm. He coolly looked at the gunmen and noticed they were amateurs by the way they were holding their guns. BayBay had sent boys to do a man's job.

He waited until they let off a burst of gunfire, then he stood up and aimed with deadly precision.

BOOM! BOOM!

The two messengers of death made their marks. One hit the gunman in the left eye and one blew into the back of his head, the only thing holding his brains was the ski mask.

He dropped. The other, realizing his gun was empty, and seeing he was fucking with a pro, took off for the back door. They had thought catching Guy at church was the perfect plan, thinking he wouldn't be armed. They didn't plan on facing the type of gangsta that even took his gun to the bathroom with him. Guy was right behind gunman, leaping over Skatter's body and out the door. He leaped down the short flight of steps leading to the exit and into the parking lot. Just as the dude was opening the door, Guy slammed it shut, put the gun to dude's head and BOOM!...BOOM! BOOM! BOOM!

The first shot killed the guy, the last three were for Skatter. Guy opened the back door and scanned the parking lot. He knew the hit squad probably had a driver nearby, and he was right. He saw the late model mini van sitting with the engine running. He couldn't see the driver's face, but once he did, he ran up to the van and put the gun in the driver's face. It was a woman, her eyes wide with surprise.

"I-I-I was just the driver!!"

BOOM!! BOOM!! CLICK!

He pumped the last two in her face. The impact threw her back so hard, she bounced and laid with her head against the horn, causing it to blow loudly like death knell. When Guy came back in the church, he checked on his family, then kneeled beside Skatter's body. Skatter gazed at the ceiling like his eyes were watching God. Guy gently closed them.

"I love you nigga, rest in peace", Guy whispered with a heavy heart.

As he stood up, Detective Atkins approached.

"You okay?" he asked Guy.

Guy nodded, still looking at Skatter.

"Listen....whatever just happened.... these guys brought it on themselves. I never saw you with a gun."

Guy looked at Atkins. Atkins extended his hand and shook Guy's in the Masonic style called the Lion's Paw. Guy knew the case would disappear, but his mind was on something else...

Kev and Ty.

Guy knew exactly where to find Ty and Kev on a Sunday afternoon at H.B Brown Park. It was a hangout spot for the hustlers that came to play basketball, show off their cars and profile for females.

Guy pulled up in his black Cadillac Sixteen, a two hundred thousand dollar car, one of only eight in existence, and got out. The sounds of DMX's "Get at Me Dog" blew loudly from someone's trunk. A few people spoke to him as he passed, but he returned no greetings, reciprocated no smiles. He walked straight onto the basketball court where Ty and Kev were playing with some other hustlers, five on five.

Everybody on the court saw Guy coming accept for Ty and Kev. Kev was checking Ty when he turned around and saw his father.

"What's-"

*Blam!*

*Guy hit Kev dead in the mouth with and over-hand right, dropping him like a sack of potatoes.*

*"Pop?!" Ty exclaimed in confusion, and in turn received a crushing left hook to the jaw that sat him on his ass, dazed and confused.*

*"GET THE FUCK OUTTA HERE!" Guy growled to anyone within earshot.*

*The court quickly emptied, Kev and Ty started to get up. "I wish the fuck ya'll would get up!" he warned.*

*"Pop! What the hell we do?!" Kev asked, his lip swollen and bloody.*

*"You almost got me killed!" Guy barked. "You almost got your mama killed! My mama killed! My daddy killed!"*

*The more he spoke the madder he got, so by the time he got to Skatter's name, he reached down and grabbed them by the collars of their sweaty tee shirts and snatched them to their feet, hissing in their face, "And you got my man, my mother-fuckin' man Skatter killed because of ya'lls bullshit!"*

*He then released them, shoving them away so hard, they almost fell back down again. When they rose, their eyes were to the ground. Guy began pacing to and fro in front of them with his hands on his hips.*

*"I oughta shoot you both in the ass and leave you on Bay-Bay's porch my goddamn self!"*

*Kev and Ty were heated with embarrassment, especially being manhandled like this in front of others. However, they began to get scared, too.*

*Ty spoke up.*

*"Pops, man...we sorry. We-"*

*"No, ya'll ain't sorry, ya'll gangstas remember? Ain't that what you wanted to be, right?" Guy sneered in disgust and pointed his finger at them.*

*"You started this and you better finish it! I ain't gonna lift one motherfuckin' finger to help you. And you better finish it, too, 'cause if ya'll left my man to die in vain, I swear to God, I'ma beat ya'll muthafuckas like a nigga in the street!" Guy*

*snarled, looking at each in the eyes. When he felt they got his*
*point, he turned away saying, "And don't ya'll come home til*
*you straighten this bullshit up!"*

For the next two days, Kev and Ty spent their time putting
together a plan regarding the Rogers' operations. They knew
that even though BayBay and his five lieutenants were in Feds,
their presence in the streets were still very heavy.

On Tuesday, they were in a motel room in Rocky Mount
with their team which included Dino, Three dudes from Wilson named Slug, A.J. and Black. Also present were five dudes
from Goldsboro.

"Yo, I say we just come through Cemetery Street and shoot
up the block," one of the dudes from Goldsboro suggested.

Ty looked at him as if he was crazy.

"So we can shoot crackheads and block runners? That
shit's stupid as fuck!."

"Naw," Kev shook his head. "We gotta get BayBay's three
brothers. They the ones runnin' shit for him. We get the head,
the body will die."

Everyone nodded or voiced their agreement.

"I know his youngest brother Ray gettin' married soon. A
muthafucka gettin' married is gonna have a bachelor party,"
surmised Slug.

"Fuck it, it'll be easier to hit the wedding," Ty reasoned.

"Naw, we hittin' the bachelor party. Slug, you find out
when and where and make that your priority, hear?"

"I got you, Kev."

Black, you find out where the main dope house is," instructed Kev.

Black nodded.

"Damn right," Ty remarked, "Might as well, they ain't
gonna need it, where they goin'."

"Naw, Ty, we ain't gonna rob it, we gonna burn it down."
Kev smirked.

*"The hell we is! All that fuckin' dope and money up in there!" objected Ty.*

*"I said we burn it. Besides, we know the spot is heavily guarded at all times. That also means some of their best shooters will be there. And we gonna make sure they don't get out." Kev began to like the idea more and more.*

*Ty reluctantly admitted to himself that it was a good plan, but he was starting to get the feeling Kev was taking over as boss of the situation and he didn't like it one bit. The crew seemed to follow Kev because he was older, but it still rankled Ty.*

*Three nights later, Ty, Kev and Slug were on their way to Pender Street in Wilson. Slug had found out where two of BayBay's pick-up men lived. Kev sat in the passenger's seat while Ty drove the late model Buick. Kev handed a gun over to Ty.*

*"Here, ya know how to use it, right?"*

*Ty tucked it inside his waist. "Fuck you, man, do I know how? Of course I do!" Ty shot back.*

*They pulled up in a quiet residential area and Kev and Ty got out. Black got behind the wheel and parked a little ways down the block. TY and Kev hid behind some hedges that ran along both sides of the front door. They waited…and waited. Ty was beginning to fall asleep and the slight snoring was getting on Kev's last nerve. He whispered, "Ty, wake the fuck up!"*

*"Huh? I wasn't asleep!" Ty grunted while wiping his eyes with the back of his gun hand.*

*After five hours hiding in the bushes, a grey BMW535 finally pulled into the driveway and the pick-up men had two women all over them. All four were drunk and the time being the wee hours of the morning made it perfect for a hit. When they opened the door and began to stumble out of the car, Kev and Ty snuck up behind them and shoved them back so hard,* one guy and the woman fell back against the other two and all four fell to the floor. Kev waisted no time. He shot the woman nearest to him in the head, blowing her wig as well as the back of her head right off. Ty raised his gun to shoot the other woman but hesitated. Kev shot her himself, thinking Ty was scared.

"Don't kill me! We already dropped the money off," begged one of the dudes. Kev placed his pistol at his head.

"Where is Ray's bachelor party supposed to be?" Kev demanded.

"I...I don't know"

BOOM!

The dude screamed in agony clutching at his thigh which was beginning to seep red.

"Okay! Okay! It's at the Marriott on Highway 301, right before you get to Rocky Mount, next Saturday night!"

"You better not be lyin' nigga!" threatened Kev.

"I'm not!"

That's all Kevin needed to hear.

BOOM! BOOM!

He opened the dude's head and spilled his thoughts all over the dingy carpet. Then he looked at Ty. "Fuck you waitin' for?"

Ty kneeled and put his gun to the head of the other dude.

"Noooo!" the dude cried out in terror.

Ty squeezed the trigger, but nothing happened.

The dude, sensing an opportunity to escape, punched Ty in the face and tried to stand. The blow didn't faze Ty, it only made him madder. He pistol-whipped the dude in the head until he was unconscious, his face so swollen he resembled the Elephant Man.

Kev watched and in frustration said, "Fuck is you doin'?? Just shoot him!"

"I tried, nigga, but this shit broke."

"Fuck you mean it's broke?"

"It's broke," Ty repeated, aiming at the dude's head and pulling the trigger. Again, nothing happened. Kev took the gun. "Let me see."

His brow knotted with concentration as he examined the gun. Then he said, "Stupid muthafucka! The safety still on!"

"Oh", repled Ty in a small voice, a little embarrassed. He snatched the gun back from Kev and unlatched the safety.

BOOM! BOOM! BOOM! BOOM! BOOM!

He pumped the five slugs into the dude's face, then looked at Kev.  "Let's be out."

Kev chuckled and shook his head in disbelief.

# CHAPTER 24

"*Pop that pussy, baby! Pop that pretty pussy!*"
And the strippers did just that.
"*Yo, Melvin. Nigga, where the fuck is Charisma?*"
*Ray demanded.*

"*Calm down lil' brah, you know the bitch wanna make an entrance,*" *Melvin replied.*

*Charisma was the baddest stripper in Wilson. Unfortunately she was currently stuffed in the trunk of her own car, her throat slit from ear to ear, eyes wide open in horror.*

"*Here she comes now!*" *Eddie Roger said, pointing to the humungous cake being pushed to the center of the room. Ray licked his lips in anticipation, imagining her emerald green eyes, almond complexion and D-cup titties. Not to mention she had a 36-inch ass.*

*Ray became hard just imagining her popping outta the cake. The music stopped for a second, then started up again, this time with R. Kelly's "Seems Like You're Ready."*

*All eyes were focused on the big cake, waiting for Charisma to come popping out. Instead of Charisma popping out, it was Ty, springing up like a jack-in-the-box.*

*Your body is my playground…..*

*BBBBRRRRRAAP! BBBRRRAAP!*

The AR-15 assault rifle ripped through the shocked crowd, blowing out backs and brains instead of kisses.

*Let me lick you up and down...*

R. Kelly sang, as the bullets peppered the bodies of all in the room, like kisses from a deadly lover. Before R. Kelly had reached his hook...*It seems like you're ready...*

Ty was already on his way out, leaving half the room panicked, injured or paralyzed. The other half everyone was dead, including all three Rogers brothers.

The small house hidden back in the woods fit Kev's plan well. Kev's crew doused the outside of the house and the area around it with gasoline. BayBay had chosen the spot because it was hidden amongst the trees. Ironically, that decision had become a disadvantage.

The Molotov Cocktails thrown through the windows set the fire, and just as expected, the crew inside sought to save the stash inside. It was only after they saw the yard and trees outside on fire did they realize they were trapped. But it was too late. Kev's team kept them pinned down until the morning. When the fire trucks, police and press arrived there was nothing left but eight dead men burnt alive and smoldering ashes. The stench was so bad, one cop muttered to his partner, "Smells like heroin burning...doesn't it?" The other cop just shrugged and sipped his coffee in the early morning light.

Guy pulled up in his Monte Carlo to the Reverend Anderson's spacious house that same night Ty and Kev were executing their plan in Wilson. He was greeted by Mrs. Anderson at the door whose lovely face brightened when she saw Guy.

"Guy! How are you? The Reverend is in the study. If you like, I'll go get him."

Guy palmed her ass through her skirt as she turned, resting his middle finger in the crack of her ass, making her jump in surprise.

"Guy!" she whispered. "Don't do that, he might see you."

Guy chuckled and removed his hand. He didn't care if the Reverend knew he was fucking his wife.

Mrs. Anderson sashayed towards the study, shaking her ass a little harder knowing Guy was right behind her. As they entered the study, the Reverend was just getting off the phone at his desk. When he saw Guy, he stood, came around the desk and shook Guy's hand warmly.

"Hey Guy, how are you? How's the family" I pray all is well after what happened last Sunday."

"I'll leave you two-" Mrs. Anderson began, but Guy cut her off.

"Naw, Evelyn, You can hear this. Have a seat." Guy smiled at her. Evelyn detected something strange in his tone and complied.

"So," Guy began. "How much is he paying you? Guy asked, still smiling. His eyes, however, were cold as steel. The Reverend scowled.

"Who paid who, Guy? I have no idea what you are talking about." Guy chuckled, though their was no mirth to it.

"Naw? Okay. Damn, Rev, do you really think I'm that slow?" Guy asked harshly, his smile all but disappeared.

"After I played it over and over in my head, I finally realized that two of the gunmen had come in through the back, but the door wasn't kicked in or broken into in any way. Therefore, they had to have had a key. I believe you are the only one with a key, Rev, right?"

The Reverend became visibly uncomfortable.

"Now, now, that's not true. I have given the key many times to one of the bishops or to my w-wife." The Reverend was stuttering and shifting nervously. His wife stared at him in a stupefied horror.

"Yeah, well," began Guy calmly looking at his nails. "You the one with a reason, Rev. I mean after all, you wash a lot of money for me. Right now, you have damn near half a mil. If I was gone, you wouldn't have to kick back nothin'."

"Guy, believe me, I would never-"

Guy interrupted. "Or is it because I'm fucking your wife?"

*"Wha-at?" Both the Reverend and he wife asked at the same time. Evelyn stood up haughtily.*

*"Bitch, you sit your ass down!" Guy hissed at her.*

*"Nigga, who do you think-" she began as Guy grabbed the Reverend by the throat and swung him right into Evelyn, knocking them both into the large armchair. Guy then grabbed the Reverend and put a gun to his head.*

*"Now, nigga, I'ma ask you one goddamn time. Did Bay-Bay pay you to set me up?"*

*"Yeah, Guy," the Reverend answered sweating profusely. "I'm sorry, man, but man, Melvin was the one who set it all up." The Reverend was a greedy man. He wanted it all. He was once a con back in the day and everybody called him Thunderfoot. He went from dope fiend to pimp and then seemed to easily transition to preacher. Everybody knew what he was about so it wasn't too hard for Guy to figure it out.*

*BOOM!*

*The Reverend's brains spilled onto the seated Evelyn's lap. She was so shocked she couldn't scream but just stared in horror at what once was her husband's head.*

*She gasped, "Guy, You know I have asthma, please....get my pump,' she began wheezing.*

*"Yeah, I'ma pump you alright," Guy responded and took her breath away permanently with two to the heart.*

*Guy then stood and looked at Evelyn's shapely figure and remembered her sex game.*

*"What a waste," he mused and then turned to leave.*

"Oh, D-a-a-ddy, mmm," the cat-eyed woman moaned. "I love that dick in my ass."

The large, heavy-set man slid his dick like a sausage in and out of the woman's puckered asshole, slow and long. The woman's body began to gyrate, making her asshole open and close convulsively. The skinny man demanded, "Open your mouth, bitch!" and slid his long skinny dick into her mouth. He grunted with pleasure as she deep-throated him and all three were in the zone. She began to finger her pussy whilst being ass-fucked and sucked both men. When she felt the skinny dude's dick start quivering, she took it out of her mouth and began jacking it off until he came all over her face and neck. The other man pulled his dick out of her ass and came all over her back.

"Oh, yesss,' she hissed and smiled, revealing her fangs. "Now you will be Vampyre's slave."

She suddenly lunged at the skinny dude and closed her mouth on his neck, the punctures causing a seepage of blood. She then turned on to the heavy set dude and did the same, this time almost ripping his throat right out. She then sat back on her heels and laughed out loud with blood dripping onto her large titties.

"And....cut!" Tre barked. The cameraman lowered his camera, as a couple of crack head-looking dudes began removing the lamps placed around the set.

"Let's go! Time is money! Meow, I want you in costume in five!" Tre commanded.

"Damn, can't I get right first?" The cat-eyed Meow huffed, as she strutted past Vee. Vee was quite amused at the elaborate set up. He had to admit, Tre sure had some top-notch chicks working for him. Tre came up to Vee and shook his hand.

"What up, Fam? How you doin'?" Tre asked cheerfully.

"Vee chuckled. "Fuckin' vampire porn? Nigga, what kinda shit you into?"

"Don't sleep, my nigga. My Vampyre Pussy series is doin' the numbers. The porn game is changin'. That bitch Pinky changed it all, now it's about a recognizable brand. My bitch Mindy Meow with them cat-eye contacts makes her look fuckin' animalistic, like a tiger!" Tre laughed.

Vee could only shake his head in admiration. He could see how the chick could be branded. Her contacts made her look cat-like for real and her body would put any woman to shame.

Wearing a robe, the skinny dude from the scene walked up to Tre.

" 'ey Tre! What up, yo? When do I get paid?"

Tre looked at the dude like he was crazy.

"Paid?? Didn't you just get your dick sucked? You got paid, so get the fuck outta my face!" Tre growled and the dude slithered off, muttering to himself. Vee laughed out loud.

"I see you're still on your gorilla shit, yo." Tre shrugged. "Old habits. Come on, I'll introduce you to Meow." Tre took Vee to a large bedroom and it seemed to Vee there were titties and ass everywhere. Six girls were sitting smoking weed and snorting coke. Two girls were tongue-kissing and fingering each other in the corner. The whole room smelled like pussy and Purple Haze.

Meow was bent over a mirror lined with coke and in one scarf, and like a vacuum, managed to snort three lines at one time. She looked up with glassy eyes.

"I'll be ready in a minute, Daddy," she chimed.

"Yo, Meow, this is my man Vee. Vee, this Meow,"

"What up, Ma?"

Meow looked Vee up and down and licked her lips. "You gonna be in the movie too, sexy?" She almost purred with lust. Vee chuckled.

"Naw, Ma."

"Stick around, baby, we can make our own movie," one of the girls kissing in the corner chimed in.

"You got your own movie, bitch! Now go get yo pussy lickin' ass on the set," growled Tre. When the girl got up with her partner to leave, she sucked her teeth and Tre reached over and grabbed her by the throat, pinning her to the wall.

"You got a goddamn problem??"

"No," she gasped, making gurgling noises whilst attempting to breathe.

"Please, Daddy," her partner begged. "She didn't mean it."

Tre kept choking until he saw her eyes begin to roll back inside her head, then abruptly let her go. She sagged against the wall, gasping for air.

"I'm sorry, Daddy," she cried.

"Just get your ass out there!" Tre demanded.

Both girls hurried out of the room.

"Matter fact, all you lazy bitches get the fuck out, now!"

Tre didn't have to say it twice. As the girls left the room Meow sashayed on past Tre and Vee. She knew she was Tre's top girl and squealed when Tre slapped her on the ass on her way out.

When the room was clear, Tre turned to Vee.

"So, what up, my nigga? I know you ain't in B'more to sightsee."

"Shit hot down my way," answered Vee.

"And?" quipped Tre.

"And...I need a new connect."

Tre shook his head in wonderment and sighed as he sat on the corner of the make-up table.

"When you say it's hot, you mean the situation hot or you is hot?"

"The circles I move in," Vee answered vaguely.

"What happened to the old connect?"

"He got murdered."

"By you?"

Vee was beginning to feel annoyed at all these questions.

"Yo, where all this goin'?"

Tre stood up and looked Vee in the eye.

"I understand you, Vee. Me and you never had problems. I like you and consider you a solid dude. But a muthafucka can never be to careful, smell me?"

"No doubt," Vee replied. "I ain't on the run or nothin', yo, just need a change of scenery."

Tre nodded. "I can dig that, but like I told you last time, porn's my hustle now. I don't rock like that no more."

"I don't need nothin' major," Vee replied. "Just a little somethin' to keep my beak wet and maybe set up something more stable."

I bet you don't even remember what I told you the last time, about bein' my partner in this shit."

Vee laughed. "Man, I don't know nothin' 'bout no porn."

"She-it, before you got on, you ain't know nothin' about heroin neither," Tre reminded him.

Vee began to see his point.

"Word, J," continued Tre. "Nigga gotta think outside the box. Porn is a billion dollar business. I film a flick for under twenty grand and move ten thousand DVDs. I make two hundred grand. And that ain't shit compared to this move I'm about to put down." Vee shrugged. "Do you but it ain't my thing." Tre quickly replied, "But it can be our thing. Check it, I gotta go to Vegas for the Porn Awards. I got major plans. Come wit me, peep the scene and see for yourself this shit is like printin' money."

"I don't know, Tre. I'll think about it."

"I'll tell you what, you gimme your word and I'll put you on to my connect if the porn thing ain't for you. Deal?"

Tre offered, holding his hand out. Vee shook on it.

"That's what it is then, yo."

*Vee kneeled at the edge of the pool, reaching out his hand to Cat. "Grab my hand, Cat! Grab my hand!"*

*Cat didn't or couldn't reach for his hand. He could see that she was drowning. Hands made of water were pulling her under and she wasn't fighting back. "Please, baby, let me save you!" begged Vee.*

*Cat turned and looked at him, but her eyes were black empty sockets.*

*"I'm already dead," she whispered and disappeared as the watery hands pulled her all the way under. Vee stood up and attempted to dive into the water, but the water had turned to glass and he ended up on top of the pool on all fours looking down as Cat sank deeper and deeper, until she completely dis-*

*appeared. "Cat!" he yelled, banging on the watery barrier. A*
*hand made of water shot up through the barrier. "The pouch",*
*the hideous voice cackled. " The pouch is all that stands be-*
*tween you!"*

*Vee fumbled in his pockets and pulled out his black pouch.*
*He started to give it to the hand but someone grabbed his arm.*
*He looked up and saw it was Ms. Sadie.*

*"Everything you ever love", she reminded him, and then*
*the pouch began to bleed in his hand as Cat disappeared from*
*view.*

"Nooooo!"

Vee sat up, breathing hard. He looked around the dark hotel room. He had that damn dream again. Every time, it was the
same thing. He got up and pulled the pouch from his pocket,
looked at it, turning it over in his hands. In the beginning,
when he was young, he didn't believe in roots. But seeing the
right situations, the unexplained ways he had cheated death
time and time again, he knew it was real. His fingers grasped
the knot that held the bag closed. He started to untie it, and
suddenly he heard Ms. Sadie's voice in his head, "Don't look
inside ever."

So he didn't and put it back in his pocket. Whatever was in
the pouch, whatever gave it its power, he truly believed was
holding him back from finding Cat. He wanted to find her...
needed to find her, but was he willing to give it up to find her?
He fell back asleep contemplating that thought.

# CHAPTER 25

"Yo Silk, What it do, dawg? This J. Love"
"J, my nigga! Where you been?!"
Vee was driving heading towards Lexington Mall.
"Shit been hectic, yo. How you?"

"Thirsty, dawg. Shit been dry since ya'll Wolf Pack niggas stopped the flow. I need to see you, yo. I need like two bricks," Silk requested.

"Whoa, playboy, How you talkin? I don't know what you talkin' about."

Vee replied.

Suddenly his inner antenna went up and he knew something just wasn't right. Silk was one of his main customers. He had called because he had copped two kilos of heroin from Tre's people and knew he could dump them on Silk on consignment. But now, Silk was coming at him sideways and he sensed the bullshit. "Naw, naw, J, we cool," Vee said, smooth as silk. "This my girl's phone. We can talk. So, what up? Where you wanna meet?"

Click!

Vee was troubled. Silk was acting real shady and talking recklessly. He wondered if Silk had some heat and was trying to give Vee up.

"Picture that," Vee mumbled, lowering his window.

Vee was right. The Durham police wanted the people involved in the slaying of the Banks family.

Silk had been caught with a gun and six bundles of heroin. When the detectives mentioned J. Love and the Wolf Pack, he sang like a bird. He didn't have Vee's phone number but when Vee called him, to Silk it was a God send. The problem was he had been too anxious and felt he tipped Vee off and cursed himself. However, he still didn't have Vee's number as it showed up as a blocked number.

Vee pulled into Lexington Market and sighed. He realized with shit so hot in N.C. he'd have to fall back from the game for a little while. At least until he could set up shop elsewhere. Suddenly, he was looking forward to his trip to Vegas. He needed a vacation. He just didn't know he'd be coming back with a whole new occupation.

Vee, Tre, Meow, a few other females and one other dude rode along Las Vegas Boulevard in the back of a stretched Hummer. The liquor flowed freely and the limo smelled of exotic blends of weed, while Jay Z's "Feelin it" emanated from the speakers. Vee had been to Vegas several times, but to him, it was a sucker's town. All the flashing lights, glam and glitter made the whole town seem like one big pickpocket. It distracts you with one hand while picking your pocket with the other.

But Vee saw things had changed. There were unfinished hotels everywhere, the concrete and steel beams abandoned, the skeletons of luxury hit by recession.

The AVA, or Adult Video Awards were being held at the Sands resort and hotel. Every year, the Who's Who of porn get together in Vegas to celebrate their own. Categories included, Best Woodsman of the Year, Best Newcomer, Best Facial and even Best Anal. The awards range from mild to outright graphic, but the participants take it as serious as recording artists take the Grammys or actors with the Oscars.

Every production company and distributer had their own booths. It was like a porn expo, where fans are able to get up close and personal with their favorite stars at the meet and greets. Porn fans can get autographs, pictures and if they're really lucky, fantasies fulfilled.

Tre had his own small booth in the sex bazaar. His company Red Light Films had its own share of fans. Tre wasn't bullshitting when he said his Vampyre series was doing well. Many horny men and women stood in line for autographs and pictures with Mindy Meow. She was dressed in a sheer red dress with her red thong showing underneath. The dress tied around her neck, but left her breasts exposed, and glitter was strategically glowing around her nipples. Vee was amused by the enthusiasm people showed meeting Meow, Pinky, Mr. Marcus and Sean Michael. They might as well have been Denzel Washington or Halle Berry, the way people were treating them.

"This is the big time, my nigga", Tre told Vee, as they walked around the Convention Center.

"I see that", Vee replied.

"You see that booth? That's Wicked Pictures, one of the largest distributers. Same as in music, same as in everything, the cracka's run this shit. The black production companies have to get distribution through the white boys," Tre explained.

"Why not start a distribution company then?" Vee asked, making eye contact with the porn star Cherokee, who blew him a kiss.

"Same reason rappers don't do it with music. The stores won't deal with you unless you come through a major distributer. But they picky about who they let in their door. That's why I'm down here", Tre told Vee. "I got a way to get a major distributer and blow this Vampyre series off the map."

Vee and Tre walked over to Mr. Man's booth. Mr. Man production was one of the biggest black porn companies in the business. Mr. Man himself was a former porn star, who came out of retirement every so often. He had some of the hottest talent signed to him, including Fiyah, a light-skin bombshell with flaming red hair on her head and pussy and a 40- inch ass.

Mr. Man had an unlit cigarette in his hand with his fedora cocked ace deuce and was standing next to Fiyah while they both took a flick with a fan. After the fan walked off, Tre approached Mr. Man, extending his hand.

"Peace man, my name's Tre. I e-mailed you about a week ago. Red Light Films", Tre said. He could tell Mr. Man didn't remember.

"Yeah, yeah, I don't remember. But anyway, what's up?" Mr. Man asked, seeming like he didn't want to be bothered. He busied himself signing autographs while listening to Tre with one ear.

"That's cool, yo. I know you busy but, I was wonderin' if I could speak with you for a minute?" Tre inquired.

"Not right now, playa. Why don't you email me and I'll get back at you?", Mr. Man said dismissively.

Vee wasn't feeling the way Mr. Man was trying to dismiss Tre, but he flexed his jaw and clamped down on his aggravation. Tre wasn't feeling it either, but he knew assholes like Mr. Man were the key to his coming up in the business, so he bit his tongue. "You ain't even get the last one", Tre chuckled, trying to lighten the mood. "Word up man, I have this hot idea on the way me and you can put together a major move."

"I'm already makin' major moves, playa", Mr. Man said impatiently and then gave Tre his full attention. "Listen…um…whatever you said your name was, this ain't how you do business. Have your people contact my people, and we go from there, awight, playa? Now, if you'll excuse me…" Mr. Man let his voice trail off, letting Tre know the conversation was over. He moved away to take a picture with another fan. Fiyah saw the anger in Tre's eyes and smiled, trying to calm him down.

"Why don't you email me?" she asked Tre, writing down her email address and handing it over. "Man's got a lot on his plate. But I'll make sure he gets it."

"Good look, Ma", Tre answered, still a little heated." And by the way, I love your movies."

Vee and Tre walked away.

"Yo Tre, I ain't feelin' how that nigga came off, yo. Word up", Vee gritted.

"If we was in the streets, I'd slap the shit outta that bitch ass nigga, but this a different game", Tre responded.

"Shit, there a nigga understand violence."

Tre abruptly stopped and smiled.

"What?" Vee asked.

"We need a nigga that move in both worlds to be our bridge. Damn, why I ain't been thought of this?"

Tre flipped open his Blackberry Pearl and dialed a number from memory.

"What you talkin' about, dawg?" Vee wanted to know.

"This nigga I grew up with. He large in the entertainment game and the streets, He-." S someone picked up, and Tre put his mouth to the phone. "Yo, what up…? Damn voice mail… yo Tito, this Tre! Get at me ASAP!"

"Ohh Baby, cum for me… Cum all in this pussy, Daddy", Debra moaned, riding Guy and gripping the head board tightly.

Guy grabbed her ass, spreading it apart to try to push himself deeper inside Debra's pussy, but she wasn't having it. She wasn't as young and flexible as she used to be. After the ninth inch, it became a tug of war to work a half inch either way.

Guy put his ass on her waist and lifted his knees, drilling deeper inside of Debra, as she clawed and scratched her way to her third orgasm, causing Guy to come, too.

Sore but satisfied, Debra collapsed on Guy's chest, throwing her leg over his and playing with his chest hair.

"Nigga, what you tryin' do? Kill me?" She snickered. "I ain't no young girl no more."

"You sure? Ain't you the fine young thang I fell in love with wit' at Sirrocco's the other night?" Guy joked.

"Fine yes, young, no", Debra giggled. "I ain't getting' no younger, hell, we ain't gettin' no younger. Matter of fact, did you go to that doctor's appointment to get your prostate checked, Guy?"

"Fuck that shit, my prostate's fine", Guy grumbled, clicking on the TV with the remote.

Debra took the remote and clicked it back off.

"Guy, you promised me", Debra reminded him.

"Deb, I'ma go to the goddamn doctor. Goddamn", Guy cursed, and got up and went to the bathroom.

"When?" Debra asked, sitting up in the bed.

"Directly", Guy answered over his shoulder, which was the southern way of saying, *when I get around to it.*

Debra shook her head. Guy flushed the toilet and washed his hands. When he came back in the bedroom, he stopped to admire Debra. Even in her late forties, she was still a dime piece. She had a smooth vanilla tone, unblemished and tight. Her breasts sagged slightly, but her stomach was flat that curved out at the hips like a Coca-Cola bottle. Her thick thighs and delectable toes made Guy's anaconda start to sit up, ready to strike again.

"Uh-uh nigga, don't even think about it", she protested, when she saw it coming to life. She pulled the covers up to her neck.

Guy laughed, leaned over and kissed her.

"And what about your promise?" Debra asked in between kisses.

Debra pulled back and looked at Guy.

"Don't play, Guy."

"What?" Guy asked, sitting on the bed.

"Retirement."

"Oh that... I am, baby... gradually."

"Guy, have I ever butted in your business?"

"No... But I can see that's about to end, huh?" Guy chuckled.

"Seriously baby, I really think you need to reconsider that thing with Sherelle's son."

Guy shook his head, but Debra framed his face with her hands.

"Baby, I know it's hard for you, but I don't think you're being fair. You're thinking with your guilt, but you don't have anything to be guilty about. Sherelle kept it from you. It ain't your fault", Debra said convincingly.

Guy sighed heavily.

"How I'm not being fair?"

"You say you're retiring and Ty is going to be in control. But you're tying his hands behind his back in a situation that he's going to have to deal with, not you", she answered.

Guy hadn't looked at it from that angle. Debra could see that she had his attention, so she went in for the kill.

"Baby, he killed Kev, he tried to kill you. What's to stop him from trying to do it again?"

"We don't know that for sure."

"Kev said he admitted it! Why would he lie?"

"He's my son, Deb. I can't just turn my back on that", Guy said sincerely.

"Remember that story Mr. Willie used to tell? About the snake?

When the man took the hurt snake home with him. The snake got better and bit the man. You know the rest", Debra concluded.

He did know. When the man asked the snake why he did that after the man had nursed him back to health, the snake said, "You knew I was a snake when you took me home."

Guy knew the story and he knew what Debra's point was. He just didn't know he was in bed with the real snake.

"Hello, Ty…come in", Karrin greeted.

Ty walked into the living room of Kev's condo. There were boxes everywhere as if Karrin was moving.

"It's good to see you", Karrin commented. She wanted to hug Ty, but she didn't know if she should. She felt awkward and she rubbed her hands on her pants. "Would you like something to drink? Are you hungry?"

Ty couldn't help but smile at Karrin's concern.

"Naw Ma, I'm good", he answered, looking around the room.

"Where you movin' to?"

"A little place in Kinston...temporarily. I just need to get out of here. Too many memories, you know?" Karrin answered.

"Why...you afraid of ghosts?" Ty quipped.

"Ghosts?" she echoed. "Why would I-",

Ty pulled his pistol from his waist and kicked off the safety with his thumb. Karrin's breath caught in her throat.

"Just tell me why, Karrin?" Ty asked, looking her in the eyes.

Karrin returned his gaze, questioningly, without responding.

"Why, Karrin?" He repeated, more intently.

"I did it for us...but at the same time, I don't know why I did it, like where the will came from, can you understand that? I just knew I couldn't *not* do it. That If there was some way for us to be together and I didn't try...I figured if I gave you what you wanted, you'd give me what I need", Karrin explained, hoping that he would understand and hear her love for him.

"What *I* wanted?" Ty asked incredulously and chuckled. "Do you think I wanted you to kill my father, My brother?"

"No, you wanted to be in charge. We both know that's where you belong, and as your woman, it's my job to do what I can to help you", she answered sincerely.

"You sound just like my mother, yo."

"We both want the best for you, Ty, and we're not afraid to do what we must to achieve it."

Ty just looked at Karrin. They say, behind every good man there is a good woman. Karrin was proving that behind every greedy nigga was an even greedier, conniving bitch. But he couldn't front, it felt good to know she was willing to do whatever it took for him. He still held his gun, but he knew he couldn't kill her.

Karrin saw the ice beginning to thaw in his eyes, so she stepped a little closer to him.

"So…are you going to kill me, Ty? Or are you going to let me love you like no other woman can?"

Karrin stepped in closer.

"You'd give me anything but your loyalty, huh?" he asked. He suddenly remembered when he saw her in her wedding dress.

"No, she said softly, kissing him hungrily, but gently.

"No baby, that was nothing… it was childish", she admitted. The passion intensified increasingly with each kiss and with every taste of his lips.

"I love you, Ty. Only you have my heart."

She kissed away his foolish pride until he began to return the kisses with a desire of his own. The gun fell to the carpet with a muffled thud. They began clawing and tearing away at each other's clothes with the urgency of lust. Ty pushed Karrin's sweat shirt over her head and lifted her bra so that her succulent melon-sized titties would fall out. He licked her areola in ticklish circles as she fumbled with his pants and belt.

"Damn, I want you so bad", she whispered harshly through gritted teeth.

Karrin stepped out of her sweatpants. Ty spun her around and bent her over the couch. His dick was throbbing so hard, he didn't even bother to pull her panties down, he just pulled them to the side and slid his manhood inside her dripping wet pussy.

"Awww, yessss, oh God, I missed you baby, I missed you sooo much", she moaned as Ty long dicked her with his hands on her hips, pulling her body into his every thrust.

"I missed you, too", Ty grunted and reached around to finger Karrin's clit. He knew her body so well he knew just what to do to make her pussy cream his dick.

Her knees went weak and she had to lean into the couch. She put one knee in the couch cushion, holding her own ass cheek spread out so Ty could go deeper.

"Promise me you won't take my dick away no more", she gasped.

"I won't."

"Pr-promise", she shivered for the love sensation.

Ty cupped her right breast and tweaked her nipple while he beat her pussy until it talked to him with squishy sounds of approval.

"I promise!"

Karrin braced herself against the back of the couch and arched her back as Ty grabbed her hair, pushing his dick all the way inside of her. He grinded her pussy until it quivered and exploded causing him to explode with her.

"I want your baby, I want your baby, I want your baby", she moaned like a mantra.

Ty wanted her to have his baby, too.

The only problem was, she was already pregnant with Kev's baby.

# CHAPTER 26

"Nine in the side", Guy mumbled, with the cigar between his lips, smoking.

He leaned across the table and gripped his stick loosely. He could bank a shot with his eyes closed.

Clack!

The cue hit the nine ball off of the side. It bounced and then rolled across the table cross- ways falling in the side pocket like it had eyes.

Hawk Bill chuckled.

"Nigga, you still got it."

Guy smiled as he came around the table.

"So Shantelle's comin' home?"

"Yeah", Hawk Bill confirmed, "Finally."

Guy nodded. He had sent Shantelle money several times over the years, but each time she had sent it back. He had decided to get a lawyer to work on her case without her knowing.

"Good thing that lawyer came out of the woodwork and took her case", Hawk Bill smirked.

He knew it was Guy's doing.

"Yeah, good thing", Guy mumbled, sinking the eight ball in the corner pocket.

"Now gimme my goddamn hundred dollars."

Hawk Bill laid his stick on the table and snickered.

"Look at it this way, as long as I owe you, you won't ever go broke."

Guy laughed.

"I know that's right."

Ty walked into the poolroom and shook Guy's hand. Hawk Bill extended his.

"What's up, nephew?"

Ty looked at him coldly, then turned away. Hawk Bill knew Ty was still upset with him. It hurt him to know the boy he had helped raise had turned so cold towards him.

"You wanted to see me?" Ty asked Guy.

Guy saw the disrespect from Ty towards Hawk Bill, but he didn't speak on it.

"Hawk, let me speak to my son."

"Yeah, I need to get back to the bar anyway", Hawk Bill answered, heading for the door. "Ty."

Ty eyed him levelly.

"What would you do?" Hawk Bill asked, and then walked out.

"What was all that about?" Guy asked, even though he already knew.

"Come on, Pop, you know. I don't care if Vee his blood. He took some of ours and lived to brag about it", Ty reminded him.

Guy sighed and sat down.

"Nobody's braggin' about nothin'. That boy's probably a million miles away. I told him what the consequences were if I ever saw him again", Guy explained.

Ty chuckled.

"You don't know Vee like I do. He thinks you soft. Now, him and them Wolf Pack niggas is gonna push back hard", Ty shook his head. "And you expect me to just twiddle my thumbs while this nigga guns for me??"

"The Wolf Pack's finished."

"How can you be so sure?"

Guy eyed him.

"Trust me…I know…anyway, I need you to go to New York."

Ty sat down across the table from him.

"Why? What's up?"

Guy rubbed his face.

"Gloria."

"Aunt Gee? What's the problem? She okay?"

"No", Guy replied. "Just like you and your mama, she stuck on this Vee situation. She went to see Tito and I know exactly what she wants."

Suddenly Ty understood. "Which is for Tito to get involved."

Guy nodded. "But I doubt he will, though. He don't want nothin' to fuck up our deal. He knows if I didn't do nothin', then there's gotta be a reason."

"True. So, what you want me to do? Make sure he workin' at it?" Ty inquired.

"Naw. I want you to make sure Gloria didn't-" Guy paused, "say too much."

At first Ty didn't understand. Then it suddenly came to him.

"Eddie? Naw, Pop, Aunt Gee been holdin' water all these years. Why would she break now?"

"Women can be emotional, you know that, Ty."

"True, but she loves you. Ain't nothin' a woman won't do for the man she loves," Ty replied, thinking of Karrin.

"But this ain't about her chico, so understand me…a woman might do anything for the man she loves, but she will do anything to protect her child. And if she gotta choose between the two…just check. Look Tito in the eye, speak of the deal, speak of family. If he knows, you'll see it in his eyes."

"And if he do?"

Guy looked away. "I'll take care of it."

Ty sighed heavily. He knew what Guy meant.

"Pop, you told me I was running the family. But each time a major decision comes up, you pull rank," Ty said, frustrated at this point, "If you don't trust my judgment, How can I run the family?"

"I trust you," Guy replied gravely. "It's just that…well, what would you do about it?"

Ty shrugged.

"Keep him close. Like you said, he wants this deal. His power base is shrinking and he's not gonna make a move 'til he feels he don't need us anymore. I would wait 'til we don't need him and leave the impression he don't need us…then I'll be waiting for him."

Guy nodded, impressed.

"Spoken like a true Simmons."

Ty cringed inwardly at the words. He knew he wasn't a Simmons, and so did Guy. Guy just doesn't know Ty knew.

"Okay, you handle it," Guy said.

"What about Vee? Pop, I'm telling you, the nigga tried to kill you. If it was up to me, he won't get a second chance." Ty said icily.

"Okay…you find that girl. The bitch that helped set me up. If she says it was Vee, then do what you gotta do."

Ty nodded solemnly. He knew where to find the girl. After all, he was in love with her.

"That was delicious, girl. I see you can still throw down," Gloria complemented Theresa's cooking.

They were in Theresa's Brownstone in Sugar Hill. The spacious dining room was tastefully decorated and even boasted an eight-tiered chandelier. Gloria, Theresa and Tito were having dinner.

It was Tito's routine to have dinner at least once a week with his mother.

"Thank you. Glo, but I have to admit, I was a little lazy tonight. I just threw that together at the last minute," Theresa said.

"Shit, if glazed Hawaiian Chicken is what you called lazy, I'm scared of you," Gloria giggled.

She and Theresa shared the giggle, then Gloria said, "I'm thinking about getting a place up here for awhile.

Theresa looked at Tito then at Gloria.

"Well, Tito has a bunch of Brownstones. He gave me this one back in the 80's, the city was basically giving these places away. Can you believe, for a dollar?" Theresa remarked.

"A dollar?"

"Hm-mmm, as long as you promised to renovate. Well, Tito snatched us a bunch of em' and now their places are going for a cool million," Theresa explained.

"That was a good move, Tito, " Gloria remarked, glad to have a reason to speak of him.

"Yeah," He mumbled, smiling eating.

"Well, Tito? Think you can find a place for your good ol' Aunt Glo? Gloria smiled.

Tito sat back, wiped his mouth, still chewing.

"How much you tryin' to spend?"

Theresa looked at Tito, wide eyed.

"Boy, I know you ain't go there??"

Gloria tried to laugh it off.

"He just playing girl. That boy know it's a recession."

Theresa laughed, but underneath, she saw the seriousness in his eyes and she wondered what was wrong.

Tito stood up.

"Excuse me, will you."

He walked out the room.

"Let me get to these dishes before I get niggerish and lay down," Theresa said, getting up.

"I'll help you," Gloria offered, standing as well.

"I wish you would try. You're my guest. Go on and relax," "You sure?"

"Of course."

Gloria went out back to the patio. Tito was sitting at the patio table, blowing Newport smoke into the night air. Gloria looked at Theresa's flower garden admiringly.

"Theresa sho got some beautiful flowers. I love pink roses."

Tito didn't even look in her direction. Gloria sat at the table and looked at him for a minute, before saying, "Tito…I wish you'd talk to me."

"And say what?" He shot back, brusquely crushing his cigarette ash in the tray. "That you was married to a snake ass nigga, and you chose his snake ass over your own fucking brother? So what does that make you?" Tito asked, looking Gloria in the eyes, stone faced.

Gloria took a deep breath.

"I won't try to justify my actions to you or nobody else, Tito. I've lived with this pain for so long, it's a part of me now. I was a fool. I know…but I was a fool in love and ….maybe you've never been in love like I've been in love…maybe you've never felt the things that I felt, but Guy was my world."

Tito inhaled his cigarette without responding, then exhaled and said," Tell me how it happened."

Gloria sat back and gazed out over the nine-foot privacy fence that encased the tiny background. Her mind took her back to a time long ago, but she remembered it like it was yesterday.

"I found out a few years later…when my mama died. We came back up for the funeral, Guy and I…there was a woman that lived across from Eddie, a friend of the family. She was at the funeral. When I saw her, we hugged and kissed, did the things you do at funerals, when she asked about Eddie's situation."

She looked like she was far away, as if she was she truly reliving the moment, right down to her facial expression.

"At first I didn't notice, understand, and then she started apologizing for not saying nothing sooner, and how she wanted to go to the police but she was scared.

She finally told me…that she had heard the commotion…the gun shots continued." Tears crystallized in the wells of her eyes.

"She said the man was holding his left side…like he had been shot. She even described what he was wearing. Guy called a few hours later and thinking back, I remember what Guy had on when he came home from the hospital, "Gloria said, then looked at Tito, seeing Eddie's face in his son." The same thing the woman described to me."

Tito flexed his jaw and stabbed the cigarette out like he was breaking a neck.

"When I confronted him, at first he denied it all, but then he admitted it", Gloria shook her head.

"And you ain't do nothing? Say nothing?" Tito couldn't understand.

"Guy was my world…he was all I had."

Tito stood up.

"You had family," he mumbled. He started to walk back inside.

"What will you do now, Tito?" Gloria wanted to know.

Tito turned back to her.

"You can't save him, Auntie," Tito replied deadpanned.

"Guy's a grown man. I'm not trying to save him," Gloria replied, even though deep down, she really wanted to.

"As far as I'm concerned, everything he has is because of my father. Therefore, it belongs to me. Once I have it…, " He eyed her coldly," I'll deal with it ALL!"

He walked back inside. Gloria understood what he said, but she wondered if what he meant by it included her as well.

The next day after the Ava Awards, Tre and Vee were driving in the black rented Ferrari to Mr. Man's mini mansion in western Las Vegas. The sounds of Fat Joe's "Lean Back" played loudly from the speakers.

*…and the bouncers don't check us*
*And we walk around the meal detectors.*

Vee turned the stereo down to a whisper. Tre, who was nodding to the beat, looked at Vee.

"Yo what up, my nigga?"

"I can't hear shit wit the radio that loud," Vee stated simply.

"Relax J, we in Vegas. Who the fuck goin' get at us on vacation?' Tre chuckled.

"You never know, yo."

Tre shook his head with a chuckle, but he knew how on point this young dude was.

"What I tell you though, eh? I told you my nigga, Tito Bell rings bells! Niggas like Puff and Frank Matthews all in one!" Tre laughed.

"That's my nigga though. I don't fuck wit him hard body like I used to since I retired, but every time I'm in New York, we do it big."

Vee nodded, unimpressed and looked out his window.

"One call from Fam and", Tre snapped his fingers, "Boom! We in the door now, I know we on 'cause I got a deal this nigga can't refuse."

Tre pulled the Ferrari through the large white sculptured marble gate. The opening split by remote, then Tre drove up the shortcut of a drive way that ran in a half circle to the front door.

Tre and Vee got out, cutting their eyes at Mr. Man's collection of cars in the garage. He had a crème colored Phantom, a beige Bentley Continental, a black Porsche Cayenne and a vintage 56' Aston Martin.

"Porn money yo," Tre commented nodding at the cars. "I'm telling you J, selling pussy is the next best thing to selling dope."

Seeing Mr. Man's lavish layout, Vee was beginning to be a believer.

Before they could knock, Fiyah answered the door.

"Good afternoon gentlemen," she smiled, "I see you got your meeting."

Fiyah was wearing a red two piece string bikini that matched her hair perfectly and barely contained her succulent C cups. On her feet were a pair of see-through 'fuck me' pumps that boosted her 5"6 frame to 6' feet even.

"If you gentlemen would follow me," she said, then turned and walked.

Tre and Vee both had their eyes glued to her bodacious ass. It was fat enough to seat a glass on and jiggled with every step.

The thong was lost so deep between her cheeks, she looked like she was wearing nothing.

Vee and Tre smiled at each other, and Vee nodded. He could tell how trick niggas would go broke trying to get a bitch with an ass like that. *Shit, some women for that matter.*

Tre came out on the patio where Mr. Man and Stan Allen were sitting at the table by the diamond shaped pool, wearing Speedos and sunglasses. On the table were drinks and cocaine and Mr. Man was in the process of sniffing a line when Tre and Vee walked up.

He finished, wiped his nose with his left hand then stood up to greet them.

"Hey, hey, glad you could make it. Have a seat," Mr. Man offered.

Tre, Vee and Fiyah sat down. Fiyah went straight for the coke.

"Thanks for having us," Tre replied

"Hey, any friend of Tito is a friend of mine," Mr. Man said.

Vee was amused by the total 360-degree turn Mr. Man did. Evidently this Tito Bell was a powerful man.

"I'm sure you know Sean Allen. Of course you do, you asked him to be at this meeting," Mr. Man chuckled. "You guys wanna drink or somethin'? A little-," Mr. Man thumbed his nose signifying sniffing.

"I'm good, "Tre said." How you doin' Mr. Allen?"

Stan just nodded with a detached smirk in his face. Vee pegged him as gay.

"Listen," Sean said, speaking in a crispy and proper manner. "If we could get down to business. Not to be rude, but I'm doing this as a favor to my man here."

"No doubt, no doubt, I'm sure we're all very busy men. Have you two heard about my Vampyre series?" He inquired.

"No", Sean answered simply.

"Can't say that I have," Mr. Man replied.

"Well, you will. My girl Mindy Meow is blowing up on the internet! We combined porn with vampire shit and Muthafuckas eatin' it up. I've already moved close to sixty thousand, but it's a bitch gettin' distribution," Tre explained.

"And I suppose that's where we come in?" Mr. Man quipped, sipping his drink.

"Naw, I ain't asking for a handout...just a hand. What I want to do is get you, Sean, Fiyah and Cherokee, and Pinky a fuckin' porn all-star series. Ya'll handle distribution and keep one hundred percent of the money," Tre paused to let what he was saying sink in, because it was his hook.

But Mr. Man and Sean looked anything but hooked.

"That's it?" Mr. Man snickered. "That's your proposal?"

"Think about it, man. My series is like an underground favorite! Like a mix-tape rapper with all the street buzz and a brand.

This Vampyre Porn shit is a brand, my brand. With ya'll names it would definitely-,"

Mr. Man cut him off and sat back.

"Not interested."

"Huh?"

Mr. Man leaned forward with a patronizing smile. "Look, I see your angle. It's a unique concept, granted. But the only person that stands to gain is you. We're already a brand!" Mr. Man laughed.

"I'll tell you what...you give me two hundred grand and I'll take you under my production umbrella. I'll get you distribution and we split the profits 50/50."

Tre was heated. He knew Mr. Man was trying to play him.

"Two hundred large and fifty percent?! You fuckin' crazy," Tre fumed.

"Hey," Mr. Man struggled, "That's my offer. And it's only because of Tito that I'm being that generous."

Tre shot to his feet followed by Mr. Man, then Vee then Fiyah. Stan Allen remained seated, the same detached smile on his face. Behind his shades he was totally wasted.

"That's bullshit!", Tre barked, but Vee restrained him.

"Now, I respected Tito because he's a good guy, but I ain't scared of him and I ain't scared of you! You want my help, those are my terms. If not, go back to the fucking corner and sling crack!" Mr. Man barked, like he was cut for a war.

"Chill Tre," Vee said calmly. "Fuck it. The man don't wanna make a deal."

"Fuck that shit J!"

"Tre," Vee said, looking Tre in his eyes. "Let…it…go!"

The look in Vee's eyes let Tre know he had something up his sleeve. Tre eyed Mr. Man.

"You on some real bitch shit, yo!" Tre huffed.

"Yeah, yeah" Mr. Man waved them off. "Fiyah, show em' the door."

When they arrived at the door, Fiyah said, "If it's any con- solation, I like the idea. I would've loved to do it," she smiled.

Vee winked at her.

"We'll, keep that in mind."

As they drove off, Tre fumed while Vee planned.

"Yo…you need distribution right?"

"Hell, yeah!"

"That's why you wanted all them stars on your shit?" Vee said. Tre looked at him, wondering where this was going.

"Yeah, with known names, distributions come to you." Vee nodded.

"So if all them Muthafuckas was signed to you, Fiyah, Pinky, shit like that, it's cake, right?"

Tre smirked.

"J…what you thinkin?"

"If I make that happen, I'll get fifty percent?"

"No doubt."

"Alright," Vee grinned. "We tried it your way…now, we gonna do it my way."

That night, Mr. Man's gate opened and his crème colored Phantom turned on to his street. The driver pulled out, unaware that he was being followed by a non-descript stolen blue Honda. As the Phantom turned the corner, the Honda rammed into the back of the Phantom.

The Phantom's driver got out and so did the Honda driver.

The Honda driver had his fitted hat pulled low and his hand up to this mouth, like he was examining his bumper.

"Hey! You fucking drunk??" The Phantom driver screamed, walking up on Vee, the Honda driver.

As soon as he was at arm's reach, Vee grabbed him and pumped two in his stomach.

Bluke! Bluke!

The shots were muffled but still echoed through the air. Vee then pulled his shirt over his nose and mouth and snatched open the Phantom's suicide door.

"Oh no!" Mr. Man gasped.

"Boom! Boom! Boom! Boom!

He gave Mr. Man and Sean Allen four shots, two apiece, one to the head and one to the heart. Vee executed them in cold blood with speed and precision. Then he pointed the gun at Fiyah.

She didn't even blink. Fiyah wasn't scared, she had been raised with death. She was from San Diego, where her neighborhood of Bloods didn't wear red, they wore green. Same place where every one of her boyfriends had been killed or had killed someone. She knew a gangsta when she saw one, and she was looking into the eyes of one right then. She figured she was safe.

"I guess I'll be getting that email now, huh?" she smirked.

Vee winked, but didn't speak. He lowered his gun then backed out of the open door. He passed the driver, who was moaning and spitting up blood on the ground. Vee pumped two slugs in his face, putting him out of his misery.

Vee jetted around the corner, where Tre was waiting for him in a used car they had just bought to drive out of Nevada in.

# CHAPTER 27

*T*y, Kev, and Slug walked into a barber shop in Rocky
Mount, a town near Wilson. It was a late Saturday evening, so there were only a few people in the shop. A pret-
ty-boy type dude named Al Clark was sitting in the chair getting a temple fade.

"What up, Al?" Kev asked, stepping in front of the car.

Al's man Cee-Lo was sitting in a waiting chair. Ty and
Slug sat down on both sides of him.

"You tell me, play," Al replied nonchalantly.

There was a short silence where all that was heard was the
buzz of the clippers and Soul 92 playing low in the back room.

"You think about our offer?" Kev inquired.

Al chucked, cool and slow, then replied, "Man, I already
told you what I thought about that shit, playa. Ain't nothin'."

Al was getting money in Rocky Mount. The heroin game
wasn't as strong as in Wilson, but Kev didn't like to have powerful neighbors that he didn't even control or supply.

Kev smiled.

"Come on Al, I'm sure we can work something
out...playa."

"I told you, I don't want no partners and I like the price I'm
getting now," Al told him.

Kev watched Al's hands. Since they were both outside the barber's smock, he knew he had caught Al slipping. Al knew it too, but he wasn't about to back down.

"You sure?"

"I'm positive."

"Fuck it then," Kev spat, then without hesitation, pulled out his .38 revolver and pumped three in Al's face and chest. The barber jumped back, the blood had splashed his face and clothes. Kev wasted no time putting a bullet in his head that splattered blood on the large mirror behind him, which ended looking as if someone had thrown a pint of paint on it.

Kev watched as Ty fired a single shot point-blank into Cee-Lo's head, killing him instantly. The only other man in the shop was the other barber. He tried to make a mad dash for the back, but Slug stopped him dead in his tracks with a bullet in his neck. When he fell, Slug stood over him like, "You don't get down," Boom! Boom! "Then you lay down!"

The blood shot out of his head and across the floor like some one had stepped on a tube of toothpaste, squirting it everywhere.

The three of them stepped carefully over Cee-Lo's dead body and exited through the back.

Once they had dumped the getaway car and left it burning on a desolate background, they made their way back to Wilson in Slug's grey Lexus LS. Goodie Mob pumped from the speakers

What ya'll niggas know about the Dirty South?!

Ty sat in the back, rolling a blunt.

"The shit ain't over big brah," Ty commented, licking the dutch then completing the roll. "Them Mexican niggas Al was gettin' that Mexican mud from? We need to rock their asses to sleep, too!"

"No doubt," Kev replied, parlaying on the passenger side. "But we'll deal wit' that later. Check this out."

He handed Ty a waxed paper packet of heroin, over his shoulder.

*No bigger than a thick piece of gum, Ty turned it over and read the stamp "Blackout" written across it. It was the name they had branded their heroin, except for one tiny difference. The "T" in Blackout had a piece missing from the right arm. The "I" was also made shorter. Kev and Ty had done that purposely, chipping the rubber stamp to create these irregularities. They had suspicions that someone in the crew was bootlegging their stamp and moving their own heroin under Kev and Ty's brand.*

*The culprit hadn't noticed the changes, and now, Ty and Kev had the proof.*

*"Yeah," Ty replied, handing it back and lighting the blunt with his lighter. "I already knew about it."*

*"You knew??" Kev asked, surprised. "Then you know it's Black. Why the fuck you ain't handle that ??"*

*"I'm trackin' it?" Ty replied.*

*"I'm trackin' it?" Kev echoed, with a chuckle. "Fuck trackin' it, we deadin' it!"*

*"Naw, brah, that ain't how to handle it. If we dead Black, then how we gonna know who supplyin' him? We won't be getting at the problem, whoever it is will only be more careful."*

*Kev shook his head.*

*"That shit don't matter, yo. Once these niggas see how we do Black, they'll think twice before tryin' us wit that bullshit again."*

*"Word," Slug added, "Make an example of his bitch ass."*

*Ty wasn't with it. He didn't care about catching a body no more than Kev did, but they had two different ways of looking at things. Kev had a kill-a-mosquito-with-an-axe mentality, while Ty would rather lay on the mosquito until he was close enough to snatch the heart out of its tiny chest.*

*"Naw Kev, I'm tellin you. I'ma handle it."*

*"Naw nigga, I'ma handle it," Kev retorted.*

*Ty chuckled.*

*"You buggin, yo."*

*"How you figure, I'm buggin? You buggin' if you think I'm letting niggas play me!" Kev shot back.*

*"Kev…you ain't the boss," Ty replied, and it was that statement that would snowball into their separation. "Pop gave us both this spot."*

*Kev huffed in exasperation.*

*"Don't never forget, you little brother, yo!" Ty reminded him.*

*The next morning, at the Holiday Inn, Kev knocked on Ty's room door. The autumn rain alternated between drizzle and shower, beating down on the cars in the parking lot. Kev was glad to be dry under the walkway.*

*After a few moments, Ty came to the door in his boxers, rubbing the cold from his eyes.*

*"What up, yo?"*

*"We gotta go meet Pop," Kev informed him.*

*"For what? Fuck time is it?"*

*"Six. You know how Pops do," Kev smirked.*

*"Man, goddamn!" Ty huffed, going back to the bathroom.*

*Kev shut the door. When he looked up, his heart dropped. Karrin was sitting up in the bed, wearing Ty's T-shirt.*

*"Hey Kev," she said weakly.*

*Kev just shook his head.*

*"You ain't gonna learn, are you?"*

*Karrin just tuned her head and looked at the TV. Kev stood looking at her, and all he saw was his mother. Just like with Guy, it seemed like Karrin was always catching him with other girls, even her cousin, and still she took him back. They'd be broke up for a few days, and then get back together. Kev would use their moments apart to speak to Karrin, masking his affection with the façade of friendship. He didn't feel guilty, because he always felt like Karrin was just another girl to Ty. If she ever left, he knew Ty wouldn't miss her. He felt Ty just* saw her as just another piece of pussy. Kev saw her as so much more.

Ty came out of the shower wearing a pair of jeans, Timberlands and a hoody, thug-fashion. He tucked his pistol and bent down to kiss Karrin.

"When you comin back?"

"I don't know, I'll call you. My car keys on the table alright?"

Ty and Kev headed for the door.

"Be safe, baby. I love you," Karrin sang.

Kev gritted his teeth.

Ty turned around, blew her a kiss then left out behind Kev.

As Kev drove, the windshield wipers were beating to their own rhythm. Ty slumped in the seat and leaned his head against the window.

"So what up wit Pop? What he got us up wit' the roosters for?"

"He wanted to talk to us. I told him about that Black situation," Kev replied.

Ty lifted his head and looked at Kev incredulously.

"You what? What you do that for, Kev? We coulda worked the shit out between us."

Ty was aggravated that Kev had gone to Guy. They weren't kids anymore, dammit.

Ty was 19 and Kev was 21, grown men in Ty's book. Besides, Ty didn't want Guy feeling like they couldn't handle their own business.

Although Ty had noticed a change in Kev, he couldn't quite figure out what it was.

He just knew he was trying to be more assertive. He didn't know that it all started with Guy leaving the house to live with Debra.

Of course, it was Gloria who had initiated the divorce, but in Kev's eyes it was like Guy just didn't care. He moved in with Debra without missing a beat. It seemed to Kev that Ty was treating Karrin exactly like Guy treated his mother. All of this created a wedge between Kev and Ty that would never be healed before Kev's death.

They met Guy in a small out-of-the-way park. At night, it was a place to park and fuck in, but in the daytime, it was always deserted. They spotted Guy's 80' white Eldorado. It was the very first car he bought and it was in immaculate condition. Like some business owners kept their first dollar they ever made, Guy kept his first Cadillac.

Guy was standing near the rusty broken-down swings. He had on a trench coat and held a black umbrella over his head.

The rain slowed, but the drizzle was still steady. Ty pulled his hoody up over his head and Kev did the same.

"What's up, Pop?" Ty greeted, yawning into his fist. "Couldn't we had done this before the crack of dawn?"

Guy smiled.

"Daddy Willie once told me, you gotta wake this game up and put it to bed", Guy remembered. "I met the man who changed my life at five o'clock in the mornin'."

Guy turned to Kev.

"Now I've heard your side, Kev. Ty what's yours?"

"It ain't like I totally disagree with Kev, Pop. I just think we should be patient. Let Black think he got over and let his connect get bolder. Then we kill the weed at the root," Ty explained.

Guy nodded. He could definitely see that Ty was the better strategist of the two and would make a better boss. But the bottom line was, Ty wasn't his son, and therefore he d never would run the family.

He saw Kev's point as well, but he was too brutal, too unyielding, and that would cause people to fear him without balance. Fear without balance becomes contempt and hate, and hate created informants.

Guy knew he would have to groom Kev better.

"Ty's right," Guy finally said, and he could see the subtle irritation in Kev's expression.

"But I think in this situation, an example needs to be made of Black immediately. Kev, make Black give up his connect with a gun to his head. Most niggas will tell you anything, then. If not, put a gun to his mama's head and every nigga'll tell you anything," Guy chucked, then looked at Ty. Follow your brother's lead in this one.

Although Ty was disappointed, he didn't show it.

"No doubt."

Guy looked at his watch.

"Anything else?"

"Naw."

"I'm good," replied Kev.

"Okay. Kev, how's your mother?" Guy questioned, as they walked back to the cars.

"Good...I guess," Kev mumbled.

Guy could see Kev was feeling off. He clamped a reassuring hand on Kev's shoulder.

"I know this is...difficult. But it's for the best. I'll always love Glo, but life goes on and people grow out of things that once fit. Your mother's grown, I haven't. I know that and I know she deserves better."

Kev opened his car door, still upset.

"Yeah."

"Ty, ride with me, okay? Let's get some breakfast," Guy said.

Ty walked around Guy's Cadillac and got in the passenger seat. Kev pulled off and Guy pulled off shortly after.

"You know...when I was growing up, I never wanted to...live my father's life," Guy explained.

Ty knew what he meant.

"So why did you?"

Guy glanced at him, shrugged, and replied, "Fate...I don't know. All I know is I had all these dreams and goals for myself. I was going to be the first man in my family to go to college, be like the Tuskegee Airmen, blaze a new trail...but those were dreams. Life woke me up real quick. I guess you could say I gave in. I wasn't strong enough to hold on to my dreams so when the opportunity came, I took it..." Guy's voice trailed off as he pulled into Denny's parking lot and turned off the ignition.

"I never wanted this for you and Kev. I guess I wanted ya'll to blaze a new trail."

Ty felt some guilt, thinking he had let his Pop down.

"College is overrated. You get cats out here with degrees and they sweeping floors. At the end of the day, it's just a piece of paper, when what it's really about is taking care of family," Ty pined, then looked at Guy. "We are blazin rolls, Pop. We the seed of a dynasty. From slavery to the new millennium. Black men that didn't bow for nobody and crated our own way in the world."

Guy smiled.

"Now see, with a mouth piece like that, you shoulda went to law school. You would've been the family lawyer."

Ty laughed.

"But you know," Guy continued, "Out of you two…I always knew you had it in you. Your brother doesn't have the foresight or sheer instinct that you do."

Even though Guy was complimenting Ty, deep down Guy was angry because Ty was Brah's son. Even though he loved Ty, he still hated the fact that Brah's seed was naturally sharper than his. Guy felt like he had to somehow make Kev better at planning and scheming.

"That's why I'm giving you your own territory."

Ty smiled proudly.

"Word?"

"Word," Guy echoed, chuckling at the usage of the young-boy slang.

"You deserve it. Now, it's a small spot and you have to build it from scratch, but I know you can do it."

Ty took it as a promotion, but it was really a demotion. Guy was putting him in Barren Land, like Abraham did Ismail, the difference being, there was no merciful God to guide Ty's footsteps.

"I'm givin you Smithfeild."

Ty shook this hand firmly.

*"I won't let you down."*
*Guy smiled.*
*"I know you won't. Now, come on, let's eat. Your mama's*
*a beautiful woman, but God knows she ain't no cook!"*
*They both laughed as they got out of the car.*

Smithfield is a small town not too far from Raleigh. Even
though it's small, the hustle was still alive. The only problem
was heroin wasn't the drug of choice. Cocaine was.

Ty, his boy AB and Karrin rode to Smithfield in AB's navy
blue Yukon, pumping the sounds of Wutang's "Triumph":

> I bomb automatically
> Socrates Philosophies and high prophecies
> Can define how I be droppin these...

The only reason Karrin was allowed to ride along was because her cousin Cat worked in Smithfield at a large department store named Harlem World Styles. This simple fact
would lead to an introduction with Vee and create the illest
team in Carolina at the time.

"Yo, I'ma make this run," Ty told Karrin, looking at his
platinum and emerald watch that matched the emerald in his
ear and the green swoosh of his Air Ones. "You good with
your cousin til then?"

"Yeah, baby," Karrin agreed. She leant over from the back-
set and kissed Ty, sucking his lip. "I'm good."

As she walked into the store, Ty watched the jiggle in her
ass in the tight fitting pink and white Lady Phat Velour suit.
Her small feet made her pink and white Air Maxes look good
on her.

Ty was definitely feeling Karrin, he considered her his
main girl, just not the only girl.

"Yo, B, I'm tellin you, we gonna blow this Muthafucka right!" AB barked in his gruff voice. He was 6'5 and his eyebrows knitted like Ice Cube's when he frowned.

AB was Ty's best friend since short pants, the only reason he didn't take AB to Wilson with him was because AB had done too much dirt in Wilson, robbed too many niggas. That added up to too many enemies and too many warrants for him there. At least in Smithfield he hadn't been caught for the dirt he had done there.

They rode to a small house around the corner from the projects. This was where Guy's people sold heroin. They parked the car and went to the door and knocked. A few moments later, a light skinned, grey eyed Amazon of a woman came to the door smoking a Newport.

"What?" she asked, looking them up and down.

At first sight, she looked like a dude. She had more waves than Ty! Her baggy clothes hung loosely on her large frame.

"I'm Ty...Guy's son."

She blew out the smoke and stepped aside so they could enter. After she closed the door, she said, "Guy said you was comin." Then she snickered.

"You musta really pissed your father off."

She sat on the couch, next to a bad ass petite redbone wearing only an oversized T-shirt. The Amazon chick reminded Ty of Latifah in 'Set it Off', minus the corn rolls.

"Pissed him off? Naw," Ty said, slightly confused.

"Yeah well, I'm Woo," she told him.

"Who she?" AB asked, eyeing the chick who rolled her ass.

"None of your goddamn business," Woo spat, French inhaling her cigarette.

"All ya'll need to know is that this is the Boonies. Heroin ain't poppin like that. Crack is. That's how I make money...with a little kickback to Guy of course."

Ty remembered Guy had said he had to build the spot from scratch, but he didn't expect this. After Woo ran it down to him how long it took for her to move ounces, forget kilos, he knew he had his work cut out for him.

He returned to the store with a lot on his mind. When he walked inside, he found Karrin with another girl and some brown-skinned dude with a Cuban linked Jesus piece. When he stepped in the circle, Karrin saw him bristle like a lion seeing another lion in the area.

"Hey, baby," she chirped, kissing him to calm his nerves, "This is my cousin Cat and this is her boyfriend, Vee."

# CHAPTER 28

B ack in B'More, Vee and Tre were on their way to building Tre's porn dream team. With Fiyah's help, they
were able to sign Mr. Man's and Sean Allen's roster of
porn stars. Tre had agreed to pay them more per scene and in
royalties. It was a deal that couldn't refuse.

Fiyah was back in Cali, but Tre was making arrangements
to get her a place in B. More.

They sat in Tre's office, a converted barber shop on Fish
Street that still had the mirror along the wall. The picture win-
dow was tinted so you couldn't see in, but they could see out.
That's how they saw the black BMW 745 pull up with two
Italians cats inside. One was short and pudgy, the other tall and
bulky. They got out of the car and headed for the door.

Inside, Tre was behind the desk, while Vee and Tre's man,
Sleep sat on the couch.

"Who the fuck is that?" Vee asked, watching the Italians
approach.

"I don't know," Tre replied, but his instincts told him to be
on point.

The short Italian tried the door, but it was locked. He
cupped his hands to try and peer inside, but couldn't, so he
knocked.

"Police?" Sleep inquired.

"Naw," Tre answered, concealing his gun in his lap. "But I gotta feelin' who it may be. Open the door."

Seeing Tre ready his weapon, Sleep did the same. He unlocked the door with his left hand and gripped the 40 caliber in his right. The only one who didn't pull a gun was Vee. He continued lounging on the couch watching 'City of Gods' on the 40-inch plasma.

The two Italians stepped through the door. When the older Italian saw the gun in Sleep's hand, he held up his hands mockingly.

"Please don't shoot. We come in peace," he chuckled, stepping closer to the desk with his bodyguard in tow. The older Italian extended his hand to Tre. "How are ya? I'm Nicky Galante. I represent the...interest of the Sarducci Family."

"What's that got to do with me?" Tre wanted to know.

Tre still hadn't shaken his hand, but Nicky still had it extended.

"Tradero." Nicky said, like a teacher mildly scolding a student, "Now is this anyway to treat you new partner?" Nicky smiled. He used his whole name to let Tre know he had him pegged.

"Partner?' Tre laughed. "The only partner I got is sitting on that couch."

Vee didn't either bother to look up.

"Oh, so you didn't get the memo?" Nicky said, mockingly. "It's in the contract you signed."

Before Tre could say anything, Nicky pulled out a folded up newspaper article. He unfolded it and laid it flat on his desk.

Tre looked down at it. The headline read: Curtain Call for Two Porn Stars

Underneath were head shots of Mr. Man and Sean Allen, and next to that, a picture of the Phantom, door open and the driver's body on the ground, under a sheet. Nicky put his finger on the picture.

"You see? Mr. Man was our partner, but since his...unfortunate demise courtesy of you gentlemen, that makes us your partner."

Nicky smiled, but his eyes were hard as granite.

"Naw, you must be mistaken. I have no idea what you're talkin' about", Tre smirked. "You got us fucked up."

Nicky dropped the smile.

"Tradero, let's not make this any harder than it has to be. Mr. Man told us Tito Bell sponsored you guys for a meeting. The next day, he's dead. Now, all his talent is signin' wit' you? You gotta be tryin' to bust my balls here, because I would hate to think you'd play with my intelligence", Nicky hissed. "Now...this is our offer...our only offer and I'm only gonna say it once. What Man owed us, you now owe us. For every release, we get thirty percent net and Mr. Sarducci is expecting a twenty five thousand dollar advance."

Tre looked at Vee, then laughed. Vee just kept watching TV. Tre then put his gun on the desk and cocked the hammer.

"Fuck you and Sarducci", Tre chuckled.

Nicky waved at the gun dismissively. "We got plenty of those. Doesn't bother me. I've been shot six times." He shrugged. "But are you sure that's the route you wanna take? Why don't you think about it, eh? You'll see it's the right thing to do. After all, you took out our money maker. So let's make it right, eh?"

"So it's ...thirty five percent on top of Man's debt? How much he owe you?" Vee asked, not taking his eyes off the screen.

"Fifty grand, give or take," Nicky smirked.

Vee chuckled.

"Of course Mr. Man ain't around to verify it either. But I'm sure you're a man of your word," Vee commented.

"Solid as a rock," Nicky answered, chin up.

"Well I am, too," Vee said, getting up slow.

When he got to his feet, he raised his head and in one smooth motion spat dead in Nicky's fucking face. His bodyguard reached for his gun but Sleep put his gun to the back of the bodyguard's head and Tre aimed his at Nicky.

"Now," Vee continued calmly, "You gonna tell Mr. Sarducci, Mr Sardine, whatever his spaghetti-eatin' name is, you tell em' suck my goddamn dick...okay? That's our offer."

Vee sat back down and looked at the TV. He motioned the bodyguard to the side because he was blocking the TV.

Nicky was furious. His face was beet red. He reached to wipe the yellowish glob from his forehead, eyes and the bridge of his nose, but Tre said, "Leave it and get the fuck out."

Nicky glared at him with unadulterated hatred. "Nigger...the next time I see you...you'll be dead." Nicky stressed so hard, the veins popped out of his neck.

He and his bodyguard walked out. Nicky angrily wiped his face as soon as he got on the sidewalk. They got in the BMW and drove off.

"We definitely ain't seen the last of them," Tre remarked.

"And they ain't even seen the first from us," Vee retorted.

Tito smiled to himself as he rode in the back of the chauffeured Phantom. He had his blue tooth in his ear and a Newport between his fingers.

"Yeah? So what brings you to New York, Fam?" Tito asked, as if he didn't know.

Ty purposely hadn't told Tito he was coming. Guy had sent him up there to see where Tito's head was and if Gloria, being under extreme emotional pressure, had let the cat out of the bag. Gloria had but Tito wasn't about to. He kept his poker face intact.

"I had to take care of a few things in Boston so I decided to stop through and check family. It's been a minute since I been to Nu Yitti," Ty cracked, using the slang name for New York.

"Indeed so, cuz. Indeed so remember all them summers when you and Kev used to come up here and when it was time to go you used to cry and beg Aunt Glo to stay?" Tito laughed, using the old memory to comfort Ty's senses and rock any suspicious to sleep. Ty chuckled.

"Can it be that it was all so simple then?" Ty remarked, singing the high pitched hook of the Wu Tang classic.

"Well yo, I'm headed over to the office on Ninth Ave, near 34th . Number 490. You know the area?"

"Naw but this GPS do," Ty shot back. "It says I'm five minutes away."

"Wit' New York traffic? Make that fifteen," Tito laughed then clicked off mumbling, "Bitch ass nigga."

"Is everything alright?" the Nigerian chick with the bright accent and look of a young Imani asked.

"No...but it will be."

Tito got back to his office. His company "Capital Music Group" was in the business of financing music labels and music publishing companies. The plush office was buzzing with activity when Tito arrived. His secretary, Jasmine, a beautiful Dominican woman gave him the heads up.

"Steve Stout called about those Pepsi endorsements and Eva Pigford's publicist reminds you the reservations are for eight.

"Cool."

"Oh and Mr. Sarducci is waiting for you in your office," she added.

Tito furled his brow.

"Sarducci? Okay, hold my calls, baby."

He didn't know what Sarducci had come to see him for. It was true that they were in a lot of business deals together, but they either handled it over the phone or Sarducci sent a lackey. If it was personal, they did lunch or Tito traveled out to Sarducci's mansion in Long Island. Truthfully, he had forgotten all about introducing Tre to Mr. Man.

When he entered his office, he saw Mr. Sarducci sitting in one of the two tight back chairs in front of the desk. His nephew Vinnie was standing near the chair.

Vito Sarducci was one of the last old school Mafia. He was over eighty years old, bald, frail and wizened. His grey bushy eyebrows made him look like a grumpy old man, and his body wracked with coughing fits. Despite his physical appearance, his mind was still sharp and he ran the Sarducci crime family with an iron fist.

Tito shook Sarducci's hand, then Vinnie's.

"How you doin' Mr. Sarducci? What brings you to my office? Tito inquired, unbuttoning his suit jacket before sitting down.

"Ehhh, a slight problem, Tito. Just hoping you can help me out," Mr. Sarducci told him.

"For my friends...anything," Tito smiled, folding his hand in the desk.

Mr. Sarducci fiddled his cane, then said, "Hey, Tito, we make a lot of money together, right?"

"Indeed."

"Music, broads, -," Mr. Sarducci thumbed his nose, indicating cocaine. "And...didn't I pour you a drink in that Vegas thing?"

"Of course," Tito replied, wondering where this was heading.

"And when your old man died, God rest his soul, didn't I take ya in?"

"Mr. Sarducci, all this is true," Tito replied a little impatiently.

"Then I wonder, what is it that I did to warrant such disrespect?" he asked, frowning with disgust.

"Disrespect?" Tito echoed. "I consider you a dear friend, why would I disrespect you?"

"You have a friend...in Baltimore. Kid named...," Mr. Sarducci snapped his fingers trying to remember then Vinnie said, "Tradero."

"Yeah that's it, Tradero. Friend of yours?"

"Indeed."

"Well this...friend of yours, the one you introduced to the porno guy, Mr. Man? This...Tradero he whacks Mr. Man!" Mr. Sarducci explained.

Now Tito understood. He remembered setting up the meeting for Tre and Mr. Man. Now Mr. Sarducci wanted to know if Tito was behind it all.

"Well I assure you, that that was never my intention. I simply introduced my man to Mr. Man. I really forgot about it until now," Tito responded.

"But that's not the end of it. A few days ago, I sent a guy to see this Tradero, with a very good business deal. Now I think that's very generous on my behalf being that the guys practically robbed us of a cash cow. It coulda went-" Mr. Sarducci drug his thumb across his throat. "But I'm a diplomat. I send him a good deal and you know what this guy does? He spits in my guy's face!" Mr. Sarducci's voice raised an octave which made him break into a fit of coughing.

Tito saw the problem. He mused about the 'good deal' Sarducci had sent. That was probably what got the guy spit on! But Tito also knew if Sarducci came to see him personally, then he was taking it personal.

"I come to you Tito, because you're my friend and because you sponsored this animal in Vegas," Mr. Sarducci stated.

"First of all, I didn't sponsor anybody. I just introduced him to the guy. He's trying to do his thing in porn, so whatever I could do, I'm there," Tito broke it down.

"So you had nothing to do with this?" Mr. Sarducci questioned.

"If I wanted in with Mr. Man I would've came to you. I knew who he worked for," Tito answered, looking him in the eyes.

"I believe you, Tito. I never doubted our friendship, just your judgment, which any man can suffer from time to time. My only concern is this disrespect. It cannot go unpunished. You agree?"

Tito knew Mr. Sarducci was asking if he would get involved if Sarducci moved on Tre.

"Let me speak to Tradero…maybe I can make things right. We only know one side of the story, the side your guy told you. I know Tre, he wouldn't spit on your message, but maybe the messenger got out of pocket," Tito reasoned.

"This is true," Mr. Sarducci nodded." "Okay Tito…you talk to your guy and get back to me soon, eh? Tomorrow evening?"

Tito nodded. Vinnie helped Mr. Sarducci up, so Tito stood as well.

"Well, I must go. My great grandson Peter, Vinnie's son, he's playin' T-ball, and I promised I'd be there," Mr. Sarducci chuckled, shaking Tito's hand. "Thank you for the ear, Tito."

"Anytime, Mr. Sarducci."

Mr. Sarducci stopped at the door and walked back.

"Tomorrow evening?"

"You have my word."

Mr. Sarducci and Vinnie walked out. As soon as they left, Tito frowned. He was pissed with Tre, not because of what Tre did, but because Tre didn't give him the heads up. Tito furiously clicked through his I-Phone until he came to Tre's number, then he hit send.

He heard a soft knock, then Jasmine stuck her head in.

"Tito, there's a Ty Simmons waiting to see you."

Tito gave her the signal to send him in.

"Speak."

"Yo, Tre," Tito gruffed, "when can you be here?"

Tre didn't have to ask. He knew what it was about.

"I can be outta here tomorrow-"

"Today," Tito cut him off.

Ty walked in but stayed quiet.

"Its that serious?" Tre probed.

"Yeah Fam, it is."

"Say no more. Me and my man J on the next thing smoking. I'll call you to tell you when the flight lands."

Tito hung up.

"Sorry cuz, shit a little hectic. Take a ride with me to meet my man Tre and some kid name Jay."

"No problem."

"Gloria!" Guy called out, stepping through her front door.

She didn't take long and was soon coming down the steps. She had just gotten back from NY a day ago, and already was packing to go back for good.

"Hello, Guy. I'm glad to see you up and around," she remarked.

Guy was using a straight black cane with a gold knob instead of the wheelchair.

"You know what I always say, you can't keep a good man down," Guy quipped.

The room grew quiet. Gloria studied Guy and felt her resolve for leaving weakening. Seeing him in the flesh wasn't like seeing him in her mind. But she knew she had to be strong.

"What do you want, Guy?"

"I wanted to see you. You said you were back from New York, so I thought I'd stop by. I mean, if you didn't want me to know you were back, why'd you call me to tell me so?"

"Force of habit," she shot back.

Gloria was so used to checkin in with Guy, it had become an old habit, one she was determined to break.

Guy moved closer to her.

"Force of habit? You tryin' to tell me my baby don't wanna see me? I damn sure wanna see my baby," he crooned, sliding his arm around her waist.

Gloria slipped out of his embrace and moved away.

"Yeah well, I'm lookin' nothin' like Debra," she stated bluntly.

"That ain't never stopped you before," he shot back.

"Believe me, that's about to change. A lot of things about to change," Gloria told him.

Guy nodded, then changed the subject.

"So...how was New York?"

"Don't beat around the bush, Guy. You know what you really want to know is, did I tell Tito about Eddie because I was upset about Kev? Isn't that what you wanna know?"

"After all this time, if you did, you gonna look like you was in on it."

"Well maybe I wanna wipe the slate clean."

"So you told him?" Guy asked casually, but inside he was taut with tension.

"What's the matter, Guy? Scared of the consequences?" Gloria quipped.

"Are you?" Guy retorted.

"I've been suffering the consequences for a long time, Guy. Ain't no fear left in me," she replied sourly. "I'm moving back to New York."

"When?" he paused. "Why?"

"As soon as I'm packed…and why not? There's nothing for me here. Kev's gone and once again you've put another woman's needs before mine," Gloria accused.

"Glo, listen, it's not about another woman's needs okay? It's about-"

She held up her hand.

"It doesn't even mater at this point. It's over, Guy."

"Over? I mean, we been divorced," Guy remarked not fully catching her meaning.

"Come on, Guy. You and I both know the divorce was only on paper…just like our marriage," she replied sadly.

Guy took her hand gently.

"Our marriage wasn't just on paper. I love you, Glo" he told her sincerely.

She pulled her hand away.

"I finally know, Guy. At first I divorced you because I figured it wouldn't hurt as much, you know? I thought it would be easier if I was the other woman. All that would be Debra's problem." Gloria shook her head. "But it wasn't easier…I don't know what I was thinkin'. All it did was give me more reason to cry, more reason to hurt." Gloria took a deep breath so the tears wouldn't fall. "And I finally realize that if I don't make a clean break, I'll spend the rest of my life like this. But I deserve better and I intend to stand in the sun and not block my blessings anymore."

She stepped around Guy, grabbed her purse and headed for the door.

"Where you goin?" he asked.

Gloria mustered her beautiful smile that made Guy re-member why he married her and regret he was losing her.

"Home…to New York."

"You packed already?"

Gloria looked around at her expensive furnishing, thought about her walk in closet full of clothes and endless rows of shoes, then simply shrugged.

"I got all I need right now. And Guy, son or no son, that boy will pay for what he did to Kev…goodbye."

Gloria closed his door quietly behind herself.

Debra pulled the phone away from her ear and looked at it like mustard was running out of it. Her lip curled with disgust.

"What the hell you need to talk to me for?"

"Look Debra, I ain't got time to argue with you. Believe me, if it wasn't important I damn sho' wouldn't be cal-lin'…but, it's about Kev," Gloria said, as she drove.

Debra felt that twinge of guilt and relented.

"Well look, I'm at Maxine's on Center Street. And you need to hurry up because I'm almost done."

Click.

Debra hung up and sighed, while the petite young girl ma-nicured her left hand.

By the time Debra was finished, she saw Gloria pull up in her Benz. She grabbed her purse and spoke to everyone on the way out, never stopping to pay. She didn't have to. She owned the salon. It was one of five different businesses she ran that no one knew about, not even Guy. Debra always planned ahead and she refused to be one of those women that ended up with nothing if her husband decided to bounce.

As Debra walked out, Gloria got out of her car. There was a bus bench a few yards away so they sat on it, watching the sun go down over downtown Goldsboro.

"Okay," Debra began, pulling her hair away from her face with her pinkie nail, "I'm here. Talk."

"I need to speak to Ty," Gloria replied.

"And for that we had to meet? You coulda just said that when you called," Debra huffed with attitude.

"You wanna discuss murder on the phone?" Gloria gritted impatiently.

"Murder?"

Gloria nodded, looking around casually to check her surroundings.

"All of a sudden, Guy's got a conscious or somethin'?" Gloria huffed. "I went all the way to New York and my own fuckin' nephew won't do shit. Too worried about this fuckin' deal."

"Yeah...Guy's got Ty on a leash, too. I talk to him and talk to him, but he won't budge." Debra replied, frustrated.

Gloria looked at her, surprised.

"You talked to him?"

Debra smiled.

"Of course I did. I want him as bad as you. Kev was like a son to me, Gloria," she admitted. She wasn't lying it was just when it came down to Ty and Kev, she had no qualms about choosing. Besides, her and Gloria's interest coincided. Gloria wanted Vee dead for revenge and Debra wanted him dead for convenience. They were on the same page abd Debra planned on using that to her advantage.

Gloria looked away, not knowing what to say.

"What? You thought I was the evil stepmother, making Kev sleep in the closet and eat Mwah?" Debra giggled.

"Close", Gloria replied and they shared a giggle.

"Well, I have to admit...I thought the same thing", Debra said. "I used to ask Ty how you treated him and he'd say Mama, Gee is cool! He said you didn't treat them any different. I always wanted to thank you for that, but never had the chance."

Gloria shrugged.

"I just figured, whatever was between me and you, didn't have anything to do with the kids, you know?"

"I agree."

"Hell, it really didn't have nothin' to do with you or I," Gloria added.

Debra snickered.

"Now you got a point there. When in actuality, he'll never be mine or yours." Debra replied wistfully.

Gloria agreed, nodding like it was the gospel.

"It took me a long time to realize that," Gloria admitted.

Debra sighed.

"Yeah well, that's somethin' I've lived with a long time," Debra returned.

Even though they had spent the better part of twenty years hating each other, they had never really known each other. Gloria, the street princess, was raised by the game and believed in fairy tales. Debra was the street chick that had gamed her way to the top and wrote the fairy tales others believed in.

The conversation had ventured away from where it initiated, but both women felt comfortable with the turn.

"Well," Gloria sighed, as she stood up, "I guess it's in God's hands now. Wherever Vee is, God bless em…but fuck em."

The sun had dipped so low, the sky turned a curious purplish hue.

Gloria started to walk away, then stopped and turned around.

"You think, if we had met under different circumstances…we coulda been friends?"

Debra shrugged, good-naturedly.

"Stranger things have happened."

Gloria paused then said, "Take care of him, Deb."

Debra nodded and Gloria got in her car and pulled off.

She sat on the bench a few moments longer thinking how crazy life really was. She got up, put her purse on her shoulder and got in her Benz. The sounds of Teena Marie's "Dear Lover" played softly as she pulled off.

Debra was totally oblivious to the fact that she was being followed by two vehicles.

"Don't lose her," the gruff voice in the passenger seat said to the driver.

They followed her onto a long stretch of road. The U-Haul truck was on her ass and high- beamed her.

"Stupid bastard!" she gritted, waving her arm telling him to go around. *People always in a damn hurry.*

The U-Haul went around, then curiously began to slow down. Debra beeped her horn in frustration, then prepared to go around it.

Suddenly, she was rammed hard from the back by an Oldsmobile '88. The impact pushed the car into the back of the U-Haul and she hit her head on the steering wheel.

"Shit!" she cursed, slightly disoriented by the accident.

But it wasn't an accident, a fact she realized when the back doors of the U-Haul flew open and a dude jumped out and onto her hood, holding a sledgehammer.

He raised it over his head and brought it crashing down on the driver's side of the windshield.

Craaccckkk!

Debra ducked for two reasons. One was out of instinct, knowing the glass would shatter and two, to grab the pearl handled .380 she kept under the seat.

It only took two blows to completely shatter the windshield, but it only took one shot from the .380 to completely shatter his face.

Boom!

He fell back dead between the hood and the U-Haul. More figures were inside and another one was on the hood. Before she could aim again, she felt the cold steel of a barrel on her temple.

"Put it down!" the dude barked.

Two more dudes came scurrying out of the truck, armed as well. She knew it was either shoot it out and die for sure, or give up and look for a better opportunity. Debra wasn't a gangsta, she was a survivor. Therefore, she opted for the second choice.

"O-okay," she mumbled.

The dude snatched the gun from her hand. The other dude ripped her from her seat and dragged her out of the car through the windshield. She put up her hands slightly on the broken glass as he dragged her into the back of the U-Haul.

One of the dudes grabbed the dude's body and the sludge hammer and put them in the truck as well. Another dude banged on the side of the truck.

"Go! Go! Go! Go!"

The driver took off followed by the second vehicle.

"Ya'll stupid niggas done fucked up!" Debra hissed. "You know that, right?? You know who the fuck I am?!"

Debra saw that this wasn't a random robbery. She just hoped it was a kidnapping.

They pulled deep into the woods, reaching a clearing that was lit by the light of the full moon. Debra looked from face to face.

"What ya'll want, money? Is that it? She asked, but no one answered.

The back doors opened and she looked at the figure standing in the door with his long dreads hanging wildly, looking like Screw Face himself. He stepped into the truck and crouched down next to Debra. She recognized him as Brah's nephew, young Hardy.

"Remember me?" he sneered, revisiting the moment.

It had took him awhile to get her, but he had found out from a hair dresser that Debra got her hair done there. He waited for the right time, and now it had finally come.

"Why are you doing this?! I didn't have anything to do with killing Brah!" she exclaimed.

"Oh you think this about Brah?" he snickered fully," Naw bitch, this about my whole fuckin' family!"

"I- I don't know nothin' about that!"

Hardy got in her face and she could smell his putrid breath.

"But your son do! Now…you wanna live? Tell me where Ty is," Hardy demanded.

Debra laughed in his face.

"Fuck you, you gonna kill me anyway!"

Hardy back handed her hard enough to draw blood.

"Wrong answer! Where is Ty!"

"Kill me!"

"Okay…gangsta bitch. We gonna see how tough you really are! Drag this bitch out!"

Two of the cronies each grabbed a leg. They dragged her out, causing her to hit her head on the hard dirt when she flopped off the truck.

"Nigga, I don't give a fuck what you do! If you think I'ma give up my son, you crazy! I hope your whole family is burning in hell!" she spat.

She was trying to provoke Hardy into just killing her and getting it over with, but he recognized the play.

"Put her on the hood", Hardy told them, grabbing the sledgehammer. They had Debra bent backwards over the hood. One was holding each arm, and two were on their knees holding her ankles.

"Now, I'ma ask you again, where's Ty?"

"Fuckin' your dead mama!" she yelled.

Hardy raised the sledgehammer and brought it crashing down on her knee, pulverizing her knee cap and making her scream out like a tortured animal. Her leg now looked grossly deformed.

"You still tough, huh?! Are you?!"

Debra continued to moan but didn't respond. Hardy swung again, this time cracking her forearm like a twig. She was in so much pain she prayed for unconsciousness, but it wouldn't happen.

"Talk, bitch!"

"F…f…fuck you," she mumbled.

Hardy pulled his nine from his waist and snatched Debra's skirt off of her. He shoved her panties aside and shoved the barrier in her pussy. She howled in agonizing pain.

"Tell me and I'll put you out of your misery."

Debra prayed silently. She knew it was over. She just asked God to forgive all her sins.

When he got no response, Hardy pulled the trigger. The bullet ripped through her womb and lodged near her spine, paralyzing her from the waist down. Mercifully, she could no longer feel anything from the waist down.

Hardy was mad as fuck that he couldn't break her. He saw now she would never give Ty up.

"Gas this bitch", he growled.

The driver of the '88 got a gas can out of the trunk which he used to douse Debra's body. Hardy then pushed her to the ground.

"Now it's your turn to burn in hell!" Hardy hissed, then sat her body ablaze, burning her alive.

The inhuman scream pierced the night air. The smell of burning flesh made one dude throw up.

"Fuck it", Hardy shrugged. "Who got her phone?"

The four dudes looked at each other confusedly.

"We…we ain't grab it."

"You what?! I told you stupid muthafuckas to get the purse!" Hardy barked. He shook his head, looking at Debra's body wiggling in the dirt. "I'ma get that nigga. I swear I'ma get him."

They burned the U-Haul and the other body, then left in the Oldsmobile 88'.

# CHAPTER 29

Tito had let his Nigerian chick take the Phantom to go shopping, so he had to ride with Ty in the rented Escalade. It was in the middle of rush hour, and traffic crept and crawled, stalled and died all the way to JFK airport. By the time they got there it was almost time for Tre's flight to land.

"That shit crazy", Ty chuckled, "A muthafucka can fly from B'More to New York faster than a muthafucka can drive through Manhattan traffic."

Tito laughed

"I know, right?"

They found a park and went in the terminal. Tito texted Tre to see if his phone was back on.

Tre looked at his phone and saw the text:

*"N front Mc D"*

The plane had just started disembarking.

"Yo, he here." Tre told Vee.

Vee didn't see why they had to come up here so urgently anyway.

What's done is done and in Vee's eyes, it was his beef, not Tito's. They got off the plane. Tre texted him back:

*"Just got n. I got u"*

Tito saw the text, then slid his I-Phone back in his pocket. "So cuz, if it's all good, we ready to make that move soon. Probably Charlotte and Greensboro in NC first, along with Charleston in SC", Tito explained.

"Anytime you ready, Tito. The Bells and the Simmons is family to the end", Ty said, looking in his eyes. "Nothing can come between us."

Tito extended his hand and they shook on it. Inside, Tito was boiling. He assumed Ty knew. *Why else would he be there?*

But even if he didn't, his words still struck Tito as ironic.

"Just like Uncle Eddie put Pop on back in the day, it's time we returned the favor."

Ty smiled, using just the right words to try and get a reaction from Tito, and it didn't fail.

If Ty had not been watching Tito's eyes he would've never seen the contraction in the pupil that indicated a person's change of moods. Ty knew right then, Tito knew.

"Yeah no doubt, cuz...no doubt", Tito replied, thinking about another favor that needed to be returned.

"You talk to Fiyah?", Tre asked, as they made their way towards McDonald's.

"Yeah I gave her a heads up", Vee confirmed.

Tito glanced at his watch.

"Damn, my man must still got the slow Bop. What's takin' him so long?"

Ty's phone rang. He saw it was Guy's number.

"Pop, What's up?"

Guy pinched the bridge of his nose. He was standing on Old Mount Olive Highway, looking at the swirling lights of the sheriff cars.

They had Debra's car highlighted under a big tarp, while the forensics team scurried in and around the car.

"It's...it's your...I need you to come home right away", Guy said, unable to get it out.

Ty's body went rigid.

"It's what? Pop, what's up? talk to"

"It's Debra, Ty. Her car was found...she's been kidnapped."

Ty clicked off, his mind in a daze. He handed the rental's keys to Tito.

"I...I gotta go."

"Cuz, what up? You okay?" Tito asked.

"My mother, yo. Somebody just fuckin' kidnapped her."

"What?! Yo, you need me, too,"

"Naw," Ty cut him off, stepping back slowly. "I got this. Just turn in the rental."

"Call me," Tito yelled after him.

Ty disappeared into the crowd to go book a fight just as Tre and Vee were emerging from the crowd to reach Tito.

Tre saw the look on his face.

"Yo, Tito, you alright?"

"Yeah, yeah, I'm good", Tito assured him, giving Tre a hug and a pound on the back. "Good to see you."

"Same here, my nigga. Yo, this my man J. Love, J, This my man Tito."

Tito and Vee shook hands firmly. As the two men sized each other up casually, Tito noticed Vee was slightly shorter than him.

"What up, J?", Tito greeted.

"Ain't nothin'", Vee shot back casually.

"Yo, we got a flight in like thirty minutes. That gonna be enough time?" Tre asked.

"Indeed. We can take a walk in the parking lot", Tito suggested.

When they got outside, the crisp winter air made them all pull their coats together.

"Now talk to me, Tre. What the fuck happened?" Tito questioned.

"Muthafucka came at me sideways, yo. Talking 'bout we owe his man's debt of 35 percent. And twenty five grand," Tre huffed. "Ain't no fuckin' way we getting' extorted."

Tito sighed heavily. He understood Tre's point, but he also knew shit could get ugly with Sarducci.

"But why the fuck you ain't tell me, yo? All you had to do was say, yo, we had a problem. I fucked with Sarducci hardbody."

Tre replied, "No doubt, my nigga. That's my bad."

"Don't get me wrong, I understand why you flipped, but goddamn!", Tito snickered, "Why you had to spit in the guinea's face?"

"He didn't", Vee spoke up. "I did."

Tito looked at him.

"J, right?"

Vee nodded.

"Spittin' in a muthafucka's face...you just can't kiss and make up. It's gonna be hard for me to set this right," Tito said.

"Tito, right?"

Tito smiled, recognizing that Vee was giving it back tit for tat.

"On the real, I don't know you, so I ain't askin' you to make it right. I came here outta respect for Tre, and he came outta respect for you. But all that makin' it right...we ain't askin' for that", Vee explained firmly.

In Vee's eyes, he saw Tito as a lackey for the Mob. The good cop to the Mob's bad cop in order to soften them up. He thought Tito was just another nigga under the Mob's thumb. He would find out in time just how wrong he was.

Tito sighed.

"Dig, this shit ain't about who's balls is biggest. Ya'll niggas made a power move and you stand to make millions. Why not give Sarducci a piece, cause in a war, nobody makes money." Tito tried to reason.

"Sarducci can eat a dick, far as I'm concerned", Tre replied.

Tito shook his head.

"Then I hope you got an army, cause you 'bout to go to war with the Mob", Tito warned.

"Naw", Vee smiled, "We just goin' to Bensonhurst.

Had Ty turned around at any point when he walked away from Tito, he would've seen Vee. But his focus was straight ahead and his mind was on his mother.

He took the first available flight to Raleigh, but still had to wait forty minutes. When he got to Raleigh, he rented another Escalade and damn near floored it down highway 40. A trooper clocked him doing 110 mph and pulled him quick. He took one look in Ty's eyes and with Ty's statement, "My mother's been hurt", the black trooper let him off with a warning. Ten minutes later, Ty was pushing 100 again.

As soon as he hit Goldsboro, he headed straight to his mother's house and found Guy's Sixteen in the driveway. He didn't have to use his key because Guy opened he door as soon as he approached.

"Anything?" Ty questioned as he entered.

Guy shook his head. His tie was loosened and he held a drink in his right hand. The sounds of the jazz saxophonist Najee, played in the background. Something Ty knew that Guy did when he was either extremely upset or straight up unnerved.

"Not any more than before", Guy responded.

"All you said was she's been kidnapped", Ty said, and just the word alone made his blood boil and his stomach queasy.

Guy sat down on the couch, resting his forearms on his knees, holding the drink with both hands.

"The police found her car in the middle of Old Mount Olive Highway, windshield totally shattered and the front and back of the car damaged. Like she had been sandwiched to make her stop... there was also blood on the hood."

"Sandwiched? Windshield busted out?" Ty mumbled, trying to fit together the pieces as he paced the floor. "Has anybody called?"

"No... not yet", Guy answered, and that's what worried him. In a kidnapping, the call would've usually been made soon after. Unless it was a bunch of young boys that kidnapped her. Which, given their propensity for violence, can only make matters worse.

Ty stopped pacing as he got hit with an idea. "Her cell phone?!" he exclaimed. "We can track her through her GPS!"

Guy sighed, downed his drink and grimaced.

"The cell phone was found in the car."

Ty deflated just as quickly as he had inflated with the idea.

"So what do we do?" Ty asked.

"We wait."

"Wait?! The longer we wait, the further they get! How many you got out there now?" Ty probed.

Guy stood up and came over to Ty. He understood what Ty was going through, because to an extent, he was, too.

"Ty...there's nothing we can do. They have to call us."

Ty's mind was in a whirl. His first thought was Young Hardy, but his arrogance wouldn't allow him to admit it to himself that the young boy could bring it to him like that. Then a thought that had been in the shadows of his subconscious began to emerge into the light of consideration.

*What if Guy had her killed?* He had tried to shake it off earlier, but the thought kept nagging at him.

It was his guilt that prompted the question in the first place.

*Suppose Guy had found out about Debra's betrayal. He would be too obvious to just have her gunned down...wouldn't it? So he would stage a kidnapping and then...*

Ty shook his head. He had to find Young Hardy.

"What's wrong?" Guy asked.

"Nothing...just thinkin'," Ty lied. He couldn't tell Guy about Young Hardy, because then he would know he killed Brah. Then he would want to know why, and if Ty told him that it was Brah who tried to kill him, then Guy would want to know why it was so hard to find the girl who set him up.

Ty sat down, holding his head. The tangled web of deception had him caught up in all its complexities.

"Where...where was she comin' from?" Ty probed.

" The hair salon in downtown Goldsboro. I talked to some people there personally. They say, Gloria met her there, then-"

"Gloria??" Ty cut him off, looking at him. "She was with Gloria?"

His mind told him, no way! They hated each other. If Gloria met her, Gloria definitely couldn't have had any good intent. Was Gloria in on it too? Did Guy use her to set Debra up? Everyone was suspect at that point.

Guy sat down with a shrug.

"She's movin' back to New York", he replied, like that was an explanation for Ty's question. He was talking more to himself, wistfully.

They sat in silence for a few moments. Guy got up to refresh his drink.

"You want one?" Guy offered.

"I'm good", Ty refused.

"Ty…I need you to…. I need you to be prepared," Guy said, proceeding carefully.

"Prepared?" Ty echoed, confused.

Guy sat on the couch across from Ty, keeping eye contact.

"They still haven't called…that's not good. I've been in this game a long time, so I know, there's a good chance that your mother…may not make it."

"You act like you already know", Ty commented bitterly, but Guy didn't pick up on the insinuation of the statement, nor the acidity of the tone.

"This is the part of the game I tried to warn you and you brother about. This game don't care who play it, the rules still apply. My wife…your mother…whoever. This is the type of shit that could happen to anyone. Nobody can catch everything. Some things just slip by you, things…you never would've saw if you didn't look hard enough. Sometimes…it's right there, right in our face…sometimes the enemy can be right in our faces."

Ty's heart dropped with Guy's last statement. He was sure Guy knew now, and any moment he'd…

Ty stood up to shake it off. His guilt was eating him up so bad, it was beginning to color his every thought.

"I'ma lay down for a minute…get my head together", Ty said.

Guy nodded and downed his drink. As Ty went up the stairs, Guy's phone rang. Ty stopped and turned around.

"Yeah", Guy answered. "This is the…" After listening for a minute, Guy grabbed his forehead and dropped his head. He hung up slowly, then looked across the room at Ty. No words passed between them, none were needed. Ty knew exactly what Guy's expression meant. His mother was gone. He slowly sank onto the carpeted stairs, and for the first time in his life, he cried.

Ty's mind was in a fog as he watched his mother's casket being lowered into the ground. He hadn't even been able to kiss her one last time because her wake had to be one with a closed casket. Her body had been burnt beyond recognition. The only way the police had identified her were her dental ·records.

Ty was numb. He felt totally disrespected and his anger was white heat, but he didn't know who to direct it at. *The Hardy family would pay dearly, whether Hardy did it or not. Never mind they were his family too. But if it had been Guy…*he didn't know what he would do.

Ty watched Guy hug Debra's mother and a few more guests at the funeral. After that, he got behind Willie's wheelchair and pushed him over to Ty.

"How you doin', boy?" Willie asked, with concern in his gruff voice. Willie was over eighty and couldn't walk anymore, but he still had his fire.

"I'm good, Grandpa", Ty answered shaking his hand.

Guy hugged Ty.

"You know I love you, right?" Guy told him.

"Yeah Pop, I love you too", Ty replied.

Guy looked at him and gripped his shoulder.

"Don't worry…We'll get to the bottom of this", Guy assured him.

"I know", Ty returned firmly. He had every intention on doing just that.

The two of them began to walk, while Guy pushed Willie's chair.

"Pop...have you heard from Karrin?" Ty inquired.

He had been trying to reach her but she wasn't answering her phone, and her voice mail was full. That made Ty both worried and suspicious.

Guy shook his head.

"Naw. I'm surprised she didn't come today. Have you heard from her?" Guy asked.

"Naw," Ty replied, "I was just as surprised she didn't come, myself."

When they had gotten further away from the crowd, Guy asked, "So what did you dig out in New York?"

Ty wasn't feeling how Guy was ready to discuss business and they had just buried his mother, but he didn't let it show.

Ty shrugged.

"He know."

Guy looked at him and stopped walking

"You sure?"

Ty looked around as he replied, "I did what you said. I looked him in the eye and spoke of family", Ty then looked at Guy, "And J saw it...he knows."

"Goddamn, Glo", he mumbled. "Okay look, make this top priority. You make sure Tito starts moving forward ASAP. I've worked too hard for some old-as-shit like Eddie to stand in my way", Guy gritted.

"Worked hard? I thought you ain't want this deal at first." Ty probed suspiciously.

"Ty, just do what I say...okay?" Guy instructed.

"Whatever you say, but it can't be top priority. Finding out who killed my mother is, remember?" Ty stated firmly, then walked away.

Guy knew Ty was upset, so he let his attitude go. He also sensed something underneath he couldn't put his finger on. There was a tension in Ty he didn't understand.

He began pushing Willie again.

"Go easy on him, Guy. The boy just buried his mama", Willie scolded.

"Yeah," Guy mumbled.

There was silence for a few moments, then Willie poke up. "So…Gloria goin' back to New York?"

"Yeah."

"Are you gonna let her?"

"What can I do?"

"Then you a goddamn fool," Willie huffed, fishing around in his inside pocket for his Trademark cigar.

"Daddy, not now, okay?" Guy shot back.

"Just gimme a light", Willie demanded.

Guy pulled out his lighter and lit the cigar. They were right in front of Guy's Caddy.

"Glo was the best thing ever happen to you, boy, and you know it. I won't speak ill of the dead, but I never trusted Debra. Neither did your Mama, God rest her soul." Willie puffed.

"What's done is done", Guy answered flatly.

"What's done is now", Willie retorted. "What's done lost you Glo, what's done lost me my grandson, but you refused to see it."

"So now this is my fault?" Guy questioned with exasperation.

Willie shook his head.

"I was with the same woman for damn near sixty years. Now, I done made my mistakes, but I know a woman's love is a precious thing. You took it for granted and it came back to bite you in the ass. Makin' babies all over the place without rhyme or reason. Family so scattered, one son don't even know his own brother!"

No matter how old Guy got, his father still knew how to get under his skin. Guy chuckled.

"Well Daddy, I may have failed as a father, but I taught my boys how to play this game. Ain't that what you wanted? I gave them what you gave me. At least we ain't uppity niggas, ain't that right, Daddy?" Guy threw back in his face.

Willie just grunted and puffed his cigar. He hated to be wrong, and deep down inside he wondered, *did it all come down to the sins of the father?*

Guy pushed him to the passenger door.

"Now let's go, before I leave yo' grumpy ass right here on the curb", Guy spat.

# CHAPTER 30

Karrin knew her way around Baltimore pretty well, because of the two and a half years she had gone to Howard University in DC. She came off I-95 on Martin Luther King Boulevard and headed towards Lexington Market. Vee had told her to meet him there because he was staying with a friend and didn't have an apartment. It was a lie. He wanted to make sure Ty wasn't trying to use Karrin to set him up. He didn't think Ty would involve Karrin in this street shit, but he wasn't taking any chances. After all, he had killed her husband.

He sat in Sleep's smoky-grey Chrysler 300 and watched every car going in and out. When he spotted Karrin get out of her white Convertible Jag , he watched her closely. She pulled her waist length Chinchilla around her tighter and entered the market. Vee waited a few minutes, then called her.

"What's up? Where are you?" Vee asked, as if he didn't know.

"I'm at the market already", she replied.

"Cool. I'm about a block away. Meet me in an hour."
Click.

He watched the next few cars pull in, scanning for Ty's face then he went in. While still keeping his eyes peeled, he began to relax a little bit, seeing Karrin's coming wasn't a set up. But the fact remained, *why did she come?*

She had called him not even two hours ago and said she was on her way to Baltimore and that she needed to see him. The fact that she had called en route was enough to send up red flags. Plus despite the fact she tried to mask it, he could sense the anxiety in her tone. She had a reason to be anxious…she thought Guy was going to kill her.

When she heard on the news about Debra Simmons' body being found burned beyond recognition in a wooded area, just one word filled her mind…*Guy.* She didn't know about Young Hardy and she knew Debra hadn't just been snatched up at random. So there was only one logical conclusion. Guy had found out about the set up and had Debra killed, no…burned. Her whole body shivered just thinking of such a torturous demise.

Karrin had started to call Ty, but stopped abruptly. *What if Ty already knew? Or even worse, a party to his mother's death?* That was when Karrin knew she didn't stand a chance. She had to get out and the only place she knew where she would be safe was with Vee.

She wasted no time grabbing clothes and shoes haphazardly and headed for Baltimore. Now that she was at the restaurant where they agreed to meet, and saw Vee approaching, she could finally exhale.

Karrin stood up and gave Vee a warm friendly hug, then they both sat down.

"Hey Karrin, How are you? You didn't have any problems finding this place, did you?" Vee asked.

Karrin giggled.

"Boy, please, as many times as me, you, and Cat used to come here and stuff our face?!"

Vee laughed as the waitress approached and brought their menus.

"Yeah, you definitely remembered", Vee chuckled, because Karrin had ordered what he used to order all the time.

As Vee ate, Karrin remarked, "I don't see how you still eat that stuff."

"Why not?" Vee asked, mouth full.

"You don't remember the time when you brought Cat to see me, then we all came to B' More so you could see that guy, I forgot his name. Dark skin, Spanish."

"Tre."

"Yeah, Tre. So ya'll left and when you got back to the room we were drunk," Karrin giggled. "I was tore up, you hear me? And you and Cat got to arguing. Then we came here and she threw up in your plate of that."

Vee snickered at the memory.

"And I still think she did that shit on purpose."

"Probably did, knowing Cat", Karrin shook her head.

Thinking of Cat made Vee's heart hurt. He suddenly lost his appetite.

"Any word on where she might be?" Karrin asked.

"No", Vee replied, pushing his plate away.

Many nights he had driven though the streets of Baltimore hoping to see her. He had been back to the hospital so many times, they knew him by face. In fact, he had been to every hospital and homeless shelter in Baltimore. He had even been to the morgue.

"It's like, she don't wanna be found", Vee surmised.

Karrin reached across the table and squeezed his hand.

"You'll find her. I know you will."

Vee rubbed his hands over his face, resetting his emotions and changing the subject.

"But you lookin' good, Rin. Gotta certain glow to you", Vee remarked.

She blushed. Of course she was glowing, she was pregnant.

"Thank you."

"So what brings you to B'More?" Vee probed, cutting to the chase.

Karrin diverted her eyes and used her fork to play with her food.

"I...I just, you know...wanted to see how things were going with Cat." She was lying and Vee knew it.

"Yeah? You coulda did that over the phone. What's goin' on Karrin?"

Karrin looked up and met his gaze. Vee could see the fear in her eyes.

"I needed to get away."

Vee looked down at the check and paid.

Once they were outside, they approached the 300.

"Talk to me, Karrin...you and I both know you didn't come up here just to check on Cat. You call me out of the blue, tellin' me you want to see me, then a couple of hours later, you here?" Vee grilled her mildly..

"It's just...I don't know."

"Did Ty send you?" Vee asked directly.

Karrin's eyes got wide.

"No! why would you-"

"Karrin don't lie to me," Vee growled. "Ty sent you to set me up!"

Karrin's eyes started to tear.

"I wouldn't do that to you, Victor. You're family!"

Vee grabbed both her arms.

"Then tell me what's goin' on?" he demanded.

The force of his voice broke her weak defense. The tears ran down her face and her body became wracked with sobs. She reached out and hugged Vee.

"Victor, I'm...I'm in trouble."

"What kind of trouble?" Vee asked, pulling away looking in her eyes.

She looked at him and told him.

"Ty's father, Guy...it was Ty's mama Debra that set him up and I was a part of it."

Vee couldn't believe his ears. This whole beef had been set off by Guy's broad? Kev had blamed him, killed Poppy and Rico, and the whole time he was sleeping with the enemy?

"Please Vee, don't be mad at me. I know we started a lot of confusion, but-"

Vee grabbed her by the arm. "Get in the car."

He looked around as he put her in the car then got in himself.

Karrin then told him the whole story from beginning to end. She felt safe telling Vee every detail, thinking he was the enemy. She just didn't know he was Guy's son, too.

He saw that Karrin had did it all for Ty, so he knew where her loyalty stood. Yet she was still Cat's cousin and if he turned his back on Karrin, it would be like turning his back on Cat in a way. He had to help her, even if his street instincts were screaming against it.

"Alright look, Rin. I'ma let you stay. But under no circumstances do you tell Ty you wit' me", he told her.

Karrin nodded.

"I don't even know who's side Ty's on right now", she mumbled dejectedly.

"Regardless, ma, you love him so if he calls, you gonna come. Don't try and deny it. Love is a magnet…but if you ever cross me, Karrin…I'll kill you and Ty", he warned her ominously, and the look in his eyes told Karrin not to take the warning lightly.

*"Ty, nooo. It's gonna hurt", Karrin whined, on her hands and knees, pussy dripping.*

*"Just chill, I'ma go slow", Ty crooned convincingly.*

*He had been banging Karrin's back out in his small Smithfield apartment. The pussy had him in a zone and her moans were exciting him and pushing his lust over the edge. Karrin had the prettiest ass of any chick he had ever fucked, so he just had to feel it.*

*He slid his dick out of Karrin's sloppy wet pussy and slid it slowly down the crack of her ass, while he fingered her clit.*

*"Mmmmm"*, Karrin moaned sensually, until her breath caught in her throat, feeling Ty's thick Mwahroom head start to penetrate her puckered asshole.

*"Ty-"* she gasped, gripping the sheets tightly.

*"Shhhh"*, he hushed her, pushing her face in the pillows as he slowly slid in deeper.

She bit into the pillow, trying her best to take it.

*"Relax your muscles, baby. You too tense."* Ty coached her.

She slowly relaxed them and the pain became less intense.

Ty was only halfway in, when Karrin felt like her asshole popped and the pain gave way to a curious feeling. She began slowing throwing it back at Ty, her muffled groans becoming less strained. The more Ty stroked, the wetter her ass got and she found out she was one of those women with a G Spot in her ass.

*"Ty, oh fuck! My pus-pussy cummin' again!"* she cried, as her pussy quivered and flowed cream.

*"Tell daddy how it feels!"* she squealed, *"You...you turning me out!"* Karrin was working her ass like a pro. It still hurt but the pleasure was one she had never experienced. She felt her ass coming at the same time as her pussy. Ty couldn't take the wet tight hotness of her asshole any longer, and he came hard deep inside her.

After showering together, Karrin rested her head on Ty's chest, while he watched Belly on DVD.

*"Do you love me Ty?"* Karrin asked out of the blue, playing in his chest hair.

*"Yeah, Ma"*, he replied, engrossed in the way the Jamaican chick made her ass dance and jingle like that.

*"Then why do you hurt me so much?"* she asked sadly.

The way she said it made Ty pause the DVD in mid jingle. Karrin was definitely his heart, but he was young and wasn't ready to settle down.

He lifted her chin gently.

*"Baby, I ain't tryin' to hurt you, okay? What I do in the street, that shit don mean nothin', yo."*

*A tear rolled down her cheek.*

*"But don't I make you happy? Why I'm not enough for you? She asked earnestly.*

*Because no one woman is, Ty thought to himself, but he said, "It ain't that you ain't enough, it's just, when a nigga in them streets...shit just happen, yo."*

*Ty's cell phone went off, and he was thankful to see AB's number.*

*"What up?"*

*"Nigga, you know what it is! Muthafuckin' Tremors is jumpin! You comin' or what?" AB barked as he sat in the parking lot, smoking a blunt.*

*Ty sucked his teeth. "Now?!" Where the fuck them niggas go? Fuck it, I'll be there."*

*AB laughed, because he knew Ty was frontin for Karrin, so he could get out and go to the club.*

*"Karrin got that ass on lock! Might as well wait til' she go to sleep and sneak out the window, pussy-whipped ass nigga."*

*Ty fought back the smile.*

*"Picture that. I'll handle it."*

*He clicked off then sat up.*

*"Ma, I gotta handle somethin' right quick."*

*"Hmm-mm," she grunted skeptically, turning over and facing the wall.*

*He leaned over her and kissed the side of her mouth.*

*"I'll be back as soon as I can", he promised.*

*"I'm goin' home. I gotta work in the morning."*

*"I'll call you", he replied as he got dressed, grabbed his gun and hit the door.*

⑧ ⑧ ⑧ ⑧ ⑧ ⑧

*Club Tremors in Smithfield was truly jumping. There were throngs of people both inside and outside the club. A lot of cats* were balling, but none of them were on the level of Ty Simmons.

Since coming to Smithfield several months ago, he had turned the spot from a desert to an oasis. There was a dyke who was now overseeing three shooting galleries instead of one, and Ty and AB were slowly expanding into surrounding towns like Selma, Clayton, Benson and Garner.

Ty had pulled it off by copping bricks of cocaine and cutting it with heroin. He was making dope fiends out of crack heads. That combined with the dope he was supplying fiends to turn potential customers out, his name was seriously ringing bells. It was Ty, who from 2000 to 2002, had started the heroin epidemic in Johnson County.

He pulled his brand new baby blue Bentley Azure up next to AB's platinum Mercedes Benz McClaren with the batman doors.

"I never seen doors go up before", a thick Mexican chick said to AB as he sat in the opened door, one foot on the ground, gutting a cigar.

Ty bounced out the car and gave AB a pound.

"Ay you shawtie, let me holla at my man real quick. But don't get lost", AB told her.

When she walked away, AB stood up and tucked the .40 caliber in his waist, handle on the outside of his Coogi sweater.

"Yo dawg, don't look now, but them niggas by the black Yukon? I think we gonna have to do them niggas real talk", AB gritted, ready to set it.

Ty nonchalantly glanced around. He saw several dudes standing by the Yukon, looking hungry and trifling. But he recognized one face. Vee's.

"Don't sweat that, B. I know one of them niggas. He fuckin Karrin's cousin. He cool", Ty told him.

"Whatever, Ty. I stick niggas too, so I know when a nigga on that bullshit", AB growled.

"Fuck it. I'ma go holla at him, see what up", Ty proposed.

"And if them niggas buck, they getting' it right where they stand", AB vowed.

*"That's what it is then", Ty agreed.*

*"Yo, I'm telling you Vee, that nigga getting it around here", Rico had told Vee, before Ty pulled up.*

*Vee looked and saw AB, blinged up, talking to the Mexican chick.*

*"I seen that nigga somewhere before", Vee remarked.*

*"You bout to see him on a milk carton, dawg. What up?" Rico probed.*

*"You know what it is, my nigga." Vee gave him a pound, "Let the wolves out!"*

*Rico threw his head back and howled. A few minutes later, Ty pulled up and parked next to AB.*

*"Yo that's that nigga Ty", Vee commented.*

*"And?" Banks wanted to know.*

*"Fall back. I'm trying to get us in wit' that nigga, yo", Vee told em.*

*"Fuck we need to be in wit' them bitch ass niggas for?" Pappy hissed.*

*"Them niggas look like a sweet lick right now!"*

*"See you the type nigga, Pap, to run down just to fuck one cow and scare the rest away. While I just walk down and fuck em' all!" Vee chuckled.*

*Mike G stood up from sitting on the bumper.*

*"They coming over here."*

*Ty and AB walked up. Ty and Vee shook hands with a gangsta hug.*

*"What up, Vee."*

*"What up, Ty. What's poppin?"*

*From the beginning, Ty and Vee had hit it off. They had double dated with Cat and Karrin a few times and kicked it as well. Vee could tell just by looking at Ty and how he moved, he was getting major paper. Ty could tell Vee was hungry and a go hard-type dude. But since both were cautious, they hadn't brought up any possible moves. Vee wanted to make sure Ty wasn't one of those rich hustlers that snitch just to stay out of jail. Ty wanted to make sure Vee wasn't a grimy nigga, that* once on, would bite the hands that fed him. They were like two dogs sniffing each other's scent.

One thing was clear to both of them, real recognized real.

"You know the drill yo, trying to stay sucka free and off the radar", Ty quipped.

"No doubt."

"Yo, I want you to meet my man AB, this Vee", Ty introduced.

Vee smirked. He knew why Ty was introducing AB. He had felt the vibe so he was letting Vee know in a subtle way that he had felt it.

"What up", Vee nodded.

"Yeah", AB returned. Neither extended their hand.

"And these my niggas, Pap, Rico, Mike, Banks and Rome", Vee introduced, letting his crew know the previous plan was dead.

"That's what's up, but look, I'm bout to roll up in this piece. If ya'll goin' in, I suggest you roll wit' me", Ty offered.

"Cool", Vee responded.

When they got to the door, Vee saw why Ty made the offer.

"What up, Ty? All them wit' you?" The bouncer asked.

Ty looked back.

"Yeah. No doubt."

The bouncer waved them through, without putting the metal detecting wand on them. The whole crew was able to roll in strapped.

"Yo, how come you gotta search us? You ain't search them", the next dude in line complained.

"Cause you ain't them! Now shut yo' bitch ass up!"

Inside the sounds of Ja Rule filled the club.

*Holla! Holla!*
*Anybody that's ready to get dollas dollas!*
*It's murrrdaaa!*

The females on the floor were going crazy to the mix of music mixed with Ecstasy. The dudes were trying to out-ball each other, until Ty came through and bought out the bar. Now they had the attention of the whole club. Females ready to fuck and niggas full of hate, ready to buck.

They already had larceny in their hearts because Ty and AB had come from Goldsboro and blew up in their town. Ty had a few local niggas on the team, but the majority were Goldsboro niggas. On top of that, they were rolling with those Durham niggas that muthafuckas hated and feared.

For the first hour, niggas just hated from the sidelines, but the mixture of alcohol and gangsta music started to make niggas feel froggy. When the DJ threw on the Three-Six Mafia's "Tear the Club up", one froggy nigga decided to leap.

The crew was on the dance floor with approximately twenty females. The dude that was dancing behind Ty with some chubby chick, elbowed Ty in the back hard.

There was no hesitation on Ty's part. He turned around and hooked dude in the mouth. That staggered him. The dude swung a lazy right. Ty dipped smoothly, then shot him a three-piece that put him to sleep.

Vee saw dude's man flinch like he wanted to help and that was all the excuse Vee needed to hit him with an upper cut so hard it made dude bite his tongue bloody.

The dude had at least five more dudes with them, but they were no match for Ty, Vee and the rest of the crew. Before it was over, one dude got his jaw broke, another got a buck fifty across the face (courtesy of Pappy's rug cutter) and three females even got knocked out. That night would be the first of many for the crew, filled with sex, drugs, money and murder.

"Hold on", AB said into his cell, then leaned out the car window and barked, "Fuck is you deaf?! I said two Big Macs,

Chicken McNuggets, two large fries and the goddamn vanilla milkshakes, stupid muthafucka!"

He put the phone back to his ear and said, "Yeah, so like I was sayin', put your ass in the air and squeeze your clit."

AB was in McDonald's drive thru, a few days after the club scene. He was phone sexing a chick he just met in the CrabTree Mall and nodding his head to Tupac's "Hail Mary", unaware that he was the topic of an intense conversation three cars back.

Two of the dudes from the club scene had spotted him turning the corner and followed him. They intended to do a drive by. When he turned into the drive thru they recognized it as the perfect opportunity.

"Pull out, pull out! I'ma blast the nigga then jump in the back seat", the passenger planned, cocking back the .380.

He hopped out of the car, went around the car in front of them and crept up on the inside of the drive thru.

"Yo, slide three fingers in the pussy", AB instructed and the girl moaned heavily like Heather Hunter:

I ain't no killer but don't push me
Revenge is like the sweetest thing next to getting' pussy

AB gripped his dick through his jeans, anxious to get to Raleigh and blow shortie's back out. It was a trip he'd never make. He moved up one car length and pulled up to the window. Turning his attention in that direction gave him the opportunity to see the shadowy figure in his side mirror.

"What the-?!" he barked, dropping the phone and lifting the 40. caliber laying in his lap. He started to turn and fire, but he caught a slug in his face that snapped his head back and knocked the gun out of his hand. The dude stood at his window and smirked. "Remember me, Pussy?!"

Boom! Boom! Boom! Boom!

The dude squeezed off twice to AB's face and twice to his chest, his body jumping and convulsing with every shot. The drive thru cashier screamed behind the gunman, alerting him to her presence. He turned around, snatched AB's order from her then hit her point blank between her eyes. She died before she hit the ground. The gunman sprinted to the get-away car and dove in the back seat as the driver screeched off.

For the next couple of weeks, Ty was sick. He had taken his first real loss in the game with the death of AB, who had been his best friend since being pee-wees. They had stayed at each other's house, even pissed in each other's beds. They had fought back to back as well as toe to toe. Now he was gone, and he had yet to catch the niggas who did it. That is, until he received a call from Vee.

"Meet me in Raleigh at gas station across the street from St. Aug", Vee told him, then hung up. Ty could tell it was serious by the way Vee brought it to him.

Ty jumped in the Azure and made a bee-line for Raleigh. When he got to the meeting spot, Vee was already there in a brown '82 Cadillac Brougham with Mike G. in the passenger seat and Pappy in the back seat. Ty pulled up to him, driver's window to driver's window, cars facing in opposite direction.

"Yo, I found them niggas that hit AB", Vee told him.

Ty was slightly surprised because he didn't know Vee was even looking for the dudes. But Vee was the type of man, that if he fucked with you, then he had your back 100 percent. Besides, Vee saw an opportunity. He knew if he held Ty down, Ty would reciprocate and be the connect Vee needed to lock down Durham.

"Where they at?" Ty wanted to know.

"You rollin' in that?" Vee inquired referring to the Bentley.

"Shit", Ty mumbled, trying to think of what to do with the car.

"Let Mike take it. You just ride with me, "Vee suggested.

Ty got out and left the car running. Mike G jumped in under the wheel and Ty got in the passenger side of the Caddy.

"Wait for us at the McDonald's on Poole Road", Vee instructed Mike.

Mike nodded and both cars pulled off heading in opposite directions.

The house was located on a street around the corner from Walnut Terrace Apartments. Vee parked the Caddy down the block and killed the engine.

"It's the brick and yellow house with the grey minivan in the driveway", Vee explained, putting on a pair of golf gloves and handing Ty a pair.

Ty put them on then pulled out his nine and checked the clip.

"Naw. Leave that here. Shells", Vee reasoned.

Shell casings at the scene was something that Vee didn't like to do if he didn't have to. He handed Ty a .357 magnum revolver.

"A-right", Ty said, gripping the .357. When they both got out, Pappy climbed over the seat and got behind the wheel.

Little kids were outside playing and riding their bikes. At the house next door, a man was watering his lawn. A perfect spring day for a murder because they'd never expect it to go down in broad daylight.

The front door was open, but the screen door was closed. Inside they could see the flickering TV and the sounds of the Young and the Restless theme song. Vee tried the screen door and found it unlocked. He and Ty stepped inside casually. A middle aged woman stepped from around the corner.

"What the hell you doin' in my house? Markie!" she hollered.

Ty raised the gun and shot her in the face, blowing away half her nose, cheek and one eye.

Markie had come out to see what the commotion was when he heard the gun shot and then found himself staring down the barrel of Vee's .357.

"What I do?" Markie exclaimed, voice cracking. He had been the driver.

Boom!

*The head shot left him twitching in the hallway. Ty looked in the bathroom door and found the dude who killed AB on the toilet taking a shit.*

*"Oh shit!" he tried to get up and push the door, but Ty hit him in the chest with a shot that would've made him back-flip but he hit the wall and slid down.*

*Boom!*

*One to the dome, finished the job.*

*Ty and Vee exited as quickly as they came. When they emerged from the house, Vee let off the last five in the air, making any potential witness drop their head or get low. The last thing on their mind was anyone seeing Vee or Ty's face.*

*Pappy pulled up in the Caddy just as they reached the curb. After they jumped in he pulled off.*

*That solidified the bond between Vee and Ty and it led to the birth of one of the most vicious drug organizations in the Eastern Carolinas.*

# CHAPTER 30

T re rested his shovel and leaned against it. The frigid New York winter air seemed to be cutting through him to the bone.

"Man, it's cold as a muthafucka tonight and we ain't even half way to the bitch yet", Tre gruffed.

He, Vee and Sleep were in a cemetery in Bension-Hurst, the final resting place of many Mob figures and their family members. All three had shovels and were furiously digging away in front of a head stone that read:

Isabella Sarducci
1963-2009

"It's a little after one", Vee said, glancing at his watch, "We can be done by four if we keep it hot.

Tre started digging again and chuckled.

"You act like you done this before", he remarked.

Vee looked at him with a curious grin but didn't say anything.

"Yo, I still don't get it," Sleep cut in, "The bitch already dead! Fuck else can we do to her?"

"War ain't always physical, dawg," Vee grunted, throwing a shovel full of dirt to the side. "We got guns, they got a billion guns, we got us, they got thousands of foot soldiers. We outnumbered and outgunned. So we gonna attack what they can't defend with guns…their honor. Show em nothing's sacred. Not their wives, their children, their priest, not even their God."

"Their God?" Sleep echoed. "What you mean by that?" Vee smirked.

"Just keep digging."

The next morning on Atlantic Avenue in Brooklyn, the police would find the decomposed body of Vito Sarducci's daughter. She had been buried for less than two months, so the state of her body made her look like a ghost off of a Thriller video. There was a deep bluish tone to her skin and the worms had been eating away at her flesh. She had a fresh shot gun blast to the chest that almost disintegrated her entire torso. Inside her coffin beside her were two dead dogs. The media had a field day and Vito Sarducci was in a rage, but Vee was only just getting started.

"Forgive me, Father, for I have sinned."

"How long has it been since your last confession?"

"Too long."

Vee sat back in the confessional and lit up a blunt.

"You can't smoke in there", the priest told him gently.

"Is it a sin?"

"Yes, because the body is a temple."

"In that case," Vee inhaled the smoke, "Add it to my list of sins. I'm the one that dug up Sarducci's daughter."

Silence.

"You still there?" Vee asked.

"Yes…yes, I'm still here. Why would you do something like that?"

"Are you judging me, Father?" Vee asked mockingly.

"No. It was just a question."

"Because nothing's sacred. Not even the fuckin' Virgin Mary can save Sarducci', Vee hissed.

"You speak blasphemy!"

"And you bless murderers", Vee chuckled. "You bless Sarducci. You even presided over the ceremony that made him Godfather of his sister's son."

"I'll pray for you my son", the priest replied, avoiding the issue.

"Pray for yourself."

Click. Crack...Boom!

The priest heard the pistol cock back and then he felt...nothing.

The bullet ripped through the confessional and split his forehead. Vee calmly picked up the shell and opened the door.

The few people at the church were in shock. Vee snatched up one of the old ladies and dragged her to the door of the confessional.

"Please, no die!" she said in broken English.

"Shut the fuck up!" Vee barked, his face covered by a bandana. He opened the door of the confessional so she could see the body of the priest. She screamed, crossed herself and began muttering prayers in Latin.

"You see this? You see it?! Vee sneered. "You tell Sarducci before I take his life, I'ma take his soul!"

The old woman looked him in the face defiantly.

"El Diablo", she hissed in Italian, then in English, "You are the Devil."

Vee smiled then walked out the church. He had one last trip to make before he left Bensonhurst.

"Okay class, now we're going to do Math", the petite blond teacher informed her 2$^{nd}$ grade class.

She received a collective moan from the class of six and seven year olds.

"Now come on, it's not that bad", she smiled motherly-like. "We'll begin wit-"

Her thought was cut off when she saw three black men walk into the classroom.

"May I help you?" she asked plainly, no trace of a smile now.

"Yeah, we need to see Anthony Sarducci", Tre informed her casually.

"And, you are?" she probed. Something didn't feel right.

"Anthony!" Vee called out.

One little brown hair boy looked up.

"Anthony, stay in your seat," the teacher told him, because now she was really getting a bad vibe. "I asked you who you are? Now, if you-"

All three pulled out .38 revolvers.

"Or what?" Vee taunted, then blew a hole through her open mouth in mid-scream. Then he blew the back of her head all over the chalk board. Her eyes stayed open as she slid to the floor.

The little kids were terrified. They screamed and cried, not knowing what was going on. Vee, Tre and Sleep showed no remorse. Vee aimed and blew little Anthony up out of his chair then hit him once more, exploding his small face into a gruesome mass of blood, bone and brains. Almost headless, his tiny leg jerked involuntarily. Sleep threw a desk through the window and the three of them climbed through it. Since the classroom was on the first floor, the three wasted no time disappearing from the scene of the crime

"Today has been a tragic one for the small community of Bensonhurst", the small Asian reporter for Channel 7 ABC reported. "Earlier today, two separate incidents occurred. First, a Catholic priest was gunned down during a confession. Then a seven-year old, Anthony Sarducci was executed in his classroom."

A picture of Anthony was put up on the screen.

"In fact, police say, both incidents involved the Sarducci family, long thought to be the most powerful Mafia family in the Nation. Reputed Mob boss, Vito Sarducci, had this to say..."

The camera cut to a scene where Sarducci was being led out of a small social club in Brooklyn by Vinnie and a bunch of bodyguards.

"Mr Sarducci, Mr. Sarducci! Is the death of your grandson and the priest the prelude to a Mob war?" one reporter shouted.

"You, people have no respect", Vito spat venomously.

"Get the fucking camera the fuck outta here!" Vinnie barked. The censor was of course bleeping out his curses.

One of the bodyguards put his hands over the lens and the screen went black. Then the camera was aimed at the ground and it looked like the ground pushed up to the lens and the screen suddenly went static and snowy.

Vinnie helped Vito into a Limo. Two bodyguards rode with them.

The rest got in Lincolns, one in the front and one in the back of the Limo.

Vito sat back in a daze.

"What kind of man...would kill a priest in church?' he asked no one in particular.

"These niggers are animals! Monkeys! " Vinnie spat.

"Anthony," Vito whispered gazing out the window.

Although Vinnie missed his son terribly, he would mourn only after those responsible were dead.

"So I had Nicky in Baltimore get the detective, the one he has in his pocket, to get in Tre's office and get some prints, right? Bingo!" Vinnie snapped his fingers, "We got names and he left them a lil' surprise at the door."

"Addresses?" Vito asked hopefully.

Vinnie shock his head.

"You never know with these fuckin' moolies, but you never know. What we do have is Tredero Verejo, Stephon Cuitler and Victor Murphy", Vinnie smiled. "Tredero's parents are still in Puerto Rico, no way to track em. But I've got a few guys going to pay them a visit as we speak. The Murphy guy is from North Carolina. His mother's in prison, father unknown. Typical nigger", Vinnie snorted. "Anyway, she's due home in few weeks. If we can't get her on the inside, the minute the bitch is free, she's dead!"

"No", Vito shook his head.

"No?" Vinnie echoed.

"Be patient. What do people usually do when they come from prison? They have a dinner, a cookout, some kind of family get together. And then we strike! My Anthony is worth a whole family of niggers!" Vito hissed, waving his finger to punctuate his statement. "And you can bet we'll get Victor, too!'

"We can get him regardless. Let me at Tito", Vinnie requested.

"No. Tito's a man of his word...a man of honor. He said he would stay out of it and I know he did", Vito replied.

"But Pop, he knows these guys. If he's really a friend, then why wouldn't he set them up?" Vinnie proposed.

Vito looked at him thoughtfully, then added, "These guys, there animals. Who needs friends like that? Tito values our friendship. He'll see it our way."

Vinnie nodded.

"Get Tito on the phone," Vito added.

As Tito and the Nigerian chick rode in the back of the Limo, slipping Hypnotique, his cell went off. He looked at the number and knew exactly what it would be about. Tito had been anticipating the call every since he'd seen Anthony's death broadcast on the news.

As soon as he saw it, he thought of Vee's words, "We just goin' to Bensonhurst."

He had smiled and shook his head. He liked the young boy he knew as Jay. Not only was he a straight-up killer, he was smart. He knew how to conduct psychological warfare. Attack what your enemy can't defend.

Now, as his "Love Supreme" ringtones filled the Phantom with a sax to match the city, he knew Vito would make him choose sides.

"Yeah," Tito answered, handing his champagne to the chick and grabbing her Blackberry out of her clutch.

"Tito? Vinnie. Pops wants to talk to ya."

"No problem", Tito replied, while at the same time texting Asia:

*"Get mommy n Aunt Glo, Get Low!"*

"Tito", Vito said, with a heavy heart.

"Mr. Sarducci, I want to extend my deepest sympathies to you and your family. Anthony will be missed", Tito replied, purposely being long winded.

Asia texted back:

*"K... Ty w/ Brooklyn in BX... "*

"Thank you, Tito, thank you. But there's something that I need to ask you."

"What?" Tito responded and texted:

*"Tell Ty my crib. Hardbody. Spagetti Heads."*

Vito sighed

"Tito, you're a smart man. You know what I want."

*"Where my dogz at?"*

Tito texted his young click of Bloods on his payroll.

*"Tito, I value our friendship."*
*"As I, Mr. Sarducci."*

*"We right here dog!"*

They texted back. Tito hit back:

*"The krib ASAP hardbody*

*Lok the blok East-West"*

"This…this Tre…he's not a man of honor like you, Tito. He's an animal! Men fight men, Tito! Only cowards kill women and children", Vito accused.

*All is fair in Love and War,* Tito thought, but he said. "I understand how you feel, Mr. Sarducci. What is it that you ask of me?"

Ty texted:

*"We on it!"*

Tito texted back.

*Send Brooklyn Home!*

"Where are they, Tito? For Anthony, where are they?" Vito asked sincerely.

Ty texted.

She said kiss her ass!

Tito sighed.

"Mr. Sarducci, Tre is my friend just like you. I told you I'd stay out of it and I kept my word."

there was a long silence. Another text came through on the blackberry. It was his young boys.

We in position.

"Tito...they can not go unpunished...nor can they be protected," Vito warned subtly.

"Be that as it may, a man must stand by his word," Tito replied firmly.

"You don't leave me much of a choice," Vito remarked dejected.

"Neither do you, Mr. Sarducci," Tito answered with disappointment neither one wanted to go to war with the other, but they had reached an impasse, that made war inevitable.

"then I guess we both gotta do what we gotta do," Vito remarked.

Ty Texted.

I see em' 4 cars deep!

Tito smiled, picturing Vito giving Vinnie hand signals to move on Tito. But Tito was more than prepared. "okay. Tito...take care."

"You too, Mr. Sarducci," Tito replied.

They hung up like two friends instead of two opponents about to clash in battle.

Tito pulled out his fully automatic and cocked it back. His Nigerian chick pulled out a 380 from the garter belt on her left thigh.

"What's up Baby?" she asked.

"We havin' Italian for dinner, he chuckled and made her giggle. Tito's block was lined with immaculate brown stones on both sides of the street except for the flower shop and the corner store. In the dark frigid air, he could see a car with exhaust smoke coming from the rear. Looking at the inside of the flower shop and corner store he could see several Italians acting like they were shopping. The bulges under their coats, a dead give away as to their true intentions.

"Here we go, baby," Tito told her.

The driver parked in the middle of the block and got out to open the door on the curb side for Tito and the female. Out of the corner of his eye, Tito saw the car from earlier turn the corner and he smiled to himself. Sarducci knew he had to send a team, and not just a few, to get Tito Bell. But even these weren't enough. The Italians came out of the flower shop and store, stepped off the curb and attempted to cross the street.

As the driver rounded the car and opened the door, he pulled his .45 caliber from his holster and, using the roof of the car as a base opened fire on the Italian hit squad. The driver took one Italian off his feet, but the other six quickly took cover behind cars on the opposite side of the street.

The car suddenly accelerated and automatic muzzles appeared in the passenger side window, front and back. The machine gun fire rocked the Phantom, busting the windows and blowing out chunks of the car, pinning Tito, the driver and the girl behind the car. The car stopped directly in front of Tito's car... a steady stream of bullets made Swiss cheese of the $200,000 car. Emboldened, the Italians across the street came up firing and approaching, thinking they had Tito right where they wanted him. In reality, they had walked into a trap.

Two of Tito's young boys popped up on the roof of Tito's brownstone and began showering the streets with fully automatic Ak-47's. The powerful projectiles ripped through one Italian's eye and blew out the base of his neck, killing him instantly. Ty and Brooklyn came out from under a brownstone's steps, across the street from Tito and behind the enemy line of Italians. They dropped three more, before the rest began to return fire. The Italians in the car had been riddled through the roof with the Ak-47's. The driver was slumped over the steering wheel and one of the back passengers was hanging half way out of the car. The other had his bloody head leaking life onto his lap. Although disoriented one was determined to survive as he stumbled out of the car. Tito crept around the trunk of the Phantom and put the gun to his head.

"Naw muthafucka, don't run now. The party's just startin'", Tito hissed. Tito spun his body around and wrapped his arm around his neck, using the guy as a human shield.

"You shoulda brought an army!" Tito boasted, firing on the remaining Italians.

They were in front of the parked cars, using the grills for cover because Brooklyn and Ty had them on one side and Tito from the other. Brooklyn tried to get a better position but one of the Italians saw her and fired three times. The first bullet missed but one found a cushy target in the left cheek of her fat ass.

"Aw fuck!!!" Brooklyn agonized.

"Brooklyn!" Ty yelled.

"I'm hit but I'm good!"

Four more of Tito's young boys rounded the corner right behind the remaining Italians. They had been positioned to lock down the east end of the block. There were four more on the west end that so far hadn't needed to fire a shot.

Tito positioned his people all around the perimeter and Vito's team was no match. Tito's young boys finished off the Italians. Everyone quickly disappeared as the sound of approaching sirens filled the air, leaving only dead Italians, smoking vehicles and major property damage in their wake.

# CHAPTER 31

"Yo J, how come you don't like to ride with the radio on?" Tre asked, reclining in the passenger seat of the rented Le Sabre.

Vee was driving and Sleep was smoking a cigarette in the backseat. They were on I-95 South, just a few miles from Baltimore.

"I done seen too many niggas get caught sleepin. I done caught niggas sleeping. Fuck that, I wanna know what's going on around me," Vee explained.

Tre's cell phone went off.

"Speak."

"What's up, Baby? How you doing? You good"? Fiyah asked.

"No doubt. How the shoot doin' in Jamaica?" Tre inquired. Tre had sent all his stars and production team to Jamaica for filming. It would be the first in the Vampyre series with an all-star lineup and it was positioned to blow. Distributors were already coming at Tre left and right. Everything was going according to plan. "Shit baby, we at Hee-doo! You know everybody on their A game at Hedonism!" Fiyah giggled.

"Yeah, for that fifteen gees a scene I'm payin' you, damn right you better be on you're A-game" Tre quipped half jokingly. "That's business, but you know, all you gotta do is say the word and you get it," Fiyah flirted.

Tre chuckled.

"Keep talkin' like that and I might just have to mix business with pleasure. I'ma hit you later," he replied, then hung up.

When they got to Baltimore City, they headed over to Vee's studio apartment first. Tre and Sleep waited downstairs, guns locked and loaded, their eyes peeled. They were taking no chances.

Vee took the stairs then opened the door with his key. The smell of garlic, butter and shrimp hit him in the face.

"Oh hey, Vic. When'd you get back?" Karrin asked, standing at the stove.

Vee could see her through the cabinet partition that separated the kitchen from the rest of the large room. The entire right wall was made up of ceiling-to-floor windows that gave a panoramic view of Baltimore Harbor. Although Vee had the place sparsely furnished because he hadn't been there long, the mahogany floor gave the place a jazzy, Neo look to it. Karrin had Opium incense burning and Jill Scott's first CD playing softly in surround sound.

"Just now. Pack up we gotta move," Vee told her.

Karrin came around the partition with concern in her gaze. "Are you okay, Vic?"

When Karrin was in the kitchen, Vee could only see her from the waist up, but when she came into the main room, he could see her head to toe. She was wearing a pair of cut off low rider jeans and a small tee-shirt that ended above her navel and hugged her firm pert softball-sized breast.

Vee shook off her beauty and stayed focused.

"Yeah, we just gotta keep it movin' for now. Go pack," Vee instructed her. Karrin nodded then walked towards the back of the room where the bed and dresser were.

Vee couldn't help but watch the slight sway in her hips as she walked. A few moments later, Karrin had her duffle bag and suitcase ready. She handed over to Vee a piece of paper.

"I made a bunch of these at Kinko's," she told him.

When Vee looked at the paper, he felt an icy hand grip his heart. It was a picture of Cat laughing into the camera. Her cat eyes in gorgeous slits. Vee knew the picture well. Karrin had cropped it but he knew it was from their trip to St. Thomas. Vee could even see the ocean behind her left ear.

"I've been driving around posting these all over town," Karrin said. "Everywhere. I had a few people tell me they had seen her but nobody knew when or where she was now," she explained, a little down because she hadn't been more success-ful.

The flyer read:
Have You Seen This Girl?

Then it gave Karrin's number and email address. Vee folded it up and put it in his pocket.

"And...Ty called today," Karrin admitted, eyes diverted.

"Did you answer?"

She shook her head.

"I wanted to so bad. He called three times and he texted me!" she explained, tears crystallizing in her eyes. "Vic I---I don't know what to do? I love him but..." her voice trailed off and she sighed heavily.

Vee held her by both her arms and looked into her eyes.

"Listen Rin, I understand you love Ty, but he tried to kill his own father and he stood by while his mother was killed for it," he stressed. "Now think. You're a loose end. Do you think he'd hesitate to clip you?"

Vee didn't know exactly what happened, but he knew what he told her would make Karrin think twice about calling Ty. Deep down, he felt she would crack, but he hoped she wouldn't do it in a way that would jeopardize him. He wouldn't hesitate to make her regret it.

"You're right, Vic. I won't contact him."

"Gimme your phone."

She complied, and then Vee punched a number in and stored it.

"Her name's Jaytiah. She in DC. Go to DC and call her, she'll help you get a place."

"You're not coming?" Karrin asked with a tinge of disappointment in her voice. "Is it because you don't trust me?"

"Naw, yo...I just gotta handle somethin'. I'll be there in a few days," Vee assured her.

"Just know Victor, I appreciate what you're doing for me and I won't forget it. I'll never do anything to break your trust," Karrin told him sincerely.

"We'll see."

Sleep was under the wheel when Vee came back to the car and they drove to McDonald's. Sleep was about to get in the drive thru, but Tre schooled him.

"Naw, don't never go to the drive thru. You trapped in."

"My bad, yo, I was slippin'," Sleep admitted.

Sleep parked.

"Ya'll straight?" Sleep asked. "Anybody want somethin?"

"I'm good."

"Yeah, I'm straight."

Sleep got out and went inside.

"Yo J, I know we don't usually do this, but I'ma need your government name for the partnership contract," Tre said, sitting with his back against the door.

Vee sat against the opposite passenger door so they could see each other comfortably.

"We don't rock like that, dawg. I know you keep it...one hundred. And if you ain't, a piece of paper ain't gonna mean shit anyway," Vee replied.

" Indeed, yo, but it ain't about keepin' it real, but doin shit legit mean doin' it right," Tre returned. "Shit gotta be proper 'cause you legit now."

Vee looked out the window, watching his surroundings.

"Temporarily."

"Naw, J," Tre shook his head, "Listen...fuck the street game yo. Let that shit go. I been in this game since the eighties, but it ain't the same. Muthafuckas got the game fucked up now. You smarter than that. We 'bout to see millions legitimately."

"Tre...on the real, this all I know. I done had a fucked up life yo. I ain't learn how to read until I went to training school when I was twelve," Vee admitted, thinking about Banks. He had been the one who had taught Vee how to read.

Tre sighed.

"But you can learn. Just give this six months. And if we ain't doin' the numbers I'll get back in the game with you," Tre vowed.

Vee smiled at his sincerity, but he wasn't ready to commit.

"Put it in my mom's name. Shantelle Braswell."

Thinking of his mother, made him think of Cat.

"'ey yo Tre, remember I came up here and we went to that club? The last time I was up here?"

"Yeah."

"That chick that was wit' me...I ain't had just met her. That was my baby's moms, yo," Vee revealed.

Tre chuckled.

"Never can be too careful, huh? I kinda-," Tre stopped and he snapped his fingers.

"That's where I seen her before! I knew I knew her!" Vee leaned up.

"You saw her again? Where?" Vee asked intently.

"It was just in passin', But I think I was in Park Heights. She wasn't lookin' too good, J. She don't fuck around wit' that shit do she?"

"Naw...I hope not," Vee mumbled. "I been-,"

Sleep came back to the car, so Vee stopped talking. Sleep knocked on the passenger window.

"You drive, nigga. Let a nigga get his chew on," Sleep remarked. Tre slid over under the wheel and Sleep got in. Tre realized why Vee stopped talking about the subject, so Tre let it go too.

"Yo," Sleep said, mouth full of fries as Tre pulled off. "Go by the office. I left like twenty stacks in the safe."

Tre drove to Fish Street. The block was quiet when they got there. Tre pulled over and parked across the street.

All three had their guns out, on point and ready for anything that may go down.

"Yo, Sleep, hurry up," Tre told him, "This the only spot them Italians don't know how to find us at," he reminded him, not knowing how wrong he was. "No doubt, yo. I'm in and out," Sleep assured him, opening the door, "and don't eat my fuckin' fries."

As soon as Sleep got out, Tre's hand was in his bag.

"But yo J, I got people in Park Heights. If she there, we'll get at her. She ain't do no foul shit, did she?"

"Naw," Vee answered, and Tre could tell he didn't want to talk about it.

Vee watched Sleep wait for a car to pass, then he crossed the street. Something inside of Vee told him, *shit wasn't right.* He peered into the office plate glass window. Even though it was tinted, he could see a dim light inside.

He squinted, then said, "Yo Tre...the bathroom light on."

Tre looked.

"Yeah," he answered, focusing on the fries.

"Tre, we ain't leave no light on," Vee remarked, gripping his nine.

"You sure?"

"Positive," Vee confirmed.

Since he was on the passenger side, Vee quickly got out on the curb. His razor sharp mind calculated the situation in milliseconds. The mob wasn't waiting for them at the office? He knew that was unlikely. He came expecting a gun fight. But the streets were deserted which could only mean one thing...

Vee popped out the door and yelled over the hood, "Yo, Sleep, don't open that door! Don't---"

Kaboooooommmm!

The moment Vee yelled was the moment when Sleep turned the key in the lock and pushed opened the door. The door had been rigged to a trip wire. The moment it was broken, it sent a signal to the explosive planted around the door. Sleep didn't feel a thing except a hot flash before his body was blown in four different directions.

The force of the blast flipped a van parked near the door and blew out car windows up and down the block, including their rental. Vee shielded himself from the blast by getting down beside the door. He felt the car rock against him and felt the shards of window glass pepper his back. The only thing he suffered was a bruised shoulder where the car rocked against him. Tre wasn't so fortunate. He turned and ducked in time not to get sprayed in the face by the window glass, but the force of the explosion blew out the ear drum of his left ear, leaving him deaf in that ear for life.

Car alarms whooped and chirped up and down the block as Vee staggered around the car to the driver's side. He looked at Tre and was relieved to see him in one piece, though his ear was bleeding and he appeared to be dazed.

"Move over, dawg," Vee told him, pushing him into the passenger seat. Vee got in and drove off with a screech.

He glanced back in his rearview and saw Sleep's headless torso burning in the middle of the street.

"Fuck!" Vee barked, punching the steering wheel.

The Sarducci Family had struck back. The only good thing that came out of it for Sleep was the fact that he didn't have to feel the pain of knowing his mother and father had been killed execution style in their own driveway.

"Yo...where's...Sleep?" Tre asked, still dazed.

Vee shook his head but didn't answer.

"Welcome home, lil' sis! That was one helluva vacation!" Hawk Bill exclaimed, bear hugging her until her feet were off the ground. "Fool, put me down!" Shantelle laughingly resisted. Though she hated to feel overpowered, she loved being in her brother's arms. They made her feel safe, free.

The Braswell family had gotten together to welcome Shantelle home. They had rented out the Rec Center in Webbtown, a spot she knew well. Back in the eighties, it had been a hangout for hustlers.

"My baby home!" her blind mother cried, feeling Shantelle's face to fix a visual in her mind.

"Well, you certainly look the same," her mother joked, and the family laughed.

It was definitely true that at 42, she didn't look a day over twenty-five. Prison preserves you, especially when you do a long stretch. She worked out to keep up her figure. She had a wasp-like waist, flat stomach and badon-kadonk ass. She had manage to tone up without losing her femininity. She had cut her hair years ago and kept it short in a style that resembled Toni Braxton's with the bang across her forehead and ice pick sharp sideburns.

She had on a pair of tight fitting Chanel Pants.

She looked so good, many of her male relatives either wished they weren't related, calculated how distant they were related or simply didn't care they were related and pushed up.

"So how does it feel to be home?" her aunt had asked.

Shantelle looked at her, searching for the words to describe how it felt. *How can you describe being suffocated and strangled under blue skies? To see freedom through a chain link fence, right at your fingertips, but just out of your grasp? To be so close but so far away. How can someone understand that's never been choked, how it feels to breathe?*

"Alive," she said with passion, but only those within earshot that had been there before, truly understood.

All her aunt could say was, "Praise God!"

There was food galore and enough children had been born, grew and had children to keep Shantelle busy catching up for hours.

The DJ Mickey D kept the old school hits spinning until he said on the mike," where my girl at? Where Shantelle?"

Shantelle had been dancing with a cousin that was steadily cracking on her.

She yelled," Right here, baby!".

"Boy, do I have a surprise for you!" Mick exclaimed, turning down the music. "What was your favorite song in 1987?"

She didn't even have to think.

"Like you don't know!" she laughed. "I used to bug you to play it at the Omni. "One Love" by Whodini!"

"Well...have you ever heard it...live?" Mick quipped, then put on the beat to the song.

Out of the back office off the dance floor, Whodini stepped out singing:

*One Love One Love*
*You're lucky just to have just one love!*

Shantelle couldn't believe her eyes. She covered her mouth with her hands and swooned like a school girl.

*Both love and life have four letters.*
*Yet they're two different words altogether*
*'cause I've liked many ladies in my day*
*But just like the wind they've all blown away*

Shantelle sang the song word for word with Whodini. They kept holding the mike out to her to finish the line. Hawk Bill videotaped the moment because he knew she'd cherish it for the rest of her life.

While Shantelle was taking pictures with Jalil and Ecstasy, she heard that smooth blackberry brandy baritone that she knew well behind her.

"You got a smile for me, too?"

The smile that she had on her face instantly disappeared. Without turning to face him, she replied, "Nigga, the only thing I got for you, you'd best duck!"

Guy laughed but Shantelle was dead serious and he saw it in her eyes. Guy turned his attention to Jalil and Ectasy and shook their hands.

"I appreciate ya'll comin' down on such short notice," Guy thanked them. "Anything for an old friend," Jalil replied, then Whodini left.

"I suppose I got you to thank for this," Shantelle huffed, arms folded across her chest.

Guy shrugged, keeping his hands in his pockets.

"Then we even, because it's you that I thank for the memories I have of that song. Remember?" Guy crooned.

Shantelle sucked her teeth.

"I was young and dumb then, but that weak shit don't work on a grown ass woman that don't believe in bedtime stories no more," she spat back. Her anger was real, but underneath, she still loved Guy. Looking at him, he was still fine, with the grey hair around his temples and down the center of his goatee, and that voice...she couldn't help but sneak a peak at the delicious print that she woke up wet dreaming about, many a night in prison.

Guy saw her subtly checking him out and he smiled to himself.

"You look good, baby...really good," he complimented her.

Before she could reply with the slick words she had on the tip of her tongue, she saw several police officers come in across the room. She frowned. Guy turned around to see what she was frowning at.

When Guy saw the police, he knew something wasn't right. Goldsboro was a small town. Guy knew the police force well because he had half of them on his payroll. None of these looked even remotely familiar. They all looked like...Italians.

"Shantelle Braswell," one of the officers called out, looking around.

"I'm Shantelle Braswell," she called back, her stomach in knots, wondering what old crime had caught up with her.

Hawk Bill sensed the same thing. He began reaching for his gun.

"Them ain't no goddamn police!" he barked.

Seeing their cover was blown, the Italians all drew weapons and began aiming for Shantelle. Guy grabbed her and dove with her behind a cement partition in the corner of the gym. Hawk Bill picked one of them off, but not before the Italian had killed Shantelle's favorite aunt. Hawk Bill got his mother to cover, while firing at the hit squad. Guy fired and picked off two Italians with headshots.

The other three made their escape as Hawk Bill followed them out the door until his chamber was empty. They jumped in a waiting van and sped away.

Guy helped Shantelle up. She was clearly shaken.

"You okay?" Guy asked with intense concern.

All she could do was shake her head but he could see the gratitude in her eyes. It had all happened so fast, but one thing was clear. Guy could've just thought of himself but he had risked his life to save hers.

Guy looked down at one of the leaking Italians on the floor and wondered why the fuck would the Mob want to kill Shantelle?

"Damn, yo! How ya'll gonna let me miss all the fun?!" Asia pouted, playfully. The Bell family, Tito, Asia, Brooklyn, Gloria and Theresa, along with Ty were in a condo Tito owned in the Poconos. The snow was thick outside and getting thicker, but the blazing fireplace kept the whole split-level home warm and toasty.

Tito sipped his warm brandy. Brooklyn leaned on the couch, because she couldn't sit on her left cheek.

"You trying to tell me all this was over pussy?" she yelped.

"Not pussy," Brooklyn spat, "You got me shot in the ass over some ass!"

Tito shrugged.

"I told you take yo' ass home, but did you listen? What you tell me?"

Brooklyn rolled her eyes.

" Ty, what she say?" Tito smirked.

Ty chuckled.

"Kiss her ass!"

Tito leaned forward in the arm chair. "Mwah! Oh I forgot, the Italians did it for me!"

He laughed.

Brooklyn leaned to get a pillow to throw at Tito, but she leaned on her left cheek and howled," Aww shit. Fuck you, Tito!"

"But on the real, cuz. The Mafia? Is this shit worth it?" Ty questioned.

Tito shrugged.

"It is what it is. Tre, my man, I had to hold him down, and now these muthafuckas came at me. I'ma give em' what they want," Tito concluded.

"Naw, don't get it twisted. I'ma hold you down, regardless. But can you bust your gun and get money at the same time?" Ty inquired.

Tito knew he was talking about the deal. It seemed like all of a sudden, Ty was pressing for the deal. This was ironic to Tito, because the sooner the deal was done, and Tito had a strong enough foothold, he planned on murdering Guy to revenge his father. He knew he'd have to kill Ty too. It seemed as if Ty was rushing his own death.

At the same time, Ty was thinking the same thing.

Nothing beats the double cross....

"This Sarducci thing won't take long, believe me," Tito remarked nonchalantly. "Tomorrow, we gonna meet my man, Nazir."

"Asia's boyfriend," Brooklyn teased and Asia gave her the finger.

"Then we goin' back up top and you can meet NY man Tre and J," Tito outlined.

"J?" Ty echoed.

Tito snickered.

"He the muthafucka that started this shit from jump. He spit in the spaghetti head's face."

Ty laughed.

"Word? I like him already," Ty cracked.

"I know, right? I do, too. Is he a cutie?" Brooklyn chimed in, knowing how he hated for his sisters to ask about his people, but he ignored her.

"Yeah, he a soldier," Tito remarked, thinking about how Vee handled Bensonhurst. "Destined to be a general."

"Ya'll bring your assess on! I ain't cooked for my health!" Theresa yelled from the kitchen.

The four of them headed to the kitchen. After dinner, Theresa was tired so Gloria volunteered to put all the dishes in the washer. Asia and Brooklyn went into the home theatre to watch "Love Thang" while Tito went into his room, talking to Nazir.

Ty stayed behind and helped Gloria.

"Mama Gee...where did you go after you talked to my mother that night at the hair salon?" Ty questioned.

Gloria looked at him.

"Excuse you? Guy send you up here to keep tabs on me? None of your damn business where I went!"

Ty looked at her, studying her reaction.

"Why the hell would you ask me that?"

"You was the last one to see her alive," Ty replied deadpan.

Gloria dropped a glass and it shattered on the floor. She covered her mouth with her hands, the diamonds on her finger dancing under the kitchen light.

"Baby, no...," she gasped.

Gloria pulled Ty to her and hugged him tightly. To Ty, the way she reacted, it seemed like this was the first she heard of Debra's death. But Ty also knew Gloria was a good actress when she needed to be.

"I'm so sorry, Tyquan," she comforted him.

When they broke the hug, she looked down at the glass all over the floor.

"Oh God, look what I done did," Gloria scolded herself.

"You ain't got no shoes on, Mama Gee. Sit down, I'll clean this up," Ty offered.

"Thank you, baby," Gloria said gratefully, while stepping gingerly over the glass to sit at the kitchen table. "How...what happened?"

As Ty swept , he replied," Somebody snatched her up, then...," Ty had to fight back the anger that rose like bile in his throat. "Then they beat her...shot her ...then burned her."

"Oh no," Gloria whispered, tears welling up in her eyes. "I am truly sorry, baby."

Ty dumped the glass in the trashcan then sat at the table with Gloria.

"Why would someone do a thing like that?" she asked, more to herself than to Ty. "Did...did you find them?"

Ty shook his head, watching her closely.

"So that's why you asked where did I go after I saw her? I guess I'm always around when the drama kicks up, huh?"

Ty knew in his heart Gloria didn't have anything to do with it, but if Guy did it, did she know? That's what he was trying to confirm, Guy's involvement not Gloria's.

"Mama Gee, I know you didn't have anything to do with it, but maybe you saw something, heard something." In his mind he added, knew something, but didn't voice it. "Anything!"

Gloria sighed.

"No ," she said, regrettably. "Actually, we had a decent conversation for the first time. Afterwards, I left but Debra was still there."

Ty nodded. It was his guilt telling him it was Guy. But his instincts were telling him it was Young Hardy. The only thing that still didn't fit was Karrin's whereabouts. She still hadn't answered the phone, or maybe she couldn't answer the phone. Ty's bottom line was, until he knew Karrin was safe, Guy still wasn't in the clear.

Vee, Tre, Karrin and Jatiah sat around the kitchen table playing spades. They were in a small apartment in southeast D.C. which Jatiah had rented the spot for Vee, at Karrin's request. The only furniture was the kitchen table and a few blow-up mattresses. Karrin had bought a small stereo but Vee wouldn't let her play it while he was there.

"I got five on it, girl," Jatiah chimed, arranging her cards.

"Well that's what we gonna bid 'cause I ain't got jack," Karrin giggled.

Vee's cell phone vibrated on his hip.

"Yo," he answered.

"How you doin? This Hawk Bill," Hawk replied.

"Yeah," Vee responded nonchalantly.

"You know your mama home?"

"Oh, word?" Vee answered with more life in his tone. "Gimme her number. I'ma hit her now."

"Naw nephew, you need to come down here. Some shit done went down," Hawk Bill explained.

Vee leaned forward, put his elbows on the table, giving his full attention, now.

"I don't really want to talk about it over the phone, you follow? Don't worry, she safe now but she need you down-,"

That's all Vee needed to hear.

"I'm on my way," Vee said. He clicked off, standing up at the same time. "Jatiah, I need you to rent me a car."

"I got you," Jatiah replied.

"Yo J, what up?" Tre asked, as he stood up, too." You good?"

"Yeah, yeah, no doubt. I just need to handle somethin, OK?"

"Ai-ight then, let's go!" Tre said, ready to roll.

Vee smiled at his man. He could see Tre really had his back.

"Naw, It's a family affair," Vee told him.

Karrin looked up at him, apprehensively.

"You good, Rin. My man gonna hold you down 'til I get back," Vee assured her.

"Okay Vee...be safe," Karrin wished him.

"Yeah, my nigga, be safe! Tre seconded.

Vee met up with Hawk Bill when he got to Goldsboro, then he followed Hawk to a tiny town called Mount Olive. All Vee could think about all the way to North Carolina was *Did Guy do it?*

He asked that very question to Hawk Bill when he got to Goldsboro.

"Naw, nephew. Guy saved her life."

They drove out to a large ranch style house set back from the road. The two-story house resembled a plantation style home that boasted a wrap-around porch that bordered two sides of the house. It also had a wrap-around veranda porch on the second floor that covered two sides as well.

The house sat on two hundred plus acres. Vee could see the horses grazing in the distance. He could also see the many armed guards that were posed strategically all around the perimeter. All carried fully automatic assault rifles, many had walkie-talkies, and a few even had Rottweilers on leashes.

Vee and Hawk Bill walked up to the front door, which was opened for them by another armed guard dressed in grey fatigues. "Mr. Simmons is in the back," the guard told them, then led them to the back.

Guy and Shantelle were sitting on the patio. When Shantelle saw Vee, she jumped up and hugged him. "Here go my baby!", she squealed, squeezing him tight. Vee tried to remain detached, but it felt good to be in his mother's arms. "Hey Shantelle, welcome home," Vee greeted.

After the hug, he turned and looked at Guy.

"'ey Shantelle, why you still fuckin' wit' this clown after all the bullshit you said he put you through?" Vee hissed.

Guy blazed inside, but kept his composure.

"Victor, watch your mouth. I'm still your mother and I'm not havin' all that fuckin' cussin'. Now, respect my presence!" Shantelle demanded.

Vee looked at Guy and they eye-boxed for a moment before Vee smirked menacingly.

"You said you ain't never wanna see my face again, you see it, right?" Vee taunted.

Guy got up slowly with his fists balled at his sides.

"Boy...somebody need to teach you some goddamn manners" Guy drawled. They had only taken one step towards each other before Hawk Bill restrained Guy and Shantelle held Vee's arm.

"Let that bullshit go! Both of you! They tried to kill my sister! Save it for them muthafuckas, 'cause ain't neither one of ya'll gonna stop me from gettin' them!" Hawk Bill barked like the bull that he was.

"Victor...sit down," Shantelle told him with motherly firmness.

Vee hesitated, then reluctantly complied.

Guy sat down as well.

"What the fuck is goin' on? First Deb, now you," Guy shook his head.

"Shantelle, why would the Mob be comin' at you?" Hawk Bill wanted to know.

"I don't know," she answered.

"The Mob?! Vee exclaimed" "You sure?"

"Positive," Hawk Bill confirmed. "They tried to come like they was the fuckin' police. Goldsboro this big," Hawk Bill snapped his fingers, "And I know every face on the force! All of em' was Italian."

Vee sat back, shocked.

"Ain't no fuckin' way," he said to himself.

"No way what?" Hawk Bill probed.

Vee shook his head.

"How the fuck did they find out?" Vee growled, fists balled up. Hawk Bill looked at Vee sternly.

"Boy, you know something about this? Talk to me!" Hawk Bill demanded.

Vee sighed, rested his forearms on his knees and said, "if it's the Mob...somehow they found out you my mother and tried to get at me through you."

"What the hell you do to them?" Guy asked.

Vee explained to them about Tre and the trip to Vegas. He didn't tell them he killed Mr. Man and Stan Allen, but all three read between the lines. Guy cut him off when he got to the part about Nick Galante's visit to Tre's office.

"You did what?" Guy chuckled.

"I spit in his fuckin' face," Vee smirked.

Guy looked at Shantelle and shook his head. That was something Vee got from her. She had been quick to do it back in the day. "Well, if they didn't' know your name, that's how they found out," Guy surmised.

"How?"

"Probably some cop they got on payroll in Baltimore. He probably came back to his office and got our fingerprints," Guy explained. He knew the tactic well because he had used it many times.

Vee nodded.

"Yeah, that'll explain the bomb they planted in the office," he told them.

"Bomb?" Shantelle echoed.

"They tried to set us up. They missed me and Tre but they got his man, Sleep!"

He went on to tell them about Bensonhurst.

"A priest, Victor? A child? A dead body?" Shantelle couldn't believe her ears.

"What do it matter? I'm cursed anyway," Vee spat.

Hawk Bill and Guy looked at each other. They didn't understand, But Shantelle did.

"Then they won't stop until you're dead," Guy told him.

"Or they are," Vee shot back defiantly.

Guy chuckled at his Vee's bravado.

"Son, you can't take on the Mob by yourself."

"Fuck them bastards! They bleed just like me!"

"And so does your momma!" Guy barked, standing up. "You see what happens when you go off half assed? The Mob ain't some niggas on the corner! They got more judges, politicians, police, a whole lot more money and guns than our black ass!"

Guy paced the floor. He had to admit, although his son had balls and brains, he was using his balls more than his brains.

Vee was fucked up over the fingerprint tactic. It made him feel like he was slipping, getting sloppy. He always prided himself on covering his tracks and watching his back. He realized he was fucking with a different breed now, but he wasn't about to back down.

"And who is it? What family is it?" Guy questioned.

"Salami, Sardini, Sardookey-,"

"Sarducci?" Guy stopped pacing and eyed him.

"Yeah. I think that's it."

"Not only do you go at a Mafia family, you go at THE Mafia family," Guy shook his head.

Vee stood up, ready to leave.

"Well yo, regardless who it is, it's my problem."

"No. You made it my problem when you almost got your mother killed!"

Vee laughed insolently. "Oh, now you wanna be her protector? Nigga, you 'bout twenty years too late."

"No, Vee," Shantelle broke in, "I have to admit, that was my fault. I was so mad with Guy, I wouldn't accept a dime from him."

"Yeah, whatever. We still don't need him, Shantelle. Come on, let's go."

"She ain't goin' nowhere and neither are you," Guy said firmly. "You not about to go do some dumb shit and get me or your mother fucked up. We goin' to meet your man, Tre...then, we gonna take care of the Sarducci shit.

Guy had a very good poker face, but inside he was amped. He knew Sarducci well. He had been one of the council's main supplier. He was also one of Po' Charlie's biggest rivals. Now, he was also Tito's main supplier. He knew if he could push Sarducci back, he could weaken Tito and he'd be closer to his goal of taking over the Bells' network.

"We leave in the mornin'," Guy informed them, then walked out of the room.

# CHAPTER 32

T he snow from the night before had turned into rain, making the streets of south Philly an icy mess, as Tito and Ty sloshed along in a pea-green hummer. Ahead of them was Nazir in a navy blue Range Rover and behind them, a nondescript brown van.

They pulled up into a series of warehouses, made a left between two more warehouses, then stopped at the retractable metal doors of another warehouse. Nazir beeped the horn twice in quick succession, then in one long one. A few seconds later, the metal doors rolled up, rattling the whole way. When all three vehicles were inside, the door rattled its way back down. The three of them parked almost side by side, then Nazir and three other Muslims got out of the Range Rover. Ty could tell they were Muslims because they all sported multicolor Kufis, had face trimmed beards and the long short favored by Muslim males called Khamisas.

A fifth Muslim got out of the van. Tito and Ty hopped out. Tito was carrying a duffle bag as he approached Nazir. The warehouse was filled with boxes and crates, but the center was clear. Inside stood three white dudes. The one in the middle stepped out and greeted Nazir. Tito could tell he was in charge by the way the other two flanked him. He was of average height, with a bald head and a crooked nose that made him look like a boxer. However, the expensive suit he wore made him look more like Don King.

"Salaam," Nazir returned, saying the same word in Arabic the white dude had said in Hebrew.

The two men embraced each other warmly, then Nazir turned to Tito. "This is my man, Sergei. He's a Russian Jew. It seems like the only time Muslims and Jews get along is when we do crime!" Nazir joked.

The whole gathering laughed.

"Sergei, this is my man, Tito. Treat him like you treat me," Nazir introduced.

Sergei and Tito shook hands.

"It's very good to meet you Tito," Sergei remarked, with a heavy Russian accent.

"Likewise," Tito returned.

Sergei glanced down at the bag in Tito's hand.

"That's a pretty big bag, eh?"

"I got a pretty big order," Tito shot back smoothly.

"So I hear. Nazir says you look for big guns, yes?"

"I need two AT4s equipped with .80 millimeter sub rounds. Two Berretta M2.50 calibers and twelve pairs of night vision goggles," Tito told him.

Sergei whistled. "I'd hate to be man you aim at. Anyone I know?"

Tito shrugged.

"I don't know who you know."

Sergei put his hands in his pockets

"Eh? I don't know much, but I do hear things. Things like maybe the Sarducci family is preparing for war. You hear any-thing like that?" Sergei signified with a smirk.

Tito tensed slightly. *How did Sergei knew about the Sar-duccis*? He knew Nazir wouldn't walk him into a trap, but Tito really didn't know who's side Sergei was really on.

"Sarducci? Naw, never heard of em'," Tito lied.

Sergei snickered.

"Excuse me, how you say...curiosity, but, I like to know who I do business with. Now, I know that Nazir and the rest of these gentlemen are our friends, But I don't know who are your enemies. Maybe...who knows, your enemies are my friends, eh?"

Nazir said something to Sergei in Russian which bugged Tito out because he already knew Nazir spoke French, Spanish and Arabic, but Russian? Sergei answered him in Russian, and laughed.

Nazir chuckled, then turned to Tito.

"I asked him, what did he think about Italians and he said it's his favorite meal," Nazir winked.

Tito knew exactly what he meant. He already knew the Russian Mob, the Grupperovka didn't like the Mafia. Hearing that confirmed by Sergei, made Tito relax slightly.

"Saarducci is thorn in my side. To see him...removed. I would like very much," Sergei said something in Russian to one of the two men behind him.

"Your order is doable, but one must wait. Come. Let's sit and talk. Are you Muslim?"

"Naw,"

"Good! Finally, Nazir brings me someone to drink with!"

The gathering laughed again as they walked to a small office in the corner.

"I'm on my way back. Shit all good?" Vee asked.

He was in the back seat of Hawk Bill's Lincoln MRX, sitting next to his mother. Hawk Bill was driving and Guy was in the passenger seat. In front and behind them four to a car were Guy's shooters.

""Yeah, yeah indeed, but I ain't in B'more, I'm in New York," Tre replied.

"What up?" Vee wanted to know.

"Peoples wanted to holla, smell me?"

Vee understood. Tito wanted to talk.

"Ai-ight. I'll hit you when I touch." Vee told him.

"JFK or LaGuardia?"

"Neither. I'm touchin' down at Newark Airport," Vee lied.

Guy glanced up in the rearview. He and Vee's eyes met, and Guy smiled. He liked the way Vee handled that.

"Cool. Hit me then."

When they got to the airport, Shantelle gave Vee a hug.

"He said Ms. Sadie's right?"

"Yep" she confirmed.

"And don't leave til' we get back," Vee cautioned her.

Shantelle put her hands on her hips.

"Am I the mother or are you the father?" she quipped, then hugged him again.

"Take care of her, Unc," Vee told Hawk Bill. "That go without saying," Hawk Bill replied, shaking his hand.

Then Guy stepped in front of Shantelle. The moment was awkward because Shantelle wanted to hug him, but so many years of mixed emotions held her back.

"Look, as soon as I get back we goin' to dinner and we gonna talk...I mean really talk, okay?" Guy suggested.

"Just make sure you get back," she told him sincerely.

Guy smiled and winked.

"The muthafucka ain't been born that can stop me from that, baby girl."

Guy shook Hawk Bill's hand, then he and Vee boarded the plane.

⑧ ⑧ ⑧ ⑧ ⑧ ⑧

*Kev couldn't believe how flexible she was. The way she could put both legs behind her head was giving him a clear shot of pure pussy.*

*"Harder Daddy, ohhh make this pussy talk to you," the cinnamon complexioned chick urged him on, massaging her titties and sucking her own nipple.*

*Kev was digging her guts out in a Best Western Hotel room. He had met her a few hours ago at a club he owned in Wilson. After a bottle of Cristal to the head and several shots* of Jack, Kev was ready to bounce with a chick to entertain him for the night. This particular chick caught his eye because she reminded him so much of Karrin. The only difference was, this chick had braids.

"What's up Ma? I'm about to breeze. What you tryin' to do?"" Kev had whispered in her ear.

Seeing it was Kev Simmons talking to her, she damn near came right there. Not only did he run Wilson's heroin trade, he was fine, too. "Leave wit' you," she replied in her best little girl/sex kitten voice.

"That's what it is then."

He imagined it was Karrin's face. Throughout all her moans of pleasure and screams of passion, he imagined Karrin calling out his name lustfully.

"Kevvvv oh goddamn Kev, you fuckin' this pussy sooo good!"

We always want what we can't have, and Kev was becoming obsessed with Karrin. He had to have her...he craved her. Thinking about her taking Ty's dick filled him with rage and he took it out on Shorty's pussy.

"Oh wait wa-," she begged digging her nails in his forearms. "Beat this - fuck!! Daddy please!"

Kev clapped his body with her, long-dicking her into a frenzy. She thought it was her pussy driving him crazy, but it was his lust for Karrin that drove him.

He felt the rubber bust. But he was too much in a zone to stop. The raw sensation of her creamy pussy made Kev arch his back and push all the way inside of her and unleash his seed.

They both lay there breathless. Shorty kissed him on the cheek.

"Damn baby, you tryin' to make a bitch fall in love or something?" she quipped.

Kev chuckled.

"I could ask you the same thing."

She took her legs from behind her head as Kev got up. His phone rang.

"Yo" he answered

Shorty got up and went to the bathroom. He watched her sway, and automatically compared her ass to Karrin's, wondering if it juggled like that when she walked.

"We got a problem," Dino told him.

"Mo' money, mo' problems," Kev sighed. "Where you?"

"The spot."

"Gimme twenty minutes."

Click.

Kev, put on his boxers and pants, then went to the bathroom door.

"Ma, I gotta handle somethin'. I gotta take you home," Kev said through the door.

"Is it going to take all night? Can I wait here 'til you get back?" she whined.

"No," he replied bluntly. He was already tired of her.

She opened the door with her lips in a full pout.

"But I want to do it again," she said, wrapping her arms around his waist," and again and again."

Kev untangled her embrace. "Ma, get dressed."

Shorty wanted to protest but she didn't want to blow it with Kev. After she was dressed, she asked, "Are you going to call me?"

I don't even know your name, who I'ma ask for? Kev thought, but instead, he handed her his phone.

"Put it in."

She quickly put her name and number and pressed Send so she'd have his number as well. Since her phone was on vibrate, Kev didn't know what she had done. She handed it back.

"Let's go," Kev told her.

After dropping her off, he drove to his restaurant. It was a small take-out spot in downtown Wilson, but at four in the morning it was closed and downtown was deserted.

He parked, then entered the restaurant to find his lieutenant Dino and captain Slug seated in the cramped kitchen.

"Them niggas in Nashville snatched up four of our workers," Dino informed him.

*"What??" Kev growled. "Who did it?"*
*Dino shrugged.*
*"Muthafuckas ain't talkin'."*
*"Then we gonna make em' talk," Kev shot back, then*
*turned to Slug.*
*"Call Toni and them. Get em' here now!" Kev demanded.*
*The next evening, the poolroom in Nashville was packed.*
*This was where the hustlers hung out and the chicks came to*
*be cashed out. The sounds of 50 Cents' "Wanksta" played from*
*the Juke box.*

*Dammmn Homie*
*In High School you was the man homie*
*The fuck happen to you?!*

*A purple escalade sitting on 22s' pulled up in front of the*
*poolroom and four visions of loveliness stepped out. The driv-*
*er was dark skinned with long hair and long shapely legs. The*
*passenger was also dark skinned, but shorter with a body like*
*Ki-Toy. The back seat passenger on the left was high-yellow*
*with emerald green eyes, a bowlegged sexy strut with a gap.*
*The fourth, was a Spanish mami that resembled Eva Mendes,*
*mole and all.*
*When they entered the pool hall, chicks were grilling them*
*just as hard as guys were eyeing them. They spread out north,*
*south east and west inside the pool room, flirting and making*
*their presence felt.*
*The dudes vied for their attention, thinking that they had*
*sex kittens, but they turned into panthers in the blink of an eye.*
*All four pulled out desert eagle .45s' and proceeded to lay the*
*room down.*
*"Everybody on the floor now!" Toni, the driver barked.*
*The room hesitated collectively until Toni let off a shot in-*
*to one dude's knee, and the Latina shot another chick in the*
*foot.*
*"Boom! Boom!*
*"She said down. Now!" Latina repeated.*

*This time the room collectively got down on their sto-*
*machs. Toni chirped her phone.*

*"We good, baby,"*

*Chirp! Chirp!*

*Kev, Dion and Slug pulled up in Dion's cocaine-white Es-*
*calade with the gold grill and sitting on 24s'. They got out and*
*came inside. When they came in, Kev snatched the plug out of*
*the wall. The room fell deathly quiet.*

*"Who the fuck is the Wolf Pack?!" Kev barked.*

*No one spoke at first.*

*"Oh now, ya'll pussies can't talk, huh?" Kev sneered, slow-*
*ly walking around the people on the floor. "You can call my*
*man tellin' us, fall back or you gonna murder my peoples, but*
*you can't say it to my face?!"*

*"Nigga, I'm Wolf Pack!"*

*Kev heard. He looked around to see Dion snatching Banks*
*up by the collar. Kev stepped to him. "Where the fuck my*
*peoples at?"*

*"How the fuck I'm 'posed to know? I'm here wit' you,"*
*Banks shot back arrogantly.*

*Kev caught him with a left that knocked him up and*
*against the pool table. He snatched Banks' cell off his pants*
*and held it up to him. "Call your peoples."*

*Banks' nose was leaking blood as he hit speed dial.*

*"Yo," Banks said into the phone before Kev snatched the*
*phone from him.*

*"Who the fuck is this?!"*

*"Who the fuck is you?" Vee retorted calmly.*

*"My peoples for your man," Kev offered, putting his gun to*
*Bank's temple. "Or you can listen to your man die right now!"*

*"Just relax playboy, it's been a misunderstandin'. Meet me*
*in Gold Rock. The motel."*

*Click.*

*Kev snatched up Banks. "Let's go."*

*While Kev talked, Toni and her crew were relieving the*
*room of their money, drugs, jewels and guns. By the time Kev*

finished the phone call, they were ready too, leaving the whole room rabbit-eared.

Both Escalades pulled up in Gold Rock at the Gold Rock motel which was visible from I-95 and familiar to anybody familiar with the interstate.

Kev saw the Yukon and the BMW 745. Standing in front of the vehicles were several dudes and Kev recognized four of them as his kidnapped workers.

They parked the Escalades a few empty rows away from the Yukon and BMW, and got out, guns locked and loaded. Slug kept his gun to the back of Bank's head, gripping him by the collar. The girls and Dion flanked Kev.

"Yo, dawg, is that really necessary?" Vee asked referring to the way Slug had his gun to Banks' head." Ain't none of us holdin' heat," Vee added, holding up his empty hands.

"Kev, let that shit go."

Kev heard the familiar voice and saw Ty step out of the passenger side of the BMW.

"Ty?" Kev barked, shocked.

"Yo ,Slug, let my man go," Ty instructed Slug.

Slug looked at Kev.

"Yo Ty, what the fuck is goin on?!" Kev wanted to know.

"First of all," Ty came over to Slug and pulled Banks from his grasp. "Nigga I'm still your boss, too."

Then he walked over to Kev.

"Second, why you ain't tell me you was movin' on Nashville?"

"Tell you?! Fuck you mean, tell you?!"

"'Cause I'm already there!...Big brah," Ty added with a smirk. "Now see if I woulda handled this your way, I woulda murdered your workers right where they stood, then me and you woulda been beefin' and not even know it." Ty huffed. "But I handled it my way. When I saw these niggas pushin' black out, my first thought was they was bootlegging our shit again so I laid on em! I decided to snatch em' up, see who they work for. That's when we called you," Ty told Dino.

"Why the fuck you ain't say somethin' then?" Kev asked.

"Cause it wasn't me on the phone and I ain't know the dude he was callin' was Dino," Ty snapped back. "But now here we are...one big happy family," Ty quipped.

Kev was still heated.

"Ty, what the fuck you doin' in Nashville anyway? I thought you were in Smithfield?"

Ty shrugged, "I'm there, too. We just been expandin'. I left you Battleboro and Spring Hope."

He had purposely taken all the little hustling spots up to the Rocky Mount Border, Raleigh and parts of Durham as well. He wanted Kev to see how hard he went.

"Nigga, you ain't gotta leave me shit! If I wanted those spots I woulda been had 'em!'"

"Suit yourself big brah," Ty replied, "I'll see you for Sunday dinner."

Ty walked away leaving Kev seething. The four workers went over to Kev and then the two crews went there separate ways.

Sunday dinner was very important to Guy, and he took it seriously if either Ty or Kev missed it without a valid reason. It was also the only time Debra and Gloria put up with each other's presence.

They always ate Sunday dinner after church at his parent's house. The big ranch-like mansion Gloria called "Six Forks" because of its resemblance to the ranch of the TV series Dallas. When Guy was married to Gloria, he still brought Debra, and when he married Debra he still made Gloria attend. He wanted both Ty and Kev to see the importance of family, no matter what the circumstances. Mrs. Simmons loved to cook for her family. Even in her elderly years, she was still sprightly and she looked forward to these Sunday gatherings.

As they ate, Guy could see something was going on between Kev and Ty. They were being themselves with everybody else, but they were being short and clipped with each other. Guy wasn't going to get involved unless they brought it to him and that's exactly what Kev did as soon as dinner was over. Ty, Kev and Guy went out on the back porch to the patio.

"Pop, I thought you gave Ty Smithfield?" Kev asked.

"I did," Guy confirmed, sipping his brandy.

"So what he doin' in Nashville?"

"I saw an opportunity, so I took it," Ty answered smugly. Guy nodded in agreement.

"So what's the problem?" Guy inquired.

"The problem is I moved on Nashville and I found him already there!" It's right next to Rocky Mount!" Kev barked.

"So why weren't you already there?" Guy asked, getting irritated.

"I mean... it's like," Kev stuttered, "I'm tryin to hold Wilson and Rocky Mount down!"

Guy shook his head and downed his drink.

"The difference between you and Ty is... you live off your name and Ty makes a name for himself..." Guy pinched the bridge of his nose then hit the table so hard with his fist. Both Ty and Kev flinched. "Goddamnit Kev, you're a Simmons and you can't hustle?! Ty moves three times the weight you do!"

Guy was angry with the fact that Brah's son was outshining his.

"Damn Pop, he's got three times as many spots!" Kev shot back.

"Look Pop, if you want, Kev can have Nashville," Ty offered. He wanted to be the best of the two, but Kev was still his brother.

"Nigga, I don't need no handouts," Kev spat, full of hurt pride, then turned to Guy. "Just give me Greenville."

"Greenville?!" Ty echoed.

Greenville was a major heroin spot, one Ty wanted for himself. By the way he was handling his business, he felt like he deserved it. He had proved himself worthy.

Guy sat back in the chair, contemplating the situation.

"How he gonna handle Greenville, Pop? He just said he can't even handle what he got now!" Ty protested.

"I ain't say no shit like that!"

"Okay," Guy sighed.

"Pop!" Ty said, shocked.

"Shut up, Ty! You want everything for yourself?! Don't be so fuckin' greedy. Greedy niggas don't last!" Guy growled.

Ty couldn't believe how Guy was trying to spin the situation!

"Greedy?? How the fuck am I greedy?!"

Guy stood up, really angry now.

"Boy, watch you goddamn mouth when you talk to me!"

"Word?" Ty smirked, shaking his head. "Whatever you say....Boss."

Ty turned around and left.

Ty was in a rage all the way to Durham. He couldn't believe what Guy had done. It seemed like every time he and Kev disagreed, Guy took Kev's side, even though he knew Ty was right.

The difference between you and Ty is…you live off your name and Ty makes a name for himself…Your brother doesn't have the instincts or foresight you have.

He praised Ty yet rewarded Kev for his weakness? The whole thing made no sense to Ty.

When he got to Durham, he found Vee and Mike G in the Fayetteville Street projects. Mike G threw a duffle bag in Ty's backseat and Vee got in the passenger seat. Ty spun the block a few times so they could talk.

"Damn, Vee you niggas ain't bullshit, huh? Ya'll moved that shit quick," Ty commented.

Vee turned the music all the way down.

"No doubt, dawg. I told you how we do. My team hungry. Fuck you think they call us wolves for?" Vee cracked. "And dig, I need you to get at Sami. We need like five more burners. We bumped heads with some niggas on Hoover, so we got bodies on three of em'."

"Just holla at Sami, he know I fuck with you."

"Man, you know, how them Arabs be actin'," Vee protested.

"Naw, he good. Just holla at him," Ty assured him.

They rode for a moment in silence until Vee said, "Yo Ty, how long we been workin' for you?"

Ty shrugged.

"Year, year and a half."

"We made you a lot of money in a year and a half," Vee commented

Ty looked at him with a sly grin.

"We both made a lot of money in a year and a half, Vee."

"So when we takin' it to the next level? When you gonna put us onto our own spot?" Vee probed.

Ty laughed.

"Damn Vee, you don't' strike me as a greedy nigga and we both know greedy niggas don't last." Ty said, using Guy's words on him.

"Come on, dawg, I'm just like you," Vee smirked, "I want it all but I ain't greedy. It ain't like we jumpin' the fence on you, but at some point every man wants to have his own," Vee said seriously.

Ty nodded.

"I agree, and when you reach that point, you'll get your own. Just be patient," Ty told him and extended his hand.

Vee shook it and looked him in the eye.

"Just don't lose track of time. That could happen when you havin' fun, you know? I'ma get at you tomorrow."

Vee hopped into the car, each man hoping that the other understood their point. Vee wasn't a patient man, and that conversation marked the beginning of the end for Ty and Vee.

# CHAPTER 33

V ee and Guy disembarked at Newark airport, then moved swiftly through the terminal. They both felt naked without a weapon, especially in the midst of a war.

"I can't stand flyin'," Guy commented as they neared Avis Rent-A-Car. Vee didn't respond.

Even though Guy had been trying to make the small talk the whole plane trip, neither had really said one word to the other. Now Guy was trying to break the silence, but Vee wouldn't comply.

When they reached the forest-green Jag they had rented, Vee finally spoke.

"Yo, Guy, there's been two white dudes following us since we left the terminal. Now they getting' in a blue Buick," Vee informed.

"I know," Guy winked, tossing Vee the key over the roof. "They wit me."

As Vee maneuvered out of Newark airport and onto the highway, Guy could tell he knew where he was going. Vee hit Tre's number on the phone.

"Where you?" Tre asked.

"I'm here."

"Meet me in the Bronx. 171$^{st}$ and College," Tre told him.

"Cool."

Click.

Tre pulled up in front of the apartment building and got out, keeping his eyes peeled and his hand near his waist. He peeped a few of Tito's men posted discreetly around the perimeter of the building so he relaxed a little bit and called Tito.

"Third floor. Take the stairs," Tito told him, then hung up.

He took the stairs two at time and reached the third floor without breathing hard. As soon as he turned into the hallway he saw several Muslims standing around. They nodded as he passed, and one opened the door for him at the end of the hall.

Inside, the place was completely devoid of furniture, except several mattresses stacked up on their ends on both sides of the living room. Tre smelled the aroma of beef sausage and onions. There were about ten guys in the apartment, not including Tito, Ty and Nazir.

"It's been a long time since we had to take it to the mattresses, huh? Tito cracked.

He had the sleeves of his silk shirt rolled up and was standing over a huge pot on the stove. "Too long, shit! We might be a little rusty," Tre joked.

"Shee-it! Like riding a bike, my nigga!" Tito laughed. "Where your man?"

"He on his way,"

Tito nodded, then said," Nazir! How long it take to cut up sausage?"

"Nigga, I ain't know when you said you had *beef.* I ain't know you meant sausage!" Nazir cracked.

They all laughed, easing the mounting tension of what was soon going to happen.

"I mean, I know this is some awkward shit, but goddamn, you ain't gonna say nothin?" Guy asked, shifting in his seat.

Vee glanced over at him.

"Say what? What's to talk about? I killed your son and you fucked my mother. Now here we are."

"That's how you see it, huh? That simple?" Guy asked.

"No, *you* see it that way. The way I see it, I ain't asked to come here. And I was in a life or death situation," Vee looked at him evenly, "What would you have done?"

Tito wiped his hands on a dish towel, stepping away from the stove, "Tell the boys it's ready."

He walked over to the window and looked down. He saw Vee getting out of the car. "I think your man here, Tre."

Tre came over and looked.

"Yeah, that's him."

Tito started to chirp his people out front until he saw someone else getting out. He couldn't see his face because of the black Stetson on his head.

"Who that?" Tito questioned.

"I don't know, But if he wit J, he good" Tre assured him.

Tito chirped his.

Chirp Chirp!!

"They wit us." Tito informed them.

The dude on the other end told Vee. "Third Floor. Take the stairs."

"Ai-ight"

When he and Guy got to the first landing, Guy stopped Vee.

"Was it you?" Guy asked. Vee knew he was talking about the attempt on Guy's life.

Vee had known all along about Ty's plot, but he figured if Guy was too blind to see the enemy in his house, then that was on him. Vee had no interest in either side of the coin.

"No, it definitely wasn't me," Vee told him.

The two locked into the gaze. When Guy saw Vee was telling the truth, he said, "Let's get upstairs."

Ty and Nazir helped fill the Styrofoam trays of the men as they filed by.

"Just like back in the pen," Ty mused.

"How long you do?" Nazir inquired.

"Four and a half."

"I did six."

Vee and Guy came into the hallway, passing the guys eating out of the Styrofoam trays. They walked in and looked around.

"J, what up, you hungry? Grab a tray." Tre told him.

When Tre called him it made Ty and Tito look up and their eyes got big as plates. Vee's and Guy's did as well.

"Uncle Guy?!"

"Tito?"

"Pop?!"

"Ty?!"

"Vee?"

"What the fuck is you doin' here?!" all four asked almost the exact same question at the same time.

"Vee?!" Tre looked at Vee," Yo J, who the hell is Vee?!"

Ty pulled his gun and Vee pulled his. They had their barrel a few feet from each other. The room grew tense. No one but Guy knew what was going on. He stepped in between them.

"No!" he barked looking at Ty then Vee. "Put it down! Both of you!"

"Yo Unck," Tito yelled. Confused, "What the hell is --,"

"This bitch ass nigga is the one who killed Kev!" Ty hissed, gripping the gun tighter. "Move, Pop! You said I could handle it!"

"Yeah Guy," Vee sneered. "*Move.*"

"Uncle Guy, talk to me!" Tito demanded.

"Not now, Tito," Guy replied then turned his body to completely face Ty. "Tyquan...I'm not gonna tell you again," Guy spoke through clenched teeth.

Ty's eyes pleaded with Guy but he wouldn't relent. Ty slowly lowered his weapon. Guy spun to face Vee.

"Now!" he gritted.

Vee lowered his pistol.

"I don't need no gun for this bitch ass nigga no how," Vee spat.

Ty didn't hesitate. He handed his gun to Tito and stepped towards Vee.

"Word?!" he smiled menacingly. "Show me I'ma bitch, pussy!"

Vee tossed his gun aside just as Ty shot a quick left hook that Vee barely dipped. Ty only caught him in the temple.

"Yo, cuz, chill!" Tito yelled, but Guy stopped him.

"Let em' go…we won't get anywhere until they get some of that off their chests."

Vee threw a left hook to Ty's rib cage, then faked a right jab that made Ty throw up his guard to block his face. leaving himself open to a crushing kidney shot. Ty took the painful blow and rolled with it, elbowing Vee in his jaw and staggering him against the wall.

Ty moved in for the kill, shooting Vee a quick three-piece to the body and one to the head. Vee shot a lazy jab that Ty slipped, then caught Vee with another three-piece, two to the head, one to the body.

Vee took it like a champ and came back with a vicious uppercut that snapped Ty's head back and sat him on his ass. Ty got back up and the two of them circled and feinted, this time with more respect and more fatigue. Ty was quicker but Vee hit harder. They stood in the middle of the floor going toe to toe, trading blows until they were both bloody and exhausted. Finally, when neither could throw another blow they rested, bending over with their hands gripping their knees.

"Ya'll finished?" Guy quizzed. "You finished trying to kill each other? Because there's a whole fuckin' mob of Italians tryin' to kill us all!"

Ty and Vee glared at each other but neither said a word.

"Ai-ight, Pay attention!"

Both slowly came over closer to the wall where Tito had a drawn out blueprint of Sarducci's house.

"Now, this is a rough sketch of Sarducci's house in Scarsdale. This is the front of the house. Here…this is the driveway that leads up to it. The house sits on a hill. These squiggly lines over here is the Long Island sound right in Sarducci's back yard."

Tito smiled. "Now this road to the left of Sarducci's house starts about twenty yards from the main road." Tito explained. He stopped just in case any one had any questions.

"Now I had a couple of chicks roll through there and they said it's swarming. That's what we expect here, in the front and here in the back by the woods. But the water," Tito smirked, "is their Achilles heel. That's where we bring the AT4's in two speed boats. Nazir you're in and out. Qua, you in the other. You're the only two that know how to fire them shits. My team will come in off the main road and move on the woods. Tre, your team will take the front. Our job is to draw their attention from the water. Make em' think we only came for a shoot-out. Nazir...Qua concentrate here, here and here. This is the study right underneath it and underneath that, in the basement is the wine cellar. When the guns start bustin', Vinnie will try and move Sarducci away from harm. That excludes the front and the left side." Tito looked at Nazir. "He'll push em' right into your arms, baby. Make it count. Two shells, one a piece, then be out. I don't want to get ya'll caught out in open waters. Feel me?"

"I got you ock," Nazir confirmed.

"Any questions?" Tito asked.

"Looks like you've got this pretty well planned, Nephew," Guy said, impressed.

"Yeah Unck, I never plan to fail nor to aim and miss," Tito replied. His smile didn't reach his eyes, which were stone cold.

Guy caught the double meaning, and smiled inwardly, knowing he was talking to him.

"But what if you do miss? If he survives then he'll go to the other families for support and they'll bring all they've got," he questioned.

"You right, Unck. That's why we *won't* fail," Tito reiterated, "Those rocket launchers will bring the whole fuckin' house to the ground."

"Then I'll just fall back and let you handle it," Guy replied, but he had something else up his sleeve.

"Ai-ight, any more questions?" Tito inquired. When no one spoke up, he added with a wink, "Then let's go make a movie."

"It's fuckin' freezing out here," one Italian said, blowing into his gloved hands. He had an M-16 slung by its strap over his shoulder as he stood with three more guys in front of the house. The night air had them all shivering.

"Aww, quit cryin' you fuckin' wuss," another said.

In all, there were at least twenty-five guys out front and around the perimeter of the house. In the back, crawling in and around the wooded area were at least twenty more all armed with M-16's or AR-15 assault rifles.

The first guy pulled out a cigarette, then pulled out his lighter. He tucked it several times before tossing it down in frustration. "Anybody got a light?"

Two seconds later he got more light than he needed as Tito's team let loose with a barrage of gunfire.

"Holy shit!" the guy exclaimed, dropping his cigarette and fumbling with the M-16.

The Italians began to return fire furiously. The ones in the back started to go help the front, until they found themselves under attack as well. The .50 caliber rounds were taking chunks out of trees, concrete and hitting the cars so hard, they rocked on their suspensions.

When the bullets found flesh, they blew holes in them the size of grape fruits, tearing off ligaments and leaving mutha-fuckas headless.

Chirp Chirp!

"On you," Tito chirped Nazir.

They had paddled halfway across the lake because of the sound. The other half, had the momentum of a 1500 HP motor until they felt they were close enough to be heard. Then they shut off the motor, coasted a bit, then paddled into position.

There were three men to a boat. The driver, a shooter with an AK46 to hold them down and Nazir in one; Qui in the other. Vee was Nazir's shooter.

Chirp Chirp!

"I'm ready," Nazir confirmed, then chirped Qua without saying anything.

The two boats were about fifty yards as they prepared their attack.

"Should I call you Vee or Jay?" Nazir quipped, loading the shell into the rocket launcher.

Vee chuckled.

"Vee."

"Yeah well, I heard alot about you, brah. I liked the way you handled that Bensonhurst shit. Ain't nobody ever took it to the Italians on that level," Nazir remarked. "When this is all over, we should talk, you know?"

"That's cool, dawg," Vee answered.

"Time for the fireworks," Nazir chuckled.

He balanced the AT4 on his shoulders and looked through the digital scope. He could see the house in his scope as the crosshairs blinked and swirled trying to lock in on the target. It only took a few seconds for the crosshairs to lock in, the target sensor to go from red to green. Nazir pulled the trigger.

The force threw Nazir back slightly as the blaze of reddish orange fire arched through the sky, illuminating the side of the house before it hit with a thunderous force.

Kaboooommm!

The shell opened up the side of the house's upper level and blew off the roof. Seconds later, Qua's shot lit up the sky and struck the foundation of the house. The shell made the whole house buckle and fold in on itself, like an elephant falling on its face. Fire began to spread throughout the whole house.

"Go!" Nazir barked.

The speed boat engines came to life and zipped away, heading for the other side of the sound. Tito's and Tre's teams, seeing the fire, withdrew as well and made their escape.

It didn't take long at all before the police and fire trucks and ambulances got to the scene. Several bodies were lying around, and numerous others had been shot or injured in the blast. But the biggest victim of all was Vinnie Sarducci. He was killed instantly by the second Sabo shell. Vinnie had been between the first and second floor on the stairs when the Sabo rocked the house and disintegrated everything in it's path, including Vinnie's body.

Vito and two of his bodyguards had made it into the basement by the time the explosion went off. They had been trapped in the basement until the rescue squad dug them out and the EMS workers whisked them away in three different ambulances.

Vito lay on the stretcher in the back of the ambulance with an oxygen mask over his face. Anthony…Vinnie…their faces flashed through his mind and his heart ached. Then Tito's face flashed through his mind and his blood boiled. Tito had not only killed his son, he had violated the sanctity of his home. The home where his family slept and his grand children played! *Tito would pay*, he vowed to himself.

"Okay Mr. Sarducci, just relax," the EMS guy told him, checking the needle for air bubbles," this won't hurt a bit."

He rubbed alcohol on Vito's forearm, then sank the needle into Vito's vein. The EMS worker leaned down and whispered in Vito's ear, "Po' Charlie and Guy Simmons send their regards."

Vito's eyes widened in horror. He hadn't heard the name Po' Charlie since he died ten years ago. Vito thought he had won their cold war type rivalry simply because he had outlived Charlie. Now he saw he was wrong. He only knew Guy vaguely. But he knew he used to be on Nicky's counsel and then had joined Po' Charlie in the south. Vito felt his energy oozing away. He'd never have a chance to avenge his son or his grandson. Po' Charlie had been dead ten years and he had still managed to beat Vito.

Vito chuckled lightly, as his consciousness turned into a dream-like state. The last mortal thought he had was, at *least*

*they let me go out in my sleep. How thoughtful...*
By the time they got to the hospital, Vito Sarducci was D.O.A, Dead on Arrival. And the EMS workers, the two guys that followed Guy and Vee from the airport, disappeared into the night.

# CHAPTER 34

"That was delicious, Theresa. Thank you," Guy said, wiping his mouth with his napkin.

"Now you know that don't make no kind of sense, Guy, "Theresa scolded him, "It took Gloria moving back up here to get you to New York?!"

"I know, I know," Guy held up his hands, in mock defense, "you're right. I've just been so busy."

"For seven years??" Theresa laughed.

Guy laughed with her.

"Our family reunion is going to be in Maui next year, and nigguh if you ain't there…" Theresa glared at him playfully.

"Well, that's up to Glo," Guy replied, looking at Gloria. "You want me to come to your family reunion?"

The three of them were having dinner at Theresa's brownstone.

"What you askin' me for?" Gloria shot back. "I damn sure ain't invite you."

Theresa recognized the tension.

"Well, let me clean up this mess and leave you two alone to talk."

"I'll help you," Gloria told her, but Guy grabbed her hand and led her away.

"No you won't," he said.

"Guy, I don't have anything to say to you," Gloria huffed.

"Who said I wanted to talk?" Guy crooned, pulling Gloria close to him and kissing her on the neck.

"Guy, stop-," she protested weakly, hating herself for always melting in his arms.

Guy kissed her just below her ear then whispered, "I miss you, Baby."

Gloria embraced him back. "Why don't you just let me go, Guy."

"I can't no more than you can," Guy said, tilting her head up and kissing her softly on the lips. It felt so good, Gloria let out a soft swoon and her pussy twitched feeling Guy pressed up against her.

"Come on home, Baby come on back to me," Guy told her softly.

"No Guy you don't want me, you just hate to lose," Gloria replied, wistfully.

Before Guy could reply, Ty and Tito came in. Gloria felt self conscious letting Tito see her in Guy's arms again. The look on his face seemed to imply she was still betraying the family. She stepped away.

"I'm going upstairs," she said.

Ty felt a way because, it seemed like Guy hadn't missed a beat to mourn his mother. He was right back at Gloria that only added to his suspicions.

"Sarducci is still alive," Tito grumbled, rubbing his temples.

"How you know?"

"They pulled him out of the basement rubble. Vinnie's a memory, but Vito…." Tito shook his head. He had planned on ending this war with the Sarducci hit. Now he saw shit was about to get deep. He was strong, but he had lost a lot of his resources, so going to war against all five families would definitely be a problem because he wasn't at full strength.

"Tito…don't worry about Sarducci…I took care of it," Guy smirked.

Tito stopped pacing and looked at Guy.

"You what?"

It's done. Sarducci's dead. Check it out," Guy told him.

Tito got on his phone. Ty approached Guy.

"Pop, now are you going to tell me what you're doing coming up here with Vee," Ty accosted him, respectfully.

"They tried to kill his mother and I was there," Guy answered.

"So?" Ty said, coldly. "What do it matter to us if she live or die?"

"Didn't you just hear me say I was there?" Guy shot back, irritated by Ty questioning him.

Ty wanted to ask why he had been there in the first place, but he didn't. Instead he commented, "and you said you never wanted to see him again, huh?" Ty shook his head. "Never say never huh, Pop?" Ty quipped then walked away.

Guy wanted to say something but he knew Ty's anger was justified. So he let it go knowing he was dead wrong.

Dro and Young Hardy drove through Goldsboro, smoking a blunt. Young Hardy was vexed. Since Ty hadn't made any attempt to revenge his mother's death, he knew Ty didn't know who was behind it. Young Hardy had expected Ty to try to get back at him by murdering one of his many relatives. That's why Young Hardy had moved the ones that mattered most to him. The rest were on their own.

But Ty hadn't done anything, and that made Hardy madder than had Ty murdered one of his crack head uncles. He wanted Ty to know he had killed Debra. He needed him to know. He had tried to get a drop on Ty but he couldn't. He knew where Guy lived at, half of Goldsboro did, but getting at him was another matter he always had bodyguards. But since the attempt on his life they kept a small army. Hardy wasn't ready for a war like that. Especially since his money was funny. Since he had stopped working for Kev, he couldn't get a decent connect. He and his crew were living off stick ups. But money was the last thing on Hardy's mind. He wanted revenge.

Which was why he was headed to Hawk Bill's Bar, The Rib Shack. He knew it would be useless to try and get Hawk Bill to give up Ty or Guy. Hawk Bill's gangsta was legendary. Hardy might as well just walk in and blow Hawk Bill away. Indeed, he wanted to deliver a message.

Dro parked the car down the block and cut off the headlights. Both of them, double checked their pistols and got out the car. They walked into the Rib Shack. The place wasn't packed only three coons nursed drinks at the bar. Hawk Bill was leaning on the counter, a towel draped over his left shoulder while he talked to the three old coons.

Hawk Bill looked up at Dro and Hardy.

"Can I help you fellas? You look a tad bit south of eighteen to be tryin' to buy drinks?! Hawk Bill chuckled.

"Naw old head, we come to pour you a drink," Hardy growled then pulled out his gun and aimed it at Hawk Bill.

Dro pulled his gun and kept an eye on the old coons.

"Keep em' where I can see em, yo," Hardy warned him.

Hawk Bill hadn't budged from the position he had been in. Really he was unfazed. But he wasn't about to underestimate the young boys either.

"You got a winner, young blood. But you picked the wrong night for a robbery," Hawk Bill cracked, referring to the fact the place was practically empty.

"This ain't no robbery. Like I said, we come to pour you a drink, so you could pour Ty one," Hardy hissed. You tell Ty muhfuckin' young Hardy killed his fuckin' mother!" Hardy barked.

Hawk Bill's whole body tensed. He wanted to kill the young boy with his bare hands. Hardy saw it and laughed.

"Come on muhfucka. Come over that counter and try and straighten it," Hardy taunted him.

Hawk Bill flexed his jaw muscles.

"You must be suicidal, nigguh," Hawk Bill seethed. "You don't want Ty to know no shit like that. Your whole Hardy family would bleed!" Hardy walked over to the counter, put the gun to Hawk Bill's forehead and grabbed him by the collar.

"Naw *he* suicidal! He signed his goddamn death warrant when he killed my mama, my son and my uncle Brah! Bitch ass nigguh shoulda killed me first, but he slipped... and I promise he gonna regret it," Hardy vowed, through clenched teeth.

Hawk Bill never lost eye contact with Hardy.

"You finished?" Hawk Bill replied, unmoved.

Hardy smiled.

"Yeah...yeah, I'm finished you just make sure Ty gets the message."

As Hardy backed out, he warned.

"First muhfucka come out this door, will be the first to meet his maker."

He and Dro backed out the door then left. Hawk Bill was pissed, but he knew it would be nothing like what Ty would feel when he told him about Hardy.

*"Kev! Oh my God, Kev," Karrin sobbed over the phone.*

*Kev was in Wilmington North Carolina, in a part called ugly town with Fathead and Kel-bino. It had been a year since Guy had given him Greenville and Kev had stepped his game up, expanding into Jacksonville and New Bern.*

*He was driving down Market Street when Karrin called.*

*"Karrin, calm down. What's wrong?" Kev asked.*

*"they got him, Kev!"*

*"Who is they?" Kev barked, ready to ride for his brother because he already knew the only "Him" Karrin would be crying for was Ty.*

*"The police," she sniffled, trying to calm down. "they just kicked in the door! They say he killed somebody!" she explained then broke down crying again.*

"Okay Karrin, listen. I'ma call Pops. You call the jail see if they gonna give him a bond, okay? But you gotta calm down. All that cryin' ain't gonna help Ty," Kev reasoned.

"o-o-okay."

Kev called Guy and broke the news. It was apart of the game to see the isnside of a county jail or prison, but murder was a serious charge, so Guy knew to be on top of it from the jump. He was locked up in Durham County jail, and was charged with two counts of first degree murder and was being held on no bond.

Kev and Guy came to see him as soon as they could.

"Ty, what the hell is goin' on?!" Guy inquired.

"It couldn't be avoided, Pop", Ty replied.

"Couldn't be avoided?! Guy echoed.

"How they know it was you?" Kev added, mouthing the words.

Ty shrugged.

"I'm clean but they still snatched me up from the crib" Ty told them, meaning he didn't leave witnesses but someone must've fingered him.

"I'll find out what's what" Kev assured him.

"Just sit tight. We gonna get you outta here," Guy vowed.

And he did sit tight for almost nine months. Every time visitors were allowed, he had a visitor. His mother and Gloria came a few times to give him encouragement, but it was Karrin that came the most.

"I love you," she told him continuously.

But Ty wasn't a fool. He knew how it went when you got locked up.

Life goes on and it's a rare chick that can do a bid with someone locked up. He wanted Karrin to be one of the few, but he wasn't about to get caught up.

He had other chicks, one he had met in the county. Her name was Tahifia and she was a C.O. at the jail. A thick chocolate sister, she already knew who Ty was. She held him down, making sure he had what he needed, even bringing him a cell phone. With that he was able to handle his business and talk freely about his case because his whole team had throw away prepaids, called burnouts.

"Yo, Vee, it's like that? Muhfuckas sayin' you pumpin a different stamp. <u>Your</u> shit wolfpack," Ty said, pacing his cell and keeping an eye out for the police.

Vee was at the mall.

"Yo, Dawg, it is what it is. I guess you lost track of time. Nigguhs gotta spread they wings," Vee replied.

"but you gonna wait til' I get locked up? That's some fucked up shit yo!" Ty was heated.

"Naw Dawg, this shit been goin' on before you got knocked. I told you I was takin' a trip to B-More. But you was so caught up in that Raleigh beef, you ain't holla back," Vee shot back.

Ty couldn't deny it. Some New York cats had come down to Raleigh, trying to stop his flow. It was two of them that he had caught slipping in Durham while he was locked up.

"But yo, you still my nigguh. Believe that. This shit just business," Vee told him. "Whatever I can do, just say the word," he vowed. When he was found guilty, his whole heart dropped. His mother, Gloria and Karrin screamed and cried. They couldn't believe it. The case was flimsy, to say the least. It hinged on two eye witnesses. A stripper chick that one of the New York dudes was fucking and her mother. They had seen the murders but Ty didn't see them.

The prosecution kept it under wraps until the trial because they were aware of the danger the wolf pack posed to the witnesses' safety and they saw Ty as the leader.

"Tyquan Simmons, I sentence you to two life sentences to be run consecutive in the North Carolina Department of Corrections. Ty kept his game face, because deep down he knew, he wouldn't be locked up long.

Ty was able to take his cell phone with him to Central Prison by smuggling in by "suitcasing." A trick inmates use when necessary. As soon as he was in his cell he called Vee.

"Yo Dawg, I heard. Cat fucked up. What you need me to do?" Vee inquired.

Ty couldn't front, Vee was a thorough nigguh. Even though they didn't see eye to eye on business, he didn't let that affect their relationship.

"We gotta find them two witnesses," Ty told him.

"Indeed."

"And look, I need you to go see Sami. I paid him like eight stacks for some ammo. I need that. Get it from him and give it to Karrin," Ty instructed.

"Done. And get me names, yo."

"No doubt. One."

Ty smirked to himself. The story about the eight stacks was a lie. He just wanted Vee to have a reason to go to Sami. Ty had already instructed Sami to start supplying Vee because Ty was supplying Sami. In this way, Ty was able to benefit from the wolf pack's hustle, and if need be, cut them off whenever he needed.

Had Vee known Sami was Ty's man, he would've never let Ty have that kind of control. Vee was a smart hustler, but Ty was, too.

While Ty was locked up, Kev got stronger. His team wasn't as serious as Ty's had been, but his name began really ringing bells. Guy was relieved that he had blossomed and it was clear that Kev was the apparent heir. Only two things came up for Kev at night. One was the wolf pack. They were quickly becoming Kev's chief rivals. Kev didn't know that they were still working for Ty and was their lifeline, so Kev looked at them as enemies. Therefore, he decided he needed a mole in their camp. Someone that could tell him the wolf pack's next move and, in the event of a beef, help Kev eliminate them.

He found his man in Banks. He was loud, boastful and wanted to be a boss, too. He was the low man on the wolf pack totem pole. Perfect for the position of mole. Kev promised him his own and hit him off from time to time with product to keep him chasing the carrot on the stick.

The other thing on Kev's mind was deeper, more serious…it was Karrin. Since Ty had been locked up, Kev had been becoming more and more forward with his feelings. Karrin hadn't encouraged him nor discouraged him either. Ty wasn't showing her affection like she thought he should. She loved Ty, but she also loved the life style he introduced her to.

Kev was sick. Guy could see it. It was like Kev was obsessed with the girl. So since he was his only son, he decided to pay Ty a visit. Ty had been locked up almost eighteen months, and he was now at Pasquotank Correctional in Elizabeth City.

When Ty came out and saw Guy, he smiled and they hugged then they sat down.

"How you doin', boy? You lookin' good," Guy remarked.

"Not as good as you," Ty chuckled, looking at Guy's Stacy Adams suit, matching gators and fedora. Guy had all the females in visitation checking out the dapper older man.

Guy leaned his elbows on the table.

"Po Charlie died," he informed Ty, sourly.

"For real?" Ty's heart dropped. Not out of love, but out of greed. He knew Po' Charlie had been the goose that laid their golden eggs.

Guy nodded.

"So, what are we gonna do?"

Guy waved him off.

"Don't worry. Po' Charlie introduced me to his people a long time ago. Now, there's no middleman we at the source."

Ty's heart went from down to beating a mile a minute. He was amped. "And those two…people," Guy said, looking at Ty so he knew what he was talking about, we found em'. That'll get handled within the week." Ty was ready to do back flips! He was sitting in prison with forever and a day being told, not only was he about to get Escobar money but, he was also getting out of prison, too?!

"Hell yeah!" Ty said, a little louder than he intended.

Then Guy got down to the real reason he had come. He told Ty the good news first to lighten the blow of the bad.

"How you and Karrin doin?" Guy questioned.

Ty shrugged like, "We ai-ight. She a good girl, do what I ask. But ain't no girlfriends in prison."

Guy nodded.

"But do you love her?"

Ty frowned up.

"Love her? Naw, Pop. It ain't that serious," Ty lied.

The truth was he wanted to love her, but he needed a reason to trust her with his heart. Ty knew the game with females. Karrin had never given him any reason to doubt her, but then again, why should she? When he met her, she was working as a waitress, getting rides to work. Now, she didn't have to work, was going to Howard on Ty's dime and pushing a BMW, jeweled up.

But now it was time she proved her love. And so far, she was doing pretty well.

"Well…your brother does,?!" Guy said, with a heavy sigh.

Ty sat straight up in the chair.

"He what?!" Ty barked.

"Now don't blame Kev. We can't help the ones we love," Guy schooled him. "that's why I asked you if you loved her. If you had said yeah, Kev would've just had to get over it. But, if she doesn't mean anything to you….",

Ty was heated. He remembered how he acted when he first met Karrin. How he always emphasized how Ty shouldn't do her wrong and cheat on her. Kev wanted the bitch for himself! He thought, then it made him wonder if they were already fucking. The thought made him sick. "Kev doesn't know anything about me bringing this to you, Ty," Guy said. "It's up to you. I know it's crazy, but Kev loves you-."

Ty cut him off like, "Pssst!"

"He does Ty, believe me. It's just…some women got a magic, and once they work it…," Guy shook his head with a smirk, thinking about Debra. "They got their hooks in you."

Ty took a deep breath. If he let Kev have Karrin but she refused then he'd know she truly loved him and that she hadn't been fucking. Then he'd be ready to give her his heart. Then, he'd be ready to marry her.

*"I am my brother's keeper," Ty said solemnly, but dead-pan. "If she mean that much to him, I'll fall back."*

*Guy breathed a sigh of relief.*

*"Thank you, son. You truly understand the importance of family."*

*Ty stood up like, "Yeah, I'll talk to you later Pop."*

*Guy was a little surprised because there was still an hour left in the visit, but he complied and stood as well.*

*"I love you son."*

*"I love you too Pop."*

*"And don't worry. This time next year you'll be back on top," Guy chuckled.*

*Ty smirked.*

*"I never fell off.*

*Guy laughed and watched Ty walk away.*

*Ty got back to his cell and called Karrin.*

*"Hey Baby! How-,"*

*"Yo Rin, I don't want to see you again."*

*"What?"*

*"You heard me," Ty replied, Doing his best to sound cold, Don't come see me. Don't call me, don't write me, don't even think about me. It's over," Ty gritted.*

*Karrin felt breathless. She was at a hair salon in D.C. waiting her turn. Her head was spinning, she couldn't think.*

*"Ty…wh-why are doing this?"*

*"Just stay the fuck away from me," he hissed, then clicked off.*

*Before the pain in her voice made him relent.*

*Karrin cried hysterically and tried to call him back four times, but he wouldn't answer. When she wrote he didn't write back and when she came to see him, he refused the visit.*

*She didn't know where it had all came from. She wasn't cheating on him so he couldn't have found out anything. She knew if it was another chick, he wouldn't just cut her off. There had always been other chicks.*

Then she thought about Kev. Had Kev said anything to Ty? Had he turned him against her? She didn't know, but she was definitely going to find out.

Kev, Dino and several other members of Kev's crew went up to Howard's homecoming. They came through, not to be out done. Balla's came from all around to get their stunt on, and even though Kev's crew was by no means the main event, they weren't a little side show either. Vee and the wolf pack were there as well. Vee had brought Cat and a few of her friends. Never the type to bring sand to the beach, Vee had to bring Cat or be forced to hear it for the next few months.

"Ain't that Ty brother?" Cat asked.

They were pulling up to Karrin's dorm in Vee's platinum Benz C-Coupe. Vee pulled besides Kev's burgundy Mercedes McClaren and beeped the horn. Kev looked at Vee with a glare. Vee looked at Kev with a smirk.

"I'll be back!" Karrin yelled.

"Girl, I ain't waitin' for you just text me when you ready," Cat told her.

"Okay. Hi Victor!" Karrin chimed.

"What up Rin?"

Kev pulled off, followed by Vee.

"Ya'll favor," Cat commented.

"Who?" Vee asked.

"You and Ty brother. Ya'll got the same nose and pretty lips," she replied.

"Fuck you doin' lookin' at his lips? You wanna kiss him or somethin?"

"Oh you ain't know?" Cat quipped, "I wanna kiss him all in the mouth!"

Vee chuckled, shaking his head.

"You got all the sense."

"But for real, ya'll do look alike."

"Kev, what did you say to Ty about me?" Karrin asked.

Kev glanced over like, "nothin. What I'ma say somethin about you for?"

"I don't understand," Karrin mumbled, tears beginning to fall. "He ...he just cut me off."

Saying the words out loud, brought the pain crashing back down and she began to cry, uncontrollably.

Kev pulled over into a convenience store parking lot and embraced her. "Karrin, talk to me baby. What's wrong?"

"It's Ty," she sobbed, "He said he didn't want to see me again...he won't accept my visits, my letters, my calls.....,"

"I understand you're in pain baby, but maybe this is for the best," Kev consoled her.

"But I love him, Kev," she sniffled, mascara running in black streaks down her cheeks.

Kev wiped her tears with his thumb.

"I've been tellin' you to let him go, Karrin. How many nights have you cried for him? How many times has he already hurt you? You think when he comes home it'll be any different?" Kev reasoned.

Karrin took a deep breath.

"I know, Kev. I know I've been a fool. But I love him so much," she stressed.

Kev tipped up her chin.

"And I love you, Karrin. I always have," he confessed.

Karrin already knew Kev had strong feelings for her, but that was the first time he had told her he loved her.

"Kev, I...I don't know what to say," Karrin replied.

"You're a Queen, Karrin. You not only deserve the best you deserve to be treated like the best...the best thing that ever happened to the man who truly loves and appreciates you," Kev crooned sincerely.

Karrin could see the love in his gaze and his words touched her. But she was stuck. Ty was her dream, but Kev wanted to be her reality. She wasn't ready to give up the lifestyle. But she refused to be Kev's plaything.

"You really love me, Kev?" she probed.

"Yes Karrin, I do."

*"Then marry me,"* she replied. *" I refuse to just be your plaything."*

Kev hadn't expected her to go all the way to the alter so quickly, but he understood her logic. Besides he intended on marrying her anyway.

Kev smiled.

*"I promise you, baby, I'ma make you the happiest woman in the world."*

Kev leaned in and quenched the thirst he'd had for her lips for so long. To him the kiss was the beginning of a beautiful life, but to Karrin, it was a simply a gesture to close the deal.

A year later, Ty was free. The two witnesses that the case had rested on, had been found…dead. The stripper was gunned down by the wolf pack at a strip club in Richmond, Virginia. Her mother, shot in the face at the front door of her sister's house in Savannah, Georgia. Kev had shot her himself for testifying against his brother.

Ty had come home, just in time for the one thing he wouldn't have missed for the world. Kev and Karrin's wedding. Karrin didn't know he was home. Ty had to see her go through it for himself.

Dressed in a black Tuxedo, he dressed the part even though he wasn't apart of the wedding. As a matter of fact, he had only caught the end.

*"I do,"* Karrin had said.

*"by the powers vested in me by the state of North Carolina, I now pronounce you man and wife. You may kiss the bride."*

As Kev lifted the veil from Karrin's face, a darker veil fell over Ty's heart.

As Kev and Karrin turned to come up the aisle, Karrin's eyes fell on the one man she wanted to see the most, but dreaded seeing the most.

Their eyes met, then slowly, Ty turned and walked out of the church.

Karrin was thinking of that very moment because Ty was calling and his picture came up whenever he called. This was the second time he had called back to back, then she received a text that simply said:

*Karrin.*

It made her think about when he made love to her and whispered her name as he long stroked her slow, and she wondered if that was how he was saying in the text. The thought made her want to call him back, tell him where she was. Go to him.

But reality struck and fear took over. His mother was dead was she next? Was he saying her name more firmly, with aggression, with a snarl? She was so confused and she wished Vee would get back soon. She felt safe around Vee and that's what she needed the most. Safety.

She heard a phone ring in the distance. She wondered where it was coming from because it sounded like it was in the room. Then she remembered the pre paid she had bought to post on Cat's flyer. Someone was calling! She sprung off the bed and grabbed her purse off the chair. The phone was still ringing when she got it out but it had stopped once she was about to answer. She couldn't return the call because it came from a blocked number. But whoever had called, left a message.

Karrin listened to her voice mail and heard:

"You have...one message. Urgent message," the computerized operator said.

"Hello?...Yo...Ummm, my name is...naw I can't tell you my name," the older male voice said. "I seen yo' poster and I see that gal 'round here a lot... is there a reward? You ain't the police is you? Anyway, I'll umm, I'll call back."

# CHAPTER 35

When Hawk Bill called Guy and told him he needed to see him and Ty a.s.a.p, Ty reluctantly agreed to come. He thought it would be something about Vee or Vee's mother, the subject he couldn't care less about never in a million years did he think it was about his mother.

Guy and Ty drove out to Hawk Bill's mother's house. Behind them was a car full of Guy's shooters.

No one was at the house because Hawk Bill had relocated his family. Guy and Ty walked in. Guy shook his hand and Hawk Bill remembering didn't even offer his hand to Ty.

All three of them sat down.

"Guy," Hawk Bill sighed heavily," you ain't gonna believe this," he said then looked at Ty. "What happened, Ty? Why you ain't kill him?

"Kill who?" Guy asked.

"Brah Hardy's nephew," Hawk Bill replied.

It hit Ty like a ton of bricks. He understood exactly what Hawk Bill was about to say.

"Fuck!" Ty blurted his bowed head with his hands.

Guy was confused.

"What does Brah Hardy's nephew have-,"

"It was him, Guy. He killed Debra," Hawk Bill told him.

Not only was Guy confused, he was dumbfounded.

"Why would..." Guy's voice trailed off, then he looked at Ty. "Ty, you knew about this?"

Ty shook his head.

"I...I know Hardy...I had a feelin' he mighta did it, but I wasn't sure," Ty admitted, leaving out the fact that he suspected Guy as well. He looked at Hawk Bill, "You sure?"

Hawk Bill nodded slowly. A hazy picture was beginning to form in his head, but he wasn't sure of what. "That's what he told me with a gun to my face. He said you killed his mother, his son and Uncle Brah. He said, Debra is just the beginning."

"Ty...," Guy began, trying to wrap his head around everything he had just heard. "Why did you kill his family for? When was this?" Ty was at a lost for words. What could he tell Guy? If he told Guy it had been Brah that had tried to kill him, then Guy would want to know why he hadn't told him so. To tell him that much could lead down a slippery slope to Pandora's Box. Once opened, the brunt of responsibility would fall in his lap, even though he hadn't been involved!

He thought of Karrin. He figured she was still alive if Hardy hadn't mentioned her. So where was she? Debra's web of deception had spun from the grave to ensnare him, as he searched for an answer.

Vee and Tre were down in Jamaica enjoying Hedo at the resort called Hedonism. The event is exactly what the name implies, Hedonistic. Anything and everything goes at Hedo.

Tre had gotten his dick sucked more times in the twenty four hours they'd been there, than the last six months. Hedo was the perfect way to unwind after the war with the mafia.

"Damn Fam, I wish Sleep could be here wit' us," Tre thought sadly, sitting on the beach in a beach chair, Colada in hand.

"He is, Dawg, he is," Vee replied.

Vee had come to relax but he hadn't gotten on the chicks like Tre had. Now that the war was over, it was time to concentrate on finding Cat.

"To Sleep, a muthafuckin' soldier," Tre said, holding up his drink and toasted against Vee's Red Stripe beer.

"Now," Tre began, downing his drink, "Do I call you Jay or Vee?" he cracked.

Vee smirked.

"Listen Dawg, I was-,"

Tre held up his hand.

"I understand my nigguh...I do. But yo, if you ain't learned nothin' else about me, you know I got your back, yo. I ain't askin' you to trust me 'cause every nigguh in the fame got that issue if they smart. All I'm askin' is that you don't *not* trust me, smell me?"

Vee smiled and nodded, then they shook on it.

"And you my nigguh, didn't I tell you we was about to blow?! We 'bout to see Hugh Hefner money!" Tre laughed. "And I couldn't have done wit' out you."

"that's why we partnas," Vee replied.

"No Doubt!"

Tre's cell rung. He looked at the number then smiled. "What up, Baby. Long time no hear from. What you got good for me?"

"Baby, I had to dig deep for this shit. Word up, you owe me ten grand *and* a pair of Manolos," the female chuckled.

"Shit sound serious. What up?"

"Remember you asked for a name?" she reminded him.

Tre had to think, then he remembered the confidential informant getting so many hustlers knocked off.

"Word! You got a name?"

"Nigguh, what's *my* name?! she giggled. "I won't say it but wait for a text. I'll see you in two days in Silver Spring. Cool?"

"No doubt mama. You never let me down. Peace."

Tre hung up and turned to Vee, excitedly.

"Yo Fam, we got that Bitch Ass nigguh.

"Who?" Vee asked, finishing his beer.

"Remember the hot nigguh I told you about? The C.I.?"
Vee's interest perked up.
"Yeah?"
Tre's phone rang with a text.
"My connect just hit me wit' it. It's gonna cost us ten stacks, but shit, it's worth it.!"
Tre popped the text, looked at it strangely then said, "Yo....this name sound familiar."
"Let me see."
He handed the phone to Vee. Vee shielded the screen from the glare of the sun. When he saw it, he couldn't believe his eyes.
The text said **GUY SIMMONS.**